The bolt slid home and the lock clicked into action

The shogun looked around the room. "We have been locked in," he said quietly.

Other than the main door and the high windows, the only way in or out of the ballroom would be through the rectangular air vents in the ceiling. But they weren't big enough for access.

One of the sec men in the far corner of the huge room, directly below an air vent, suddenly began to cough. Ryan spun, seeing that two more soldiers had been stricken with coughing fits. He looked up at the air vents, a sudden dreadful suspicion filling his mind.

It was Mashashige who voiced the danger. "It is an attack with gas," he said with an almost insane calm.

"The *rodin* have trapped us like foxes in their den and will kill us with poison gas."

Also available in the Deathlands saga:

JAMES AXLER

DEATH LANDS®

Keepers of the Sun

A GOLD EAGLE BOOK FROM

WORLDWIDE®

TORONTO • NEW YORK • LONDON
AMSTERDAM • PARIS • SYDNEY • HAMBURG
STOCKHOLM • ATHENS • TOKYO • MILAN
MADRID • WARSAW • BUDAPEST • AUCKLAND

This one is for Sue and Ann, connoisseurs of teashops and very good friends. In hope that they both succeed in finding the elusive gold at the rainbow's end.

First edition April 1996

ISBN 0-373-62531-6

KEEPERS OF THE SUN

There are those who believe that the mysteries of Japan were discovered in the nineteenth century. This is fallacious thinking. The true mysteries of Japan have not yet been discovered. Nor will they ever be.

—From *Scouting in the East,*
by Sir Arthur Bowden-Powell,
Crest Press, Norwich, 1895

Chapter One

The gateway chamber, a few miles north of Glenwood Springs in old Colorado, was flooded to knee height.

Ryan stood in the pink-walled armaglass hexagonal chamber, holding hands with Krysty Wroth. Doc Tanner was next to her, close to Jak Lauren. The albino teenager was leaning back, soaking wet from a fall into the water. Next to him stood J. B. Dix, folding his glasses and putting them into a pocket of his coat, preparing for the expected matter-transfer jump that would take them to an unknown and uncontrollable destination. The last of the six friends, Mildred Wyeth, was trembling with the cold, the beads in her plaited hair whispering against one another.

The door was firmly closed, which should have triggered the jump mechanism, but it seemed as if the flooding had done serious damage to the electrics.

They waited for the disks in the floor and ceiling to start glowing—the former just visible under the water—and for the mist to gather about their heads.

"Has anyone considered that if we fall unconscious, we might drown during the jump?" Doc asked.

But nothing happened.

Ryan opened and closed the door again.

A flash of silver light blazed from the control room, and every one of the lamps went out.

In the silent dark, the water was still rising.

"WE TRAPPED?" Jak's voice sounded hollow and flat, muffled by the water in the chamber.

"No. Door opens," Ryan said. "Worst is we can still get out and climb back to the surface. Move on from there. Be a real pain in the ass."

"Try it again," J.B. suggested.

"Think the power's all down," Ryan said. But he remembered the words of the Trader, his old commander on the war wags: *Keep on trying until something better happens on by.*

He picked his way across the floor, water lapping at his groin, and fumbled for the handle. He pushed it open a little way, conscious of the resistance from the flood, and pulled it shut as hard as he could.

At the third try, Ryan thought that he heard a more positive click from the lock, but he couldn't be sure because of the noise of the water sloshing around inside the chamber.

"Quiet," he said. "Think it might be working."

Doc coughed. "Has anyone considered what I said a few moments ago?"

J.B. looked down at the water, almost invisible in the darkness. "Comes up past my knees," he said. "Two feet. Two and a half feet. Plenty to drown in."

"It's starting," Krysty warned. "Jump's beginning. Feel it like a feather behind my eyes."

"Everyone sit down, backs against the wall!" Ryan raised his voice, aware of the ceiling disks beginning to glow brightly, the ones below the water showing more dimly. "Arms around each other for support."

Mildred exclaimed as she sat down, "Water's colder by the second," her voice already beginning to sound slurred and distant. "Comes up to my chin."

"Hang on tight, friends." Ryan sat and clutched at Krysty, his arm around her, pressing his back to the armaglass wall. The chill struck halfway up his chest. There was no longer any point in trying to save the blasters from the water.

A mist formed at the top of the hexagonal chamber, filtering down over them.

The usual feeling of having his brains curdled and whipped into oatmeal mush started to overcome Ryan as the mat-trans unit began to swing into grudging, reluctant life.

His last thought was to wonder if the flooding was going to affect the mysterious mechanics of the jump, take them to some other place or time.

Or take them nowhere, so that their molecules were sprinkled through the universe.

Ryan closed his eyes.

Chapter Two

Ryan opened his eye.

His first conscious thought was that the floodwater had disappeared. Secondly he saw that the color of the armaglass walls had changed from the pale salmon pink of the Colorado redoubt to a fiery orange that glowed like the rising sun.

He took several long, deep breaths, amazed at how well he felt. Normally a jump left everyone sick and prostrate, and sometimes generated hideous nightmares. This time he had no sense of time passing. His eye had closed, and there had been a kind of period of blackness. Then he opened his eye again, and the jump appeared to have been successfully completed.

Ryan was the first to come around and he sat motionless, resting, his arm still around Krysty, her long red hair brushing his wrist.

He glanced sideways at her, seeing an attractive woman in her midtwenties. As she was still unconscious, her bright emerald eyes were hidden. She was close to six feet tall, strongly built, and wore a blue jacket and a white shirt over dark blue pants.

Across the chamber, J.B. was stirring. John Barrymore Dix, hailing originally from Cripple Creek, was known throughout Deathlands as the Armorer because of his unique knowledge and skills with all weaponry.

J.B.'s first act on recovering was to check that his beloved fedora hat was still in place, then to take his spectacles from his pocket and place them on the bridge of his bony nose. He peered across at Ryan.

"Not a bad jump." J.B. had always been a man of few words.

He was Ryan's oldest friend. They had met as young men, full of gall and sand, and rode with the Trader in his war wags. They'd traveled and fought all across Deathlands for more than ten years, learning the manifold skills of killing at the hands of the notorious master.

J.B.'s next move was to check his blasters, the Uzi machine pistol with twenty 9 mm full-metal jacket rounds and the brutal Smith & Wesson M-4000 shotgun. The weapon had been designed to hold eight rounds of Remington fléchettes, each round containing twenty inch-long, needle-pointed darts.

"Not bad," Ryan agreed.

It wasn't just that the flood had vanished from the gateway chamber. The six friends had been sitting chest deep in the water. Now they all seemed to be bone-dry, and there wasn't a trace of moisture on the floor.

Ryan closed his good, right eye and opened it again. He automatically checked his own hardware—the Steyr SSG-70 hunting rifle, which fired a 7.62 mm bullet, its accuracy increased with a Starlight nightscope and a laser image enhancer. On his right hip he carried his trusty SIG-Sauer P-226 automatic pistol, which fired fifteen rounds of 9 mm ammunition. Everything was in place and bone-dry. Finally Ryan's hand poised along the taped hilt of his eighteen-inch panga, sheathed on his left hip.

Jak Lauren was next to recover.

The teenager blinked open his ruby eyes, running fingers through his shoulder-length white hair. He swallowed hard. "Don't feel bad."

Jak was only five feet four inches tall, and barely pushed the scales over one hundred pounds. But he was a fine acrobat and the finest hand-to-hand fighter that Ryan had ever known. He was also a genius with the leaf-bladed throwing knives that he kept hidden all about him.

Despite his age, Jak had lived several lifetimes. He'd been a married man and a father before tragedy had robbed him of that happiness.

Krysty had come around from the jump without Ryan noticing. He felt her stir against him and turned to kiss her lightly on the cheek. "Welcome to somewhere else, lover," he said quietly. "How is it?"

She sighed. "Felt better. Then again, I've surely felt a whole lot worse. That was one of the better jumps."

Ryan nodded. "Mildred's coming out of it," he said. "Leaves Doc to last."

"As usual," the black woman muttered, still sitting with her eyes closed.

Ryan grinned at Krysty, squeezing her fingers. Ever since the thirty-six-year-old doctor had joined them, she and Doc Tanner had always teased each other.

Mildred Winonia Wyeth was born in December 1964, more than a century earlier. She had been one of the world's greatest authorities on the science of medical freezing, which turned seriously ironic when she went into hospital for minor abdominal surgery in late December of the year 2000. Something went wrong with the operation, and to save her life the doctors decided to freeze her.

Only a few days later and the world exploded.

The nuclear holocaust that had been feared for nearly sixty years finally happened. The heavens were blackened with missiles, at the time that was later to be called "skydark." Tens of millions died in the massive blasts of the first couple of days. Then came the predicted period of the long winters, with the insidious radiation chilling off hundreds of millions of the survivors of the first strikes.

And through all the endless years of bleakness, Mildred Wyeth slept dreamlessly on. Gradually a form of civilization crept back to what had once been the United States of America—what was now Deathlands.

There were isolated communities called villes, many with their own rulers, who named themselves barons. It was a world of violence, ruled by the gun and the knife; a world where science and industry were almost gone; a world with virtually no airplanes and few motorized vehicles, adapted to run on crudely processed gasoline; a world with only rudimentary power, no television or telephones.

Ryan and his friends had finally awakened Mildred from her long sleep, and she was now an integral member of their small group.

"I don't remember feeling so well after a jump," she said. "Not ever."

Her right hand reached down for the comfort of the butt of her ZKR 551 Czech target revolver. The 6-shot revolver had been chambered to take a Smith & Wesson .38-caliber round. Mildred, other than being a specialist in cryogenics, had been a member of the U.S. pistol-shooting team in the last-ever Olympics, in Atlanta in 1996.

She was, quite simply, the finest shot that Ryan had ever seen.

"Doc hasn't even got his usual nosebleed," she observed, standing up a little unsteadily. "And where in the name of Mary and Joseph did all the water go? Even my clothes are dust dry."

Ryan shook his head. "Don't know. Must've sort of drained away during the jump. Who knows?"

The truth was, nobody knew.

All they knew was that in the last months before skydark, the government had poured billions of dollars into what was memorably called an aggressive defense. The master plan was christened the Totality Concept, of which the Strategic Defense Initiative had been one small part. Operation Chronos had been ultrasecret research into time-trawling, which plucked people from their own past and dragged them helplessly forward into the militaristic present.

Then there had been Overproject Whisper, and a crucial segment of this had been code-named Cerberus—matter transfer.

Highly secret installations had been buried deep within a number of military complexes, which were called redoubts. Most were built in the last five years of the previous century, many in isolated parts of national parks to the pointless disgust of the conservationist lobby. Opposition to the siting of the many redoubts was ruthlessly crushed, with most of the leading protagonists mysteriously disappearing.

But the system worked.

You entered a gateway in Portland, Maine, for example, pressed in the code and woke up sometime later in say, Portland, Oregon.

Ryan and his companions had stumbled on one of the gateways many months ago, and triggered the start mechanism by simply closing the door. But they had no idea of how to control the system. As far as was known, all of the intricate coding instructions for the mat-trans units had been destroyed during the skydark and the long winters—which meant that you got into a gateway to make a jump from Portland, Maine, for example, and you might end up anywhere: Florida, Montana, west Texas, Oregon, New York, Moscow, Louisiana, the Amazon jungle, Pocatello, Bucksnort....

Anywhere.

Five of them were up on their feet now, stretching, waiting for the sixth member of the group to lurch back out of the mind-crushing numbness of the jump.

Dr. Theophilus Algernon Tanner was the only surviving subject trawled forward in time during Operation Chronos.

He'd been born in the beautiful hamlet of South Strafford in Vermont on Valentine's day in 1868. Highly intelligent, successful, traveled and cultured, he had been married in June of 1891 to Emily Chandler. In the next four years they had two adorable children, Rachel and little Jolyon.

In November 1896 Doc Tanner was trawled forward in time to 1998. During the next two years, he made himself intolerably awkward, constantly trying everything he could to return to his own time and to his wife and children, or to sabotage the detested Chronos operation. In the end he became such a running sore, the whitecoats got rid of him by pushing him forward nearly a hundred years, into Deathlands where he met up with Ryan Cawdor. It was an event that almost certainly saved the old man's life.

The experiences of being trawled had toppled the balance of his fine brain, and he clung to sanity by ragged nails. Now he was generally in good mental health, though sometimes a few cogs failed to connect and he would slip away for a few seconds. But he always came back.

Doc was as tall as Ryan at six-three, but as skinny as a lath. He had silvery hair, which hung to his shoulders, and wore an ancient frock coat, so old that it showed patches of dull green mold, though the garment was in slightly better condition than his cracked knee-boots. His weapon of choice was a unique gold-plated commemorative J.E.B. Stuart 9-shot LeMat revolver, which also fired a single 18-gauge scattergun round.

He also carried an ebony cane with a silver lion's-head hilt that concealed a slender rapier of finest Toledo steel.

"By the Three Kennedys! What a fine jump that was. I'm ready now for any roister-doistering that you may care to mention. Be it drinking snapdragons or jumping jointed stools."

"Hi, Doc," Krysty said, reaching down to help him to his feet. "Glad to see you're back with us."

"I never really left, did I, my dear?" He looked around the chamber and brushed at his clothes. "I have two comments to make on our location. Firstly to point out that the color of the walls is by far the most hideous that I can remember. Like the agonizing feeling at the back of the eyes after a long night's drinking of porter at O'Flaherty's Irish bar, down on the Tenderloin in old Boston."

Everyone waited, and Ryan finally asked the old man. "You said you had two comments, Doc?"

"Ah, yes. Indeed I have. Perhaps it's my failing memory, but I seem to recall that we commenced the jump while sitting neck deep in floodwater. Does anyone have any suggestions where it might have gone?"

"We were just talking about that," J.B. said. "And the answer, Doc, is that nobody has any idea. Somewhere in the middle of the jump it just sort of vanished."

"Well enough, John Barrymore. I shed no tears for its departure. There are few things more unpleasant than walking around with wet underwear."

"Guess you know about that, Doc." Mildred grinned. "Not one of my problems."

He shook his cane at her in mock anger. "Aroint thee, rump-fed runyon."

"Would if I knew how," she retorted. "But I don't, so I guess I won't."

"If you two have finished, then I reckon we should think about moving out of here." Ryan drew the SIG-Sauer, examining it carefully, working the action a couple of times. "Everyone onto double red, as usual."

"Suggest we all check blasters," J.B. said. "All been soaked in the water, so it's better to test them."

The gateway chamber was filled with the sound of guns being cocked and cartridges ejected, tinkling on the metal disks in the floor.

Ryan waited until everyone was happy before reaching out to the handle of the heavy door. "Right. Here we go."

The armaglass door swung open more easily than usual, totally silent. Ryan paused in the entrance, peering at the deep-set steel hinges. "Been properly oiled," he said. "Within the last few weeks, I'd say."

"Think someone's been using chamber?" Jak asked as he looked out into the anteroom. "Something there."

Ryan stepped out, aware immediately that the flavor of the air was different. "What does...?" he began.

But the others noticed it, except Doc, whose sense of smell was never that good.

"Not a redoubt smell," J.B. commented.

"Too fresh," Mildred agreed. "Sort of an odd flavor to the air. Like a mixture of town and country. Kind of warm smell, as well."

"Swamp and desert," Jak offered. "But not like any swamp or desert I ever knew."

"I cannot notice anything at all unusual in the scent of the air." Doc sniffed vigorously, making himself sneeze, so that he had to blow his nose into his swallow's-eye kerchief.

Jak pointed again into the anteroom. "On table," he said. "Look."

Most of the rooms adjoining gateways were stripped bare, though occasionally one might have a small chair or some shelves. This one had a rectangular table with bamboo legs and a glass top.

On it was a crumpled silk scarf. Ryan picked it up and unfolded it, revealing a pattern of crimson flowers.

"Chrysanthemums," Krysty said. "That's beautiful."

"Looks oddly Oriental." Doc took the scarf and held it to the overhead lights. "Hand-printed design, I believe. What a lovely thing to leave in a gateway."

"Table doesn't look American, either," Mildred observed. "That looks maybe Japanese or Chinese."

A small seed of suspicion was growing fast at the back of Ryan's mind, growing and bursting into flower, an idea that might make a lot of sense of many of the things that had been happening in the previous weeks.

"You feel anything, lover?" he asked Krysty.

"I can't feel anyone close. But..." She looked at him in the eye. "You got the same idea as me, Ryan. I can see it in your face."

The others stared at them in bewilderment. "Can we all share this?" J.B. asked.

"If we're right, then we'll soon know it," Ryan replied.

Chapter Three

The control room to the matter-transfer unit was more or less similar in its design to the others they'd seen, although it was markedly smaller.

Ryan paused, looking at the rows of desks with their flickering comp screens and ever-changing data, the display panels of dancing colored lights and coded digital readouts.

The ceiling was lower than in most redoubts, and the lighting was different.

"Some of the neon strips have been replaced," J.B. said. "You can see that some of them are a different design. Never seen that before."

"Does that mean that someone's been down here and using the gateway since skydark?" Mildred asked.

"Lot more recent than that," Ryan replied, running his finger across a light film of dust on the clear plastic tops of the consoles.

Doc had walked on past him, stopping at the nearest desk. "Look at this! Someone's stuck paper labels on a few of the screens."

"So what?" Jak asked.

"So they're in Japanese."

It was what both Ryan and Krysty had begun to suspect. The fact that the redoubt showed signs of having been used, combined with the beautiful scarf and the design of the table, pointed in only one direction—to Japan.

Months ago they had begun to hear rumors of occasional small bands of Oriental warriors, armed with bows and swords, raiding and then vanishing silently into the backcountry wilderness.

Then, they had encountered a pair of these mysterious samurai killers themselves. One of them had been chilled by Ryan, and the other had fled, wounded, when Mildred broke his longbow with a brilliant shot from her revolver.

It had become obvious that they had found a way of using the gateways, perhaps even understood something of how they worked.

But for all that to be happening, one of two things had occurred. A party of the Japanese had to have made their way north, perhaps to the Kamchatka peninsula in the extreme northwest of old Russia, crossed the Bering Strait into Alaska, then jumped from a redoubt up there.

Or what seemed slightly more likely, the Americans had managed, in those perilous, predark days, to build a gateway somewhere in Japan.

They'd done it successfully on the outskirts of Moscow. Ryan and some of the others had been there, so they knew about that. So why not in Japan?

The sec door at the far side of the comp-control room was smaller than usual, but it was obviously made of the usual armored vanadium steel.

The green lever was in the down, closed position.

Everyone looked at it in a deep, meditative silence, which was broken finally by J.B. "If we're really in Japan, then there could be thousands of screaming slant-eyes waiting behind that door."

"I'm not sure that 'slant-eyes' is a very politically correct, as we used to say, phrase to use, John. Though, in the world of Deathlands, it may be perfectly acceptable."

"Used to call them Johnny Chinamen in my day," Doc offered. "They all used to go along with big pigtails and little black caps, and the women had tiny bound feet and shuffled everywhere. Never made much of a distinction between Chinese and Japanese back when I was a stripling."

"Don't know difference now," Jak said.

"Should be moving," Ryan told them, taking a couple of steps toward the main sec-door control, stopping at a strange noise from behind him.

Every head swung around.

"It's the gateway," Krysty said. "Someone's operating the gateway and making an incoming jump."

Just for a moment in the control room, there was something that was definitely confusion and could almost have trembled on the edge of panic.

Doc started for the green lever, intending to lift the ponderous sec doors so that they could get out into the rest of the redoubt; Jak immediately dropped to his knees behind one of the desks, drawing his .357 magnum Colt Python; J.B. unslung the Uzi and looked around for a good defensive fire position; Mildred, for reasons best known to herself, started moving toward the actual door to the gateway, revolver tight in her right hand; Krysty and Ryan stood where they were, looking at each other in shock.

The air inside the actual gateway chamber had become clouded, with the mist circling thicker at the top, near the metal disks recessed into the flaming orange armaglass. There was a faint humming sound, and the lights in the comp-control area dimmed visibly, indicating the prodigious amounts of power that the mattrans jump drew on.

Doc's gnarled hand was on the green lever before Ryan called out for him to stop.

"Hold it. Could be jumping out of the burning ship into the shark's mouth."

"Frying pan into fire," Mildred muttered, standing in the doorway to the anteroom, staring fixedly at what was happening inside the armaglass walls.

"We could ambush them as they step out," J.B. suggested. "Chill them all, easy as winking. They won't expect that. What do you reckon, bro?"

Ryan considered all the options.

Three options.

The Trader always used to say that almost any situation you were likely to encounter offered three basic choices. You could run or fight or hide.

To run meant opening the sec doors, which always took a little time, and involved risking who or what lay outside.

To fight meant taking on an unknown force as they emerged from the chamber. J.B. was right that it could hardly fail to be a successful ambush. But there was almost a good possibility that whoever was making the jump might not be actively hostile. In fact, whoever lay behind the sec door might be prepared to be fairly friendly.

One way of turning friends into enemies was to chill a few of them.

"Hide," he said. "Doc, leave the door where it is. Mildred, come away from the gateway before anyone spots you moving out here. Rest of you, get behind the comp desks at the far end there. Triple red."

"If they see us?" Jak asked.

"Then we'll have about one-hundredth of a second to decide whether they're hostile. But they could easy walk on through and out the doors and never look too careful. Seems the best idea at the moment."

"Think the jump's nearly done," J.B. said. "Fog's clearing."

"Quick." Ryan led the way between the desks, crouching out of sight at the far end of the room, the SIG-Sauer cleared and cocked in his right hand.

Everyone joined him, moving with reasonable speed and silence, except for Doc and the pistol-shot explosions from his kneejoints.

"Doc, shut it up!" Ryan hissed.

"My dear fellow, I can hardly be held responsible for the conditions of the cartilage and tendons and bony tissue at the center of my knees, can I? It seems most unfair that—"

He stopped suddenly as J.B. dug him hard in the ribs with the muzzle of the Uzi.

"Door's opening," whispered Krysty, who probably had the best hearing of them all.

Ryan closed his eye for a quiet moment, controlling his breathing, calming himself, ready for what might be sudden, explosive movement.

There was the click of the gateway door opening, followed by someone groaning, as though they had a fearful headache. Ryan found himself almost grinning sympathetically, knowing only too well the feeling of coming around from a jump.

He waited for the sound of talking, which would give them a clue as to where they might have landed. But all he could hear was someone groaning and someone getting to his or her feet, then a sharp metallic sound as though something had scraped against the armaglass wall, and footsteps.

Three people, he guessed.

Ryan strained to hear, guessing from the noise of their walking that they were either small-built men or teenagers or, possibly, women.

Shadows moved quickly by, thrown against the wall behind him. The footsteps never paused until they reached the control lever for the sec door. Ryan risked a quick glance around the edge of the desk, desperate to know what these jumpers looked like, but the angle of the consoles blocked them from view.

Someone threw the lever, triggering the familiar sound of concealed gears whirring as they lifted the great weight of the sec door.

Out of the corner of his eye, Ryan could see Jak trembling with the suppressed tension, his red eyes seeming to glow like molten rubies.

The whirring stopped, and the footsteps moved on and out. The sec door dropped slowly back into place again.

Everyone waited for Ryan to take the lead, but he kept them there, counting two hundred heartbeats, concentrating on trying to catch the least movement or breathing. But the control room was as silent as a midnight tomb.

He inched out on his belly, moving like a hunting rattler, crawling on the floor until he was able to see around the farther corner of the row of desks, seeing that the room was completely empty.

"Right," he said, standing, brushing himself down and holstering the blaster. "Whoever they were, they've gone now." He pushed back an errant curl of dark hair from his forehead. "Anyone see them at all or hear anything?"

Everyone shook their heads.

Krysty made an undetermined gesture with her hand. "Nothing much," she said. "But I thought I heard a kind of metal-rubbing-on-metal noise. Might be wrong. And I don't reckon that they were wearing combat boots. Something softer and quieter."

Jak was sniffing the air like a possum hound, head back, eyes closed. "Smell like..." he began. "Like don't know what. Not like us."

"What kind of smell?" Ryan asked. "Can't detect anything myself."

"You couldn't smell if your pants were on fire, lover," Krysty teased. "I can catch something kind of different. Sort of spicy scent. Or herbs like I don't know."

"What do we do now?" Doc asked, rising to his feet with a positive eruption of noise from his knees.

Jak had gone quickly to check out the chamber. "Nothing in there," he called. "Except smell's stronger."

Ryan looked around. "Best give them a little time to get out of this section and into the main redoubt. Then we might as well move ourselves. Can't wait here forever."

"Give them five minutes?" the Armorer suggested. "Should be long enough."

"Make it ten," Ryan said. "No point hurrying to shove our necks into the noose."

RYAN LOOKED DOWN at his wrist chron, waiting for the crystal display of flickering digits to turn over. "Right," he said. "That's the ten."

"Want me to take the control lever, Ryan?" Doc asked. "Without Dean here, it falls to the oldest member of the party to take the responsibility. I assure you that I am confident of handling the handle, if I can get a handle on it. Be handy if I could. Handy and Andy. What happened to the Kingfish? Play some Handel for the handle." His eyes had glazed over, and he seemed a thousand miles away.

Ryan clapped his hands smartly together, making the old man jump. "Ready, then, Doc. Know the way. This time I only want it a couple of inches off the ground. No more than that, so I can take a squint under it.''

"What do you think you'll see, Ryan?'' Mildred asked. ''The teahouse of the August moon, perhaps?'' She saw the look of incomprehension on his face. ''Sorry, period reference. Getting nearly as bad as Doc.''

Ryan ignored her. ''If I shout a warning, then you drop the door, Doc, instantly.''

''If not sooner, my dear fellow.''

''And we all run like smoke to the gateway, pile in and try and jump out of here before the swift and evil enemy comes in after us. No arguments and no hesitation.''

J.B. readied the Uzi again. ''Don't forget we're still on triple red until we're safe out of here.''

''Right. Places, everyone. Ready on the green lever, Doc.'' Ryan lay flat on the concrete floor, pressing his face against the bottom of the sec door.

Mildred and J.B. went to the left of the door, Krysty and Jak to the right.

''Now,'' Ryan said quietly.

Doc slowly and carefully inched up the green lever, biting his lip with concentration, listening for the clicking of the operating mechanism. Ryan actually felt the slight tremble through the floor as the vanadium-steel sec door began its slow upward progress.

Doc had moved the lever only enough to start the door moving very slowly, and he now placed one hand elegantly on his hip, posing like a Regency dandy.

"Watch it, Doc," Ryan warned, trying to see through the tiny gap as it increased with infinitesimal slowness. "Don't let it go too high."

But Doc was off in a world of his own, waving one hand dreamily in the air as though conducting an invisible string quartet, the other hand leaning negligently on the green lever, his whole body swaying to and fro.

The door was moving up a little faster, already three or four inches from the floor. Ryan hadn't yet been able to see anything under it and he looked away, calling out another warning to Doc. "Stop it . . . now!"

The sudden shout, echoing flatly through the mattrans unit, made Doc jump. He grabbed down at the lever, off-balance, and his boots slipped, throwing him to the floor.

Out of his control, the sec door began to rise inexorably and more rapidly into the air, leaving Ryan sprawled helplessly beneath it.

Chapter Four

Most people would have lost their nerve and tried to roll back inside the control room to a specious safety. But once Ryan saw that the sec door was rising out of control, he immediately rolled outside into the passage, blaster ready, head turning both ways to face the danger.

The corridor wasn't like most of the others he'd seen. It was much more narrow, with a lower ceiling, and the lights were of a different design.

More importantly there was nobody there.

Behind him, Ryan could hear Doc's voice, high and plaintive. "I'm most frightfully sorry, my dear friend. My foot slipped, and then my hand lost contact with the piece of apparatus that controls the door and . . ."

"Quiet, Doc. Doesn't matter. No harm done."

"Nobody there?" J.B. said, who'd moved quickly beneath the ascending door, ready to back up Ryan in any firefight.

"No. Krysty, you feel anyone?"

"Yeah. Close by. Not on top of us but . . ." She hesitated. "Moving slowly away."

The others had joined Ryan.

"Different sort of setup here," Mildred commented. "Those overhead lights aren't the same as in the other redoubts we've jumped to."

"Smaller," Jak said, stooping to look at the floor. "Been used a lot. Got sort of reddish dust." He straightened and sniffed. "Air's different, too."

Ryan had already noticed that. He stood and dusted himself down. "No air-conditioning working down here," he said. "Could be that the redoubt machinery has partly malfunctioned. Though all the consoles were operating properly."

To the left, the corridor ended in a blank wall, which was a feature of almost every mat-trans unit that they'd encountered. The passage itself was no more than eight feet wide and about the same height with a slightly curved roof.

There was a number of scratches and deeper gouges in the rough stone of the walls.

"It doesn't feel right," Krysty said. "Not usual."

"That just because of the size or the air or what?" Ryan looked at her. "You feel something else?"

Krysty nodded slowly. "Can't quite put my finger on it, lover. Nearest I felt was that dacha in the woods outside Moscow. Not a redoubt."

J.B. licked his lips. "That would tie in with the possibility that we've somehow jumped to Japan."

Doc coughed. "Did I offer my apologies for muddling the opening of the security portal, Ryan? If not, then please accept my heartfelt..."

Ryan shook his head brusquely. "Let it lie where it fell, Doc. Past's past. Next time be more careful. Learn from the mistake. You can't do more than that."

"I do have some thoughts in the chances of this being old Japan."

"What?"

"During the time that the whitecoats held me prisoner, I was involved in some of the Totality Concept's war games. A large house in Wyoming. Very hush-hush."

"What's any of this crap got to do with Japan, Doc?" Mildred asked.

"Oh, a great deal, my dear Doctor. During these games they would program their computers with all sorts of data for a potential nuclear holocaust. What it might do to the various parts of the world." He laughed. "Needless to say, none of these doomsday scenarios included the possibility that the United States would find itself among the losers."

Ryan was eager to get moving out of the corridor. "What about Japan?"

"Indeed, yes, my dear friend. What about Japan?" Doc blinked his milky blue eyes, recovering himself. "Ah, yes. Their prediction for the Far East was that virtually the whole of Japan would be wiped away by quakes and eruptions and swamped by tsunamis, the tidal waves triggered by massive undersea quakes along the known tectonic fault lines."

"The whole country destroyed?" J.B. asked.

"They predicted that there would be some slight damage to California," Doc said.

Ryan laughed, the sound quickly muffled. "Slight damage. California disappeared overnight. Just the western islands there now, with cliffs rising straight up into the big Sierras. Real good prediction, Doc."

"As far as Japan was concerned, my somewhat blurred recollection was that they expected massive destruction. Hokkaido at the north would vanish, as would Kyushu and Shikoku in the south. Much of the main island of Honshu lies abreast classic fault lines and would be devastated. Their computer plan showed just the western section of Honshu being spared, with Hiroshima the main center of the population."

They considered that for some time.

It was common knowledge what had happened to the old United States that had become Deathlands. Massive structural and climatic changes had taken place, with whole slices of the West Coast falling into the Pacific. Deserts had become mountains, and peaks turned into lakes.

But there was little knowledge of what had happened in the rest of the world.

Europe was supposed to be a plague-ridden pesthole, covered in rad hot spots, some of them rumored to last for ten thousand years or more.

"So, if your whitecoats were correct, then we're probably in that bit of Japan that's left. What did you say that it was called, Doc?"

"Honshu, Ryan. The western section of Honshu Island. But I would never place much credence on the diseased frothings of a whitecoat."

"Me neither, Doc. Rather put my dick in a rattler's mouth."

"Nice image, lover," Krysty said, grinning.

"You could say it was short and to the point, sister," Mildred said, sniggering.

"You might say that, Mildred, but you can't possibly expect me to comment on it."

Both women giggled, while Ryan felt his cheeks flush with embarrassment, which he covered by becoming businesslike and efficient. "Can't stay here fooling around," he said. "Best we get to carrying out a careful recce. I'll lead the way. Jak, come second but stay a safe distance back. No way of knowing what we might find once we start to explore."

THE EXPLORATION DIDN'T take long. Ryan walked around the curving passage for about thirty paces, until he came to a small elevator that blocked it off, with a comp-control panel set into the wall at its side. The door was closed.

Six digits were neatly printed on the pale concrete, at chest height, in peculiarly angular numbering: six, two, eight, three, four and one.

"Entry code," the Armorer said. "Has to be."

Ryan nodded. He looked around in the hope of finding a staircase of some sort that would remove the need to take the elevator, but there was nothing at all.

"Don't like it," he said. "Get in there, and we're like salmon in a beer keg."

"Could go and jump out of here," Mildred suggested, but there was little conviction in her voice, and she got no response from the others. Smiling to herself, she added, "Then again, Mildred, maybe we can just go and get ourselves chilled by a band of nice samurai warriors with big swords."

"Long as only got swords, can chill them first," Jak said, running his fingers through his snowy hair.

"One way to find out." Ryan looked around. "Ready as you can ever be," he said, pressing the index finger of his left hand against the small number pad and reading the numbers out loud. "Six and two and eight and three and four and one."

For several seconds nothing happened, then a red light flashed on above the door. But there was no sound of gears. Jak pressed his ear to the smooth metal of the door and shook his head.

"Nothing," he said.

"No sign of how many floors there are in this redoubt." Krysty looked at the red light. "Always assuming that it *is* a redoubt."

"Mebbe the code simply activates the elevator. And there's some other kind of signal to actually make it go up and down." Ryan peered at the panel. "Ah, stupes!"

"Who?" Mildred asked.

"Us. There's two arrows on the control panel. One pointing up and the other one pointing down." He pushed it. "Yeah, here she comes."

They could all hear the high, characteristic whine of the elevator's motor. In less than fifteen seconds there was a dull thump, the whirring stopped and the door slid back.

"Get in and look for something to hold the doors," Ryan said. "Quick, Krysty."

The redheaded woman darted inside the metal cubicle, looking to her left, seeing nothing and checking the other side. "Got it," she said. "Nice and simple. 'Door Open' it says."

There was just enough room for them all. A neat notice on the back said that the Rumplemeyer Elevator and Moving Walkway Company of Detroit, Michigan, recommended that no more than six adult persons should be on board at any one time, with a maximum combined weight of no more than twelve hundred pounds.

"Stand clear of the door," said a tinny little voice from a small speaker in the ceiling.

"Let go of the Hold button," Ryan said, positioning himself at the front of the cabin, the SIG-Sauer steady in his right hand. J.B. stood at his side, with the Uzi set on full-auto, ready to blow away any of the ungodly.

There was the hissing of pneumatic gears as the door slid closed, then a slight jolt before the elevator began to climb. It was always difficult to judge the speed of an elevator, except for the effect it had on your stomach. Ryan figured it wasn't going very fast, and it certainly wasn't going very far, either. After no more than about a hundred feet, and passing no intermediate floors on the way up, it jolted to a stop at the top of the shaft.

"Candlewick bedspreads, children's toys and haberdashery," Doc said quietly.

"Stand clear of the door," repeated the tinny little voice.

Ryan's finger tightened on the trigger of the SIG-Sauer, taking up the first pressure.

The door opened a little way, less than six inches, then changed its mind and closed again before Ryan could even glimpse anything outside. Then, after a moment's hesitation, it finally slid back all the way.

They were in another corridor, but this was much more like something in a small office block. It was painted off-white, with a darker ceiling. Neon lights glittered at regular intervals, and doors opened on either side. In neat bronze pots, standing on low bench tables, were a number of tiny trees with twisted branches.

"Those are bonsai trees," Doc hissed in a piercing stage whisper.

Ryan was standing still, listening, gesturing as a sudden afterthought for Krysty to again press the control that held the door open.

The place was completely silent. A painting hung on one wall. From where he stood, Ryan couldn't make it out clearly, but it looked like a strange, stylized picture of a foaming wave breaking on a shore. A short distance along the corridor was what seemed to be some kind of shrine.

Ryan stepped out into the passage, followed by J.B., with the others at their heels. Krysty let go of the control, and the door hissed shut.

The doors revealed empty offices, most without windows. One had heavy sec-steel shutters across what looked like a casement, and Jak slipped in to try it, shaking his head when he found it firmly locked.

"Not even slit see through," he reported in a whisper.

The shrine was a little altar, recessed into the wall. A tiny statue of a squatting Buddha was at its center, with a few dried flowers scattered in front of it. But most significant was a bundle of rose-scented joss sticks that were smoking in front of the altar. About a third of them were unburned.

"Must've been lit in the last few minutes," Mildred said. "The guys who came out of the gateway."

Ryan nodded. "Has to be. Means they can't be all that far away from us."

"Exit door," the Armorer said, pointing with the barrel of the Uzi.

It was an ordinary door set at right angles to the passage. It looked like white-painted wood, but as soon as Ryan touched it he realized that it was actually a disguised sec door. At its upper corner a small sec camera was moving back and forth, a bright green light showing that it was operating.

"Anyone watching that'll know we're here," Krysty said. "Could mean a reception committee."

"Nothing we can do about that. There's no reason for them to expect visitors, so they probably don't have a watch set on the vid screens." Ryan tested the door handle. "It's open."

"Looks a good fit," J.B. observed. "Almost vacuum tight around the edges."

Ryan eased it open and peered around the corner.

"Still nobody," he said.

They were in a small, brightly lit anteroom, about ten feet square, with no windows and another disguised sec door facing them at its far side.

Doc was carefully examining the door that they'd just passed through. "This reminds me strangely of an air lock," he said. "Have you noticed that it has rubber seals all around the edges to make it tight?"

"Not like any redoubt ever saw," Jak commented.

Ryan reached for the handle of the second door. With every barrier they reached, it was obvious they were getting closer to the heart of the mystery.

"We could still go back, lover." Krysty laid a hand on his sleeve, biting her lip.

"Bad feeling?"

She shook her head. Ryan noticed that her mane of sentient red hair was packed tightly against her skull instead of flowing freely across her shoulders.

"Not bad. Just different. When I can't see clearly, it worries me, Ryan."

"We've come this far. Might as well go that last step and see what's what."

He turned the handle and eased open the last door.

Chapter Five

"Dark night!" At Ryan's shoulder, J.B. peeked out past the edge of the open door.

Doc, looming over Jak, also expressed his surprise. "By the Three Kennedys! We are transmogrified from a mat-trans unit into an ordinary house."

"Not many houses got a gateway hidden away in a deep root cellar," Mildred said.

The door opened into a hallway of what looked, as Doc had said, like a perfectly ordinary American house. It was sparsely furnished in a style that seemed a little out-of-date for the end of predark times, with a three-legged semicircular table holding some dried flowers and a high-backed bench seat with a red padded chair on either side of it.

There were a couple of spaces on the wall where the paint was a distinctly different, brighter color, showing that paintings or mirrors had hung there at some time.

Ryan could see that the hallway veered to the right in a sharp right angle, and he moved cautiously toward it. He glanced into the open doors on both sides, seeing that the place was more or less fully furnished, though odd gaps showed where things had been moved or removed.

J.B. glanced behind them. "That door used to have a curtain or a tapestry in front of it to hide it," he said. "See the rail above it?"

Ryan looked back, seeing that the Armorer was right. "Seems more and more that this is like that house in Russia," he said. "Might've been a sort of diplomatic home, and they used it to secretly build a gateway."

The angle in the hall revealed the front door of the mansion and a flight of stairs.

Ryan stood still and held up his hand. "Quiet a moment."

It was totally silent.

All of the outer windows had the impenetrable shutters bolted over them, making it impossible to see out. But the patterned glass in the front door of the house was clear, showing bright sunlight. The light streamed through the stylized stained glass, with a picture of waves of cherry-tree blossom and a long-legged stork with a fan of feathers in its tail.

"Should check upstairs," Jak said, his brilliantly white hair catching the soft pinks and greens of the filtered sun through the glass.

Ryan was at the bottom of the wide flight of uncarpeted stairs. He stooped to look at them, running his finger through a layer of reddish dust. "No need, Jak. Nobody been up or down in a good few days."

"Or months," Doc said. "As a great man once said, you don't have to worry about dusting after five years, since the dust gets no thicker."

"What great man?" Krysty asked distrustfully, suspecting that the old man had made the quote up himself.

"I forget."

Mildred smiled. "I know. For once Doc's actually telling the truth. It was an amazing person called Quentin Crisp. A gay Englishman and style guru. Used to live in New York."

Ryan shook his head, lifting the hand with the SIG-Sauer. "Enough chat," he said.

There was another little Buddhist shrine just inside the door, with its own clump of smoking incense sticks tucked into a pierced copper bowl—musk flavored, this time—and a tiny bronze model of a grasshopper.

"We really going to be in Japan when you open that door, lover?" Krysty breathed. "Sure this isn't all some kind of a jump dream?"

"If it is but a dream, madam, then it is a dream which we all share." Doc rapped on the floor with the ferrule of his swordstick. "Solid enough, I believe. No ectoplasmic imitation of reality."

Ryan took the doorknob and turned it slowly. He eased the heavy front door open an inch, his good eye to the crack and checked outside.

"Looks like we're on top of a hill," he said. "Fireblast! The air doesn't taste all that clean."

The others could smell it now.

"Prefer the musk," Mildred said. "You know that's a sort of familiar stink. Like L.A. on a hot, smoggy afternoon when the air turns orange and your eyes sting and your breath catches in your throat. Sort of polluted smell. All my time in Deathlands, I never did smell anything like that before.''

Ryan blinked again, feeling a sharp prickling behind his right eye. ''Formal garden that could do with weeding. Lot of stones, as well.''

He opened the door a little wider, feeling more secure now that there was no sign of human life outside. ''Trees. Pine and some little apple and plums. Few big oaks and . . . Don't know what that sort of weepy tree is.''

''Cypress,'' Mildred told him. ''And those are beautiful azaleas beyond the dry fountain.''

A rectangular area of raked gravel was covered with dead leaves and patterns of larger stones, some of them as large as a man's head.

''I believe it's a Zen garden,'' Doc said. ''Though certainly a little neglected.''

''Can't see anything beyond the trees and bushes.'' J.B. took off his glasses and wiped them, then put them on and sniffed. ''Doesn't make it much better. Definitely a nasty sort of haze in the air.''

Ryan finally stepped out, finding himself on a narrow porch that ran the whole considerable length of the front of the house. There was a wickerwork sofa, designed as a garden swing, at one end, though it had ripped away from one of the rusted couplings and scraped back and forth in the light breeze.

All the windows along that flank of the property were concealed by shutters, and when Ryan stepped down onto the garden path, he was able to look back and up and see that all the second-floor windows were also sec shuttered.

He also noticed that there had once been a flagpole fitted above the door, though wind, weather and time had contrived together to remove it.

"I bet your fedora full of fresh-minted jack that this place used to be some kind of official U.S. residence," he said. "And Old Glory must have flown from up there. See where the pole used to be fixed?"

"Makes sense." The Armorer took off his spectacles again and rubbed at his eyes with a linen kerchief. "This air sure stings," he said.

"I believe that Japan, in the last years of predark, was one of the most polluted places on the face of this noble planet." Doc also wiped at his eyes. "Industry run rampant. Asthma and all manner of respiratory ailments plagued a significant section of the population." He coughed. "But enough of this merry persiflage, my friends."

"What's persiflage, Doc?" Jak asked.

"Raillery and jolly banter, my sweet, ice-topped youth. Not all that appropriate, considering our somewhat parlous position here, I fear."

Ryan started to walk away from the house, his combat boots crunching through the leaf-littered gravel, the SIG-Sauer still cocked in his right hand. The dry fountain had a dead animal in it, what looked like a mutie rat, with unusually floppy ears and a feathery tuft on the end of its extremely long tail. The statue at the center of the moss-crusted stone bowl was a kneeling woman in a flowing gown, covered in pale green verdigris.

"Come on, folks," he said. "Let's keep it on double red for a while."

The tumbled remains of what might have been a watchtower stood in a corner of the garden, up against a high wall of creamy stone, with residual loops of razored wire laid along its top.

"Quite a fortress," J.B. commented.

Ryan turned back to gaze once more at the big house. There was something about the design that was definitely not true American, something in the angle of the peaks of the roof and the shape of the windows.

At the end of the driveway was a pair of double gates, at least twenty-five feet high and forty feet wide. They were made of wrought-iron, the gaps filled with corroded sec-steel panels. Sharp spikes were set along the top.

Ryan looked at the formidable obstacle, thinking how appropriate J.B.'s comment had been. The place really had been a fortress.

"Something's going down, lover," Krysty said, tugging at Ryan's sleeve.

"What? Danger?"

"There's people around. Quite a few of them. Close to us. Not sure whether they're a threat."

"Might I proffer a suggestion?" Doc asked.

"Yeah." Ryan had reached the gate, hesitating, fingers reaching out for the ornate handle.

"Dear John Barrymore hasn't yet utilized his miniature sextant. It might be of some assistance to know for certain where we are, might it not?"

"Guess so. J.B., give it a try."

The sun was smiling down from a sky of almost unsullied blue, with just a few tiny wisps of pinkish cloud gathering at the far north.

The Armorer reached into one of his many deep pockets and plucked out the little scientific instrument. Built in predark times, it was of a degree of technical sophistication that it would now be impossible to reproduce. He aimed it at the sun, turning the little milled wheel on its side, checking the angle and reading off the measurement, his lips moving silently.

"Tell you one thing," he said.

Ryan raised an eyebrow. "What?"

"Not in Deathlands. Reading's about one thirty-two by thirty-five. Near as I can recall from the old-world maps, that definitely puts us the other side of the Cific Ocean."

"Japan, John?" Mildred asked as J.B. folded the sextant and put it back in his pocket.

"Probably. Yeah. Close as I can tell, but I don't have the least idea where precisely we've ended up."

"There was a lot of political tension between us and the Japanese in the last few years before skydark," Mildred said. "Trade wars at a high level, as well as threats about tariffs and boycotts and cutting off supplies and aid. I don't think that the sores of the Second World War and the atom bombs have ever really been properly healed."

"But they started it at Pearl Harbor," the Armorer protested. "They only got what they deserved."

"I'm not sure it was quite as clear-cut as that," she replied. "I remember reading magazine articles saying that we didn't need to drop the bombs on Hiroshima and Nagasaki. The Japanese were ready to quit."

J.B. sniffed meaningfully, making it obvious he didn't place much belief in what Mildred was saying.

On the far side of the sec gates, it was possible to see the tops of some slender conifers. A murder of crows suddenly flew noisily into the air, circling, etching their black shadows against the sky.

Ryan opened the gate and looked through the gap. They were on top of a steepish hill, the road winding away, lined with a dark mass of pines.

The others joined him.

"Lovely view," he said, his words punctuated by a hissing sound as two unusually long arrows thunked into the turf a yard in front of him.

Chapter Six

"Ho, *gaijin!*" The voice had an odd, hollow quality to it, sounding high and strained.

"Nobody move," Ryan said. "Got us cold."

"Might only be two of them," Jak whispered, dropping into a shootist's crouch, his red eyes darting around the blank walls of the forest.

"Might be two hundred," Ryan replied. "Best wait and see before we commit suicide."

"Ho, *gaijin.* We wish you to accept the hospitality of our lord, Mashashige."

"What's he calling us?" J.B. asked, his finger white on the trigger of the Uzi.

"*Gaijin.*" Mildred had fallen naturally into the classic two-eyed stance of the shootist—legs slightly apart, sideways on to where the voice came from, right arm extended, the muzzle of the revolver describing slow circles, back and forth. "Means a foreigner. An outlander."

"How come you by such esoteric knowledge, madam? Is there no end to your wisdom?"

"Shared a room at med school with a Japanese woman. Suki Hokashani. Father was a baseball ace. She taught me a few words. *Gaijin* was what she used to call me when I did something she thought was stupid."

Doc had turned and walked a couple of paces toward the half-open gates of the house. There was a barked word of command, and two more of the long feathered shafts crossed in front of him, missing him by a scant couple of feet.

"Upon my soul! They nearly kabobed me. Dangerous fellows, these samurai."

"I said to stand still," Ryan hissed. "Make a wrong move, and it's pincushion time all around."

"I have not heard any reply to let us know whether you wish to encounter the hospitality of our lord, Mashashige. Or whether you wish to take the dark journey to meet up with the spirits of your ancestors."

"He means kill us," Krysty whispered.

"I got the picture." Ryan looked to both sides, shaking his head at the hopelessness of the situation. The consoling feature was that the hidden archers could almost certainly have chilled them all without once showing themselves.

And they hadn't.

"Got any good Japanese words to accept their kind offer, Mildred?"

"Afraid not. All I know is that they wrap things up a lot when they speak. Sort of flowery."

"What does the *kokujin* woman say?" the voice called. "She should keep silent. This is the business of men. Of warriors. Tell her, One-Eye."

Ryan turned to face Mildred. "*Kokujin* mean what I think?" he asked quietly.

"Yeah. They got a special word for us black folks, Ryan."

"Well, since they got the drop on us, I guess we better do like they say. Sorry about this."

"Rage ahead, boss," she said, lowering her head submissively. "I can take it."

He pointed a finger at her, raising his voice. "You must keep quiet when men speak, Mildred, or I will have to sternly discipline you."

"Promises, promises," she breathed, without moving her lips or changing the penitent expression on her face.

Ryan managed not to smile. "We will be pleased to accept the kind offer of your baron, Mashashige. Will you show yourselves to us?"

He was waiting for the hidden enemy to order them to lay their blasters in the dirt and was trying to think up some convincing arguments for not complying.

"Your guns interest us, *gaijin*."

"Yeah."

"When we reach the—" There was a slight hesitation as though the speaker wasn't sure of the right word "—the fortress of my master, he will wish to see them. He has a small collection of the unclean weapons himself."

"Unclean?" Ryan questioned.

A laugh shimmered all around them on both sides of the trail. "Only the *katana*—the sword—is the truly pure weapon to us samurai."

Ryan nodded, turning to the others. "Might as well holster the blasters, friends. Saves the bastards taking them away from us. But keep your hands close."

"That is well done, One-Eye. If you had not done that, then I would have come out alone and fought you all and taken away those impure toys and thrown them into the shit heap. So, you have behaved with wisdom."

"Thanks," Ryan said laconically. "You ready to come out and show yourselves?"

They heard a single barked word of command.

Jak whistled under his breath as the pine woods around them seemed to come to instant life. Ryan's joking estimate of two hundred men ambushing them was suddenly not at all funny.

At a quick count, Ryan made it well over a hundred, and he wondered about the iron discipline that had kept them silent and patiently waiting. Most were what he guessed to be ordinary foot soldiers for the local baron, wearing identical crimson blouses and baggy white pants, with thonged sandals on their feet. Half a dozen of them carried huge rectangular banners on bamboo poles, with Japanese lettering on them.

All carried long daggers or short swords, and most held the enormously powerful bows, each with a five-foot arrow notched and ready.

A few also carried the "impure" firearms.

"Semiautomatic New Nambu 9 mm," J.B. stated. "Interesting. Eight rounds. Based on the old U.S. M-1911 pistol."

"What's the rifle?"

"It's a 7.62 mm NATO blaster. Twenty rounds. Safety selector on the right, above the trigger. Safe, single-shot and full-auto. Comes with a tripod. No, a bipod. Looks like they've all been well cared for."

Ryan was more interested in the small group of horsemen who had walked their animals out from under the trees.

They were dressed much like the samurai that they'd already encountered in Deathlands, with horned helmets and full body armor. None of them carried blasters, but they all wore long swords on the left hip and all of them had the long bows, ready strung, fastened to their ornate saddles.

The horses were stocky mountain ponies, all wearing slatted armor across their chests and with rich silken blankets covering their flanks.

The leader of the warriors heeled his animal forward, stopping about twenty yards from the group of outlanders, scowling down at them.

"Two women, a white-haired boy, an old man, a weakling with glasses and a leader who has only one eye. What can you know of *otoko no michi?*"

Ryan grinned pleasantly. "Well, if we knew what that was, we could tell you what we know of it."

"*Otoko no michi.* It is the manly and honorable way of the samurai."

"Then I guess you're right. We don't know diddley about that stuff."

The scowl deepened. "You find all of this risible, do you, *gaijin?*"

The man had a slight problem with pronouncing the letters *l* and *r,* and Ryan struggled for a moment to try to work out what was being said.

"Risible," Doc prompted. "Means he wonders why you think it's all funny."

"Yeah, I just got it, Doc. Thanks."

He turned to the leader of the Japanese miniarmy. "We don't think all this is funny. Absolutely not."

"You came through the gateway?"

"Sure. But we never expected to end up here in Japan. No control over the way the gateways make jumps."

The man didn't try to hide his disappointment. "You do not understand how it works?"

"No."

"Honto desu ne?"

"Wants to know if you're telling him the truth," Mildred mouthed.

"Since the skydark time and the long winters, all records have been lost," Ryan said.

"Hai, hai, wakarimashita, wakarimashita." He shook his head. "I should not speak in our language, which you cannot comprehend. I was saying just that I understood what you said."

"But you've been making jumps out of here into Deathlands, haven't you?"

"That is possible." It was as though a mask had dropped, veiling the man's eyes.

"You said that your baron was offering us his hospitality," Ryan said. "We're tired and hungry, and would very much like to accept his generosity."

The leader of the samurai was obviously having difficulty in trying to decide just what his attitude should be toward the alien invaders. Should he treat them as enemies, peasants or honored guests? It was safer and would run less risk of losing face if he was cautious.

He bowed in the saddle. "Forgive me. I am called Toyotomi Hideyoshi." He stared at them as if he anticipated some kind of response at the mention of the name. "You are not familiar with the name. It is a greatly honored one. One of the greatest generals that our country has ever known."

"I'm sure you bear the honored name with honor," Ryan said, inclining his head, surprised at how easy he was finding this archaic way of speaking.

"If any man wishes to challenge the name and the respect that sits upon my helmet, he must face my sword and will die slowly at my hands."

Ryan simply nodded.

The warrior was still not happy. "My lord, Mashashige, will not welcome—" he touched his eyes under the helmet "—*metsuke*. One who attaches their eyes as an enemy."

"Spy?" Krysty asked.

He smiled at her, then immediately turned it into a frown. "Yes, but it is not for a woman to tell a samurai what is a word meaning."

"Sure," she muttered.

During the conversations, the rest of the horsemen and the army of retainers had all stood motionless, their faces betraying no emotion. The bowmen had their arrows notched, but had made no effort to draw the longbows. Ryan knew more than a little about archery, and he couldn't imagine what kind of a powerful pull would be needed to loose a shaft. To string the bows would probably take at least three men.

"But we stand here while the cranes fly south and the demons gather at the northeastern gate. Kimon. The gate of demons," he added.

"Did you know we were there in the house?" Ryan asked, gesturing behind him at the tall gates and the peaked roof of the mansion.

"Of course. Our brothers had been traveling into Deathlands. They could tell that the gateway had been used recently."

"How did they know that it wasn't one of you who had used it?"

"The sticks of incense had not been lit on the altar."

"Of course. Elementary, my dear Watson," Doc muttered. "The dog that didn't bark. The joss sticks that weren't lit. Obvious when you know how."

"Is it far to your home?" Ryan asked.

The man stared. "Every journey begins with a single step," he replied.

Ryan was becoming tired of the verbal games. He was hungry, the stink of pollution in the air was getting to his throat and his eye was watering. "Can't argue with that, but it's fuck-all use at answering my question."

The Japanese leader shook his head sorrowfully. "The man who speaks with words of fire might discover that he has burned his own mouth."

"Gently, lover," Krysty whispered, her hand touching Ryan's arm.

He nodded, taking long and slow breaths. "You either tell us how far it is to your ville, or we turn around and go back into the house and jump out of here."

The man laughed, striking himself on the chest. "My heart swells with pride that a *gaijin* of such courage is to be our guest. You speak to me like that, though you know that I might lift one hand and a thousand times a thousand arrows would feather themselves in your corpse."

"And you'd be falling off your horse with a 9 mm bullet through your skull," Ryan replied calmly. "So, let's cut away the shit, shall we?"

"The shit? Ah, yes, the bullshit that we know of. Of course. It is an education to hear you speak pure American. We have heard it when in Deathlands."

"You speak it well," Doc said. "How can that be? Why American and not Japanese?"

"Our lord will answer all questions," Hideyoshi said, his face splitting into a smile of satisfaction. "But I thank you, Grandfather, for your kind words." One of his comrades leaned across and whispered to him. "It is about four miles to our...what was your Deathlands word? Ville? You can walk that far? Perhaps we should send transport for the women."

"We can walk you off your feet," Mildred replied, "any day of the week."

The smile disappeared and he pointed a finger at her. "You are a guest in our land, not strutting and flaunting yourself in your own second-rate country. It will lead to sadness if you do not remember that."

Mildred stared at him for several long seconds before dropping him a curtsey. "Sure thing."

"NEVER SEEN DISCIPLINE like it," Ryan said to J.B. as they watched the army quickly assemble itself into columns of four, their banners flapping in the light breeze as the foot soldiers fell in behind the horsemen. Toyotomi Hideyoshi had given a string of commands, then walked his horse to the head of the sec men, ignoring the outlanders as though they didn't exist.

But a space opened in the center of the armed men, and Ryan led the others into it.

There wasn't a lot of choice.

Chapter Seven

The scenery that they walked through was an odd mixture of the familiar and the bizarre: apple trees and plum trees in neat orchards, their branches tied out to iron posts; a small forest of oaks, but with foliage that was scarred and discolored by the ravages of the polluted air, and everywhere banks of slender cherry trees dripping with exquisite blossoms.

The group walked down the road from the house, leaving the main forest behind them, the trail leveling out as it passed between some tiny hovels.

"Looks like the sea in the distance." Ryan pointed, catching the glint of sun off water.

"Or a lake," Krysty said. "Can't tell at this distance. Gaia, but the air's so fouled."

Away to the north they could see what looked like some kind of factory complex, with a thick pall of orange smoke billowing out of it.

Ryan turned to one of the blank-faced sec men marching at their side. "What goes on there?" he asked, pointing toward the cloud of stinking smoke.

But the man ignored him, staring stolidly ahead, swinging his arms in a slightly exaggerated motion.

"They do not speak American," said one of the horsemen, reining back when he heard Ryan's question.

"Only the samurai speak it?" Doc asked. "Is that the way it divides up?"

"Every answer from the lord, Mashashige," was all that the man would say.

It was noticeable that his grasp of English wasn't as good as that of his leader, Hideyoshi.

Krysty was at Ryan's side, talking quietly as they walked along the dusty road. "What happens if they try and divide me and Mildred from the rest of you?"

Ryan coughed. "Trader used to say that there was no point wondering where the bullet had gone until you'd already squeezed the trigger."

"You mean we have to wait and see?"

"Yeah."

"The way they seem to treat women, it could easily happen, lover."

Ryan nodded. "Fireblast! This bastard dust chokes you! Yeah, I'm sure it might happen. But from what we've seen, they're not at all hostile to us. Considering that we're foreigners in their country, that's surprising."

"Just hope they stay friendly."

At the front of the squad, Hideyoshi suddenly punched his fist in the air and shouted something in a guttural voice. Instantly, the men around Ryan and his companions echoed the cry, waving their hands as they marched in perfect unison.

"What does *banzai* mean, Mildred?" Jak asked. "That's what word sounds like."

"Sort of victory cry," J.B. answered. "Read a book about the Japanese in the Second World War. They had lots of young men who were kamikaze pilots of planes filled with explosives. And they had enough fuel to get them to their target and crash on the American ships. Death in battle brought honor to them and their families. *Kamikaze* meant 'divine wind.' I remember that. Stuck in my mind what a different kind of worldview they must have."

It was an unusually long speech for the normally taciturn Armorer, and its implications silenced the others for a good quarter-mile or more.

The long column wound its way up and down, over a range of small hills, passing more of the crude huts. A few of the locals came out and stood at the roadside, bowing so low their heads almost reached their knees. One or two glimpsed the round-eye foreigners, including the unique sights of a black woman, a tall, fiery redhead and a slender youth with a great veil of snow white hair tumbling to his shoulders.

And their shock was all too evident as they stood slack jawed and wide-eyed.

"Never seen nothing like us," Mildred said out of a corner of her mouth.

One of the peasants, a withered old man, stooped and picked up a handful of dung from the edge of the road and shaped to throw it at the outlanders.

Without even breaking step, the nearest of the guards drew his short sword and clubbed him across the side of the head with the flat of the blade. Blood gushed down the old man's neck as he fell senseless to the ground.

"They look after their guests," Ryan said.

The road wound on, seemingly forever, past a large artificial lake. Ryan leaned over the low stone wall into the muddied depths, seeing vague, huge shapes moving ponderously below the surface.

"Carp," Doc said.

"Have them in temple gardens," Mildred added. "The Japanese regard them as a symbol of courage and determination. Big and slow is what I reckon."

"Looks like home," Jak said, pointing ahead of them, where they could now see high turreted roofs peaking over a stand of neat conifers.

Almost simultaneously they heard a welcoming cacophony of drums and gongs, followed by several loud explosions. A cloud of black powder smoke drifted toward them, carried on the light breeze, adding to the pollution in the air.

"Sounds like the stickies have taken over," Ryan said, knowing, as they all did, the love that those particular muties had for all fires and explosives.

The blacktop finally straightened out across an embankment, between the trees, ending in a pair of gates even larger than those that had guarded the house with the mat-trans unit hidden in its subbasement. And beyond them was their destination itself.

"Now, that's what I call a fortress ville," J.B. said, casting his admiring, professional eye over it. "Built like an old citadel."

Ryan had seen pictures in books of the medieval strongholds with moats, drawbridges and portcullises, and had to admit that the home of Lord Mashashige did look similar.

A river had been diverted so that it flowed completely around the high perimeter walls. The main difference between the fortress of Mashashige and the castles of old Europe was that European fortresses were built almost entirely from stone. This was built from wood, great balks of seasoned oak with overlaid yew for extra strength.

There was a bridge across the river that could be raised and lowered by thick chains of iron, and beyond that was a heavily barred set of gates. The walls were high, topped with battlements, with numerous slits for archers.

"The home of our lord, impregnable," Hideyoshi called, turning in his high saddle to look down on them. "It can withstand a siege of a thousand years."

"The Nazis said that about Adolf's Reich," Doc muttered.

"All the armies of the world would wither and die outside these strong walls."

"One little antitank nukehead would blow it way out of sight," J.B. said just loud enough for his friends to hear.

The drums and gongs were still flailing away from somewhere inside the walls, but they were quieter now.

Ryan looked up at the amazing array of bright silk flags that strained at their poles every few yards, each with a line of angular Japanese symbols on them.

"Look at all carved wolves," Jak said, pointing to the wooden animals that seemed to decorate every post and tower of the fortress.

Hideyoshi smiled at the albino teenager. "Not wolves, young man. They are foxes, the messengers of the god of rice, blessed Inari."

"What are those kind of beautiful swirly patterns called?" Krysty asked, gesturing toward the delicately carved panels on the outer walls.

The samurai hesitated for several long moments before replying, as though his temperament forbade a response to a question from a mere woman. His expression, shadowed under the helmet, showed the conflict.

Finally his fear of losing face by showing ill nature to one of his lord's guests won out.

"They are called *tatsumaki*. This means 'the twist of the dragon.' They are whirlwinds of flame."

"Thank you," Krysty said. "I'm very grateful to you for telling me that."

"You are welcome."

They bowed to each other.

"I think this could be the start of a beautiful friendship," Mildred whispered.

As soon as they were across the echoing bridge and inside the cool walls of the castle, the foot soldiers disappeared. It was a sign of the vastness of the fortress that more than a hundred men vanished completely in less than a minute.

Grooms and servants scurried forward to take charge of the horses, leading them away under another archway, toward the rear of the building. The samurai all stalked off, walking with a splay-legged gait under the weight of their armor, the tips of the sword scabbards scraping on the cobbled floor.

Only Toyotomi Hideyoshi waited with them in the huge courtyard.

He removed his helmet and handed it to one of the bowing, scraping servants, revealing a broad face, with thinning hair and a deep scar across his cheek that puckered the corner of his mouth into a permanent sly grin.

"It is hot work," he said, wiping sweat from his forehead with a brilliant vermilion silk kerchief. "We will dine and refresh ourselves after you have had the great honor of meeting with Lord Mashashige."

"He knows we're coming?" Ryan asked.

"Of course. What a stupe question. Lord Mashashige knows everything."

"Everything?" Doc asked innocently. "Does he know the EMF of a Leclanché cell?"

The warrior scowled. "It is a mistake that could bring serious punishment to try and make a fool of Lord Mashashige or of any of his heroic samurai."

"Yes, I am sure that you are right," Doc said, putting his hands together and bowing.

The drums and gongs had finally ceased, though they could all hear the plaintive keening of a number of flutes, floating through an open window.

Ryan looked around awed at the sheer size of the place. The roof towered over them, made from tens of thousands of handmade tiles, with subtle changes in color. He could see through to some of the internal walls, which appeared to be formed from sliding panels of some sort of thin, translucent material.

"What are they made from?" he asked the samurai, pointing across the courtyard.

"It is oiled-and-waxed paper on some walls. Those of the higher ranked, such as myself, have embroidered silks and satins around them."

"Can we go in?" Jak asked.

"No. Not until the lord sends for you. I will go and report to him. You wait here."

He swaggered off, disappearing into the shadowed interior between a row of bowing servants, who bobbed up and down like stringed puppets.

"Reminds me amazingly of some old Japanese art movies I saw when I was at college," Mildred said. "Ichikawa and Mizoguchi. Like stepping back five hundred years."

"Think it's safe, Ryan?" J.B. asked. "Got so many men here we'd be wiped away like flies if they decide to do some serious swatting of the infidels."

"I haven't felt any threat."

He turned to Krysty. "You feel anything, lover?"

She shook her head. "Apart from some serious unpolitical antifeminist emotions."

"Amen to that, sister," Mildred echoed. "Going to be difficult here for me and Krysty to keep a tight rein on ourselves. Triple hard."

Ryan pointed a finger at her, his voice low and urgent. "I know that. Fireblast, we all know that! But we can't afford to upset them. Trader used to say that there were times you had to play the game by the other man's rules."

"Yeah, men's rules," Krysty said.

"I know. Easier for us than for you two. But this seems to be a place where a wrong word could get you three feet of razored steel through your guts."

Four young women in brilliantly colored silk kimonos tottered by on little clogs, their tiny feet bound tight with strips of linen. Their heavily painted faces were mainly hidden under the hoods, and they waved painted fans to aid the concealment. As they went by, they were giggling together, sounding like a quartet of caged budgerigars.

"Pretty looking," J.B. commented, wiping his glasses on his sleeve.

"My college roommate used to quote me some old Japanese saying. 'This morning's pretty face is this evening's corpse.' Kind of grim, huh?" Mildred watched the young women until they were out of sight.

"Gaia knows what kind of a miserable life they have here," Krysty said.

Doc cleared his throat. "I do not dispute there is a certain male-chauvinist attitude in these warriors, but I could not help noticing that those delicate little dolls had every appearance of happiness."

"Because they don't know any better, you silly old goat," Mildred snapped.

"When it comes to—" Doc stopped speaking abruptly when Ryan shot him an angry glance.

He'd spotted a small door opening in one corner of the courtyard, and a slender Japanese man appeared. He was barely five feet tall, as skinny as a lath and dressed in a plain black gown that brushed the ground over his sandaled feet. He had a sword tucked into his waistband, but its silver hilt was totally without any ornamentation. His face was narrow, with heavy brows over hooded eyes, and his long black hair was sleeked into a neat ponytail tied with a single strand of black silk.

He walked briskly toward them, and Ryan noticed how easily he moved, like a trained athlete.

"Must be a messenger," J.B. said, "bringing us the invitation to dinner."

The man stopped in front of them, inclining his head in what was no more than a token bow, surprising Ryan with his slightly offhand manner.

"You come to take us in to meet this Lord Mashashige?" Ryan asked.

The voice was quiet and cold as Sierra meltwater, each word given equal value. "No. I am Lord Mashashige."

Chapter Eight

Jak picked halfheartedly at a round dish of something pale and pink that looked a little like large prawns. "What these?" he asked.

"Sea slugs," replied Hideyoshi, who was the only samurai sitting with them, cross-legged around a long, shallow table in the great hall of the fortress ville. Silent servants in scarlet-and-white livery stood around the paper-thin walls.

"Sea slugs." The teenager stared unhappily at them, finally poking at the largest specimen with one of the ivory chopsticks that they'd all been given. He gasped. "Holy Judas! It's moving."

The sly grin widened on the face of the warrior. "Of course it is alive. Did you think we would serve to you sea slugs that were already dead?"

Lord Mashashige was sitting at the end of the table, quietly eating from a bowl of plain boiled rice that contained some strands of boiled vegetables.

"There is other food, Jak," he said. "The sushi is good and it is dead."

"But not cooked, Jak," Mildred warned. "It's raw fish, maybe in a vinegar sauce."

"No burgers, beans and fries?" the young man asked. "Real food?"

Hideyoshi slapped his hand on his thigh and roared with laughter. "We many times eat old, predark-times American food. But we knew that we would have strangers here for the first time in more years than an old man might remember. And our cooks have worked hard to make dishes that are truly of our country. If you would wish for Yankee food..."

Ryan shook his head. "That's all right. This rice, fish and stuff's fine."

Lord Mashashige lifted a small porcelain cup filled with the blood-heat sake that they had been drinking. "We wish you happiness and health. All of you. Even the women."

All of them lifted their cups and drank. Krysty dabbed at her mouth with a corner of the snow white linen napkin at her side, covering her whisper with it. "Tastes like scented piss to me, lover."

"Wouldn't know," he responded quietly. "Never knowingly drunk scented piss."

He had made several attempts to find out more about what had happened in Japan after the nukecaust of nearly a century earlier, as well as trying to get information about how and why they had been able to use the gateways. But each time he asked a question, Mashashige would deflect it as easily as a swordsman parrying a clumsy lunge.

"How many times have your people made jumps into Deathlands?"

The dark eyes drilled into his face. "How many leaves are there in a forest, Ryan Cawdor?" Like his second-in-command, Lord Mashashige had slight problems with his pronunciation, so Ryan's name came out more like "Lion."

While young women servants fluttered in carrying steaming-hot towels to wipe their hands and faces, Mashashige promised to answer all their questions a little later, after the meal.

"Food should not be sullied with impertinent questions. Do you not share that belief in your world?"

Ryan nodded. "Yeah. Oh, sure, yeah."

Doc was looking suspiciously at his towel, peering at it by the light of the oil lamps, sniffing.

"You do not like the idea of the cleansing, Doctor?" Hideyoshi asked.

The old man coughed, rubbing at his eyes with the back of his hand. "I have read that it was the practice of your ancestors, when they wished to remove troublesome enemies, to give them towels like this to wipe their faces in the middle of a meal. But those towels would have been rubbed first over the open sores of a leper or smeared over the running wounds of a smallpox victim. Is that not correct?"

Mashashige came as close to smiling as he had since their first meeting. "It is a refreshing change to encounter the minds of *gaijin*."

After plates of succulent flavored ices and crystallized fruits had been circulated, the Japanese baron of the ville clapped his hands. "Tea," he said.

Tea wasn't all that common in Deathlands, generally made from a dubious combination of brown herbs, often with molasses stirred in.

Ryan was on the point of refusing the offer when he caught a subtle shake of the head from Mildred, warning him to keep quiet.

Simultaneously a dozen more of the elegant young women came silently into the hall, shuffling along in tiny steps, all of them carrying either trays of handleless cups or steaming earthenware pots.

The detritus of the meal had been cleared away by other servants, and the women went to one end, all dropping into a kneeling position.

"This ceremony of the making of tea is a very ancient and honorable tradition," Mashashige said. "It goes back many hundred years before time of skydark. Our young girls learned it from their mothers."

"After we've drunk the tea," Ryan said, "can we then ask some questions?"

Mashashige bowed. "But, of course."

"And get answers?"

A hint of a thin smile flickered across the stone face. "Of course."

Watching the women begin the ritual of tea making, Ryan felt that he'd slipped through a tear in the fabric of time, traveled back to the lost heart of the Middle Ages. It didn't seem possible that they were all living at the dark end of the twenty-first century.

It appeared to be an endless ceremony.

A careful mix of gray green herbs was sprinkled into each of the white porcelain cups that were so thin that you could see light through them. Hot water at precisely the right temperature was poured into each cup and stirred furiously with a short-handled bamboo whisk. The resulting liquid was a vaporous green color, steaming gently, filling the air with a delicate scent that overlaid the ever-present harshness of pollution.

It was swirled around in the hand-painted cups by the women, then whisked again until it frothed, followed by more hot water and more whisking.

The first cup was offered by the tallest of the women, on her knees, to Mashashige, who gestured to Ryan and the others. "Serve it to our honored guests."

The servant looked directly at Krysty and then at Mildred, whispering something to the Japanese baron, who looked down the table at the women.

"Yes," he pronounced. "To every one of our honored guests. Omit nobody."

"This will be one of the most ace-on-the-line experiences of your lives," Hideyoshi boasted. "No food or drink from Deathlands is anything like this. The wonder of green tea. *O-cha,* as we call it. Try these small cakes made from bean paste. They are a perfect accompaniment."

Ryan nibbled at one of the little confections, avoiding pulling a face, although he found it unbearably sickly.

He had been watching Mashashige, noticing that the little man held the bowl in his cupped hand, bringing it to his nose and inhaling the steam with a beatific expression on his face, then sipping at it with an infinite slowness.

Ryan tried to copy him, finding the smell pleasant enough, like a herbal infusion. But when he brought the round cup to his mouth, he grimaced, finding it deeply bitter.

Jak barely touched it to his lips, pulling a face and replacing it on the table. "Sorry," he said. "Don't like."

Mildred was the only one who didn't find the *o-cha* unpleasant, smacking her lips appreciatively. "Excellent," she said. "Most refreshing."

"Only the woman enjoys it," Hideyoshi said. "What manner of barbarians they are."

"Our guests," Mashashige replied softly, but the samurai recoiled as though he'd been slapped.

He bowed so low that his forehead touched the table between the cups. "Forgive my foolish babbling tongue that ran away with my brains, Lord," he said.

"Yes." He waved to the women servants, barking a command to them in his own tongue.

They rose together from the wooden floor. Ryan watched the peculiar way they fought the restrictions of the tight, heavy kimonos. They rocked forward on their knees first, then back on their heels, then straightened upright. In a flowing, triple movement, they shuffled away in a line, carrying the remains of the tea ceremony with them.

Mashashige yawned, adjusting the angle of his sword. "Now you wish to have your questions answered. Perhaps it might be easier and short in time if I give you a . . . what is the word for a schoolmasterly talk?"

"Lecture?" Doc suggested.

"Thank you, Doctor."

"Welcome."

"A lecture. I will tell you what has happened to my country, about the discovery of the gateway and my plans for what you call Deathlands. There is much that will interest you all very greatly, I promise you."

"This going to take long?" J.B. asked. "Only my knees are getting cramped."

"Mine also," Doc said. "Forgive my standing, Lord Mashashige." He unfolded his lean body, joints cracking like firecrackers. "The repast was of fine quality, and I am indebted to you for it. Perhaps next time we might eat in Western chairs?"

The baron nodded, also standing, uncoiling with a serpentine grace. "I will do anything in my power to assist you in your request, Doctor."

"From my experience that's just a fancy way of saying no, to avoid losing face," Mildred whispered as she, too, rose from the uncomfortable kneeling position.

"We will go into one of the rooms where we can relax more, and all will be made clear to you."

Outside they heard a sudden blaring of trumpets, gongs and drums.

Mashashige turned toward the noise. "That means that my right-hand man has returned from his day's hunting."

"I thought," Ryan said, pointing to Hideyoshi, "he was your second-in-command."

"I have the honor to be in charge of all sec matters for the ville," the samurai said, adjusting his sword in its sheath. "I am number three here."

"He will join us and we will hear of his hunting success. He has been several times to your Deathlands,

though one visit brought great pain and sadness."
Mashashige paused a moment, staring at the group of
friends as though a thought were nagging at the back of
his mind. Then he shook his head and carried on. "But
he will tell you all of this himself. Now, follow me."

He strode off at great speed, never once looking
back. Hideyoshi beckoned for the others to follow
quickly, along a corridor, between paneled walls of fine
silk that showed butterflies, dragons and rural scenes
with lakes, giant carp and square-rigged ships.

They came to a large room with a fire burning at its
center, with couches all around it, covered in cushions.
In one corner a young woman sat demurely, plucking at
a long-necked stringed instrument, producing a series
of melancholy tones, dissonant to the occidental ears of
Ryan and the others.

"You are familiar with the music of the *shamisen?*"
Lord Mashashige asked as he made his way to the largest of the couches, which stood on a slightly raised dais
at the farther end of the long room.

"No," Ryan said.

"Like a sitar with most of the strings missing," Doc
commented. "Hardly appropriate for a good ceilidh or
a hoedown or a serendipity hootenanny, I think. Or
even for a bar mitzvah or a hunt ball. Oh, I hear myself rambling, and I do not care for the sound."

The two Japanese ignored him.

"Sit where you wish," the baron said, lying down
and resting his elbow on one of the pillows. "I will have
more sake brought."

Outside the room they sensed some sort of disturbance. A man's voice, hoarse, shouted loudly in Japanese, and in a flurry of movement servants ran quickly past the open doorway.

"He wishes it known that he has returned," Mashashige said, picking up an ivory fan and covering his smile with it.

"He will be surprised to see you *gaijin* here," Hideyoshi said, settling himself comfortably. "The scum from the village outside our walls will have told him of your arrival and of your looks."

The disturbance outside was increasing, with a woman screaming and a man's voice, thunderous and angry.

The door slid open so violently it was torn from its hinges, and everyone turned to look at the newcomer, the second-in-command of the ville.

"Fuck," Doc said.

Chapter Nine

At that moment of highest drama, Ryan found himself distracted for a second while he tried hard to remember the last time that Doc had used a four-letter obscenity, tried to remember whether he had *ever* heard the old man swear like that.

He decided instantly that he thought Doc had never said the word *fuck* before, but agreed privately that there was a very good and cogent reason for it right now.

The samurai who stood in the doorway was in a towering rage, his sword drawn in his right hand, eyes glaring, spittle clinging to his chin. He wasn't wearing full armor, like Toyotomi Hideyoshi, but contented himself with a light breastplate, his helmet in his left hand.

A deep scar slashed across his face disfigured him, half-closing one eye, pocking his cheek and seaming down toward his ear.

He was pointing at Ryan with the sword.

"You, *sodai gomi gaijin*. You slew my dear brother!"

Mashashige didn't seem that surprised at the interruption. Standing slowly from his couch, he hardly raised his voice. "You should not draw your *katana* in the presence of your lord, my friend, unless you fear that my life has been threatened.''

"What did he call me?" said Ryan, trying to buy a few moments that might calm the situation.

"He said that you were outlander rubbish."

"But he said that I killed his brother."

"You did." The samurai shuffled a few sideways steps across the floor toward Ryan, the point of the long sword held low. "You cannot say you have not." He hurled his helmet across the room in his rage, so that it ripped through the thin wall and vanished into the next chamber.

"This is Takei Yashimoto," said Doc, who had recovered most of his composure, though the big Le Mat had magically appeared in his fist.

"Who?" Ryan said.

"We met him and his brother close to the ruins of the old city of Washington. I believe it is better known now in Deathlands as Washington Hole, as that is all that remains."

It all flooded back to Ryan. "I killed his brother. Tokimasha was his name."

"I broke his bow with the revolver," Mildred said. "One of my better shots, though I do say so myself."

"*Kokujin* bitch!"

"The scar's down to old Betsy here," Doc said quietly, tapping the chamber of the Le Mat with his other hand. "Can see why he's in such a temper." He hesitated and bowed to Krysty and Mildred. "And I apologize for my grossly intemperate and obscene expletive, ladies. I was taken a little by surprise."

Ryan rested his hand on the butt of the SIG-Sauer, wondering whether the newcomer was about to suffer an apoplectic fit. His mouth worked uncontrollably, and his eyes stared at the six Westerners, the sword waving in the air as though he couldn't decide which of them to attack first.

"These are the ones you spoke of, moons ago, when you returned from Deathlands?" Hideyoshi asked. "The lord had said to me that he wondered if it was so."

"Honor demands their deaths," the enraged samurai spluttered, "at my hands."

"They are the guests of Lord Mashashige," responded Hideyoshi, whose hand, Ryan noticed, had dropped to the hilt of his inlaid sword.

"My guests," Mashashige stated. He was the embodiment of calm, standing by his couch, physically insignificant yet imbued with an amazing sense of power.

Gradually the newcomer regained control over himself. He licked his lips nervously as he realized how badly he had behaved in front of his lord.

"Put away the *katana*," Mashashige said, "and sit and become quiet."

"I could slay them all as easily as a butcher wringing the necks of six feeble little chickens," Yashimoto insisted. But he sheathed his sword in a whisper of steel.

"Talk's cheap," Ryan said, feeling the sudden throbbing of anger, the pulse that beat in his temple, making his own deep scar burn. "I don't like being threatened by a cheap little killer like you!" He pointed at the warrior.

"Cool it, lover," Krysty breathed.

"He speaks the truth about his brother, our dear cousin, Tokimasha Yashimoto. You did kill him, did you not, Ryan Cawdor?"

"Killed him before he killed me. We'd have killed him—" he gestured toward Takei Yashimoto "—if we'd had the chance. He got lucky. He wants to try for revenge, then him and me can step outside, across that bridge. Go into the woods for a few minutes and see who comes back."

"He insulted me to my face in front of you, Lord!" the samurai protested, his voice rising to a squeak in his reborn rage. "I demand satisfaction, Lord."

"You might ask, cousin. You might not, I think, demand. Unless there has been a change here that I did not realize. Perhaps you are now the lord and I must kneel to obey you. If that has happened, then I am sorry for not having observed it."

There was a deathly silence in the room at the stinging rebuke, so mildly administered. Ryan noticed a moon-shaped face appear for a moment in the hole in the far wall, where the samurai had thrown his helmet. The face stared at the tableau, then disappeared just as suddenly as it had appeared.

Mashashige sat again and nodded to the newcomer. "Join us, cousin. You and I will talk later of the outlanders and how the situation might most honorably be resolved. But not here and not now." He clapped his hands. "Bring us sake. Or we have *mizuwari,* if you prefer."

"What's that?" J.B. asked.

"Whiskey and water, Mr. Dix. Perhaps it would be more suitable for your palate."

There was general agreement among the six friends that it would indeed be a great deal more acceptable to them than the lukewarm sake.

Another line of shuffling maidens in their constricting kimonos brought in the amber liquid, using silver trays and cut-crystal goblets.

Doc sniffed at his drink, tasting it and beaming. "This is more than passingly delicious. I swear that it reminds me of the very best liquor from bonny Scotland that I drank as a young man in Iron Mary's tavern in Boston."

"It was made five miles from here, by the sea, in the distillery," Hideyoshi said, getting his tongue in a tangle over the last word.

Mashashige nodded. "The price we pay is the fumes when the wind is northerly."

"That the only thing that pollutes?" Mildred asked.

"Sadly not. After the disasters that destroyed our land, as much of your country was laid waste, we have had to use what resources we can. The old skills have been lost, and iron-making and food processing is not...efficient? That is the word? There is much smell and waste. And women give birth to monsters."

"Can't it be stopped?"

"The wheel has rolled too far."

"Crap. That's a poor excuse for not bothering to try to make things better."

"Many would die if our poor industry was stopped." The shogun Mashashige seemed to have totally forgotten that he was arguing in his own fortress with a poor, weak woman. A *gaijin* woman.

"Many are dying as it is. I'm a doctor... Well, I was a doctor, but that's a long story. I can taste the toxins in the air—Sulfur, carbon dioxide, hydrogen sulfide and something bitter that could be aluminum or zinc. There're garbage heaps everywhere you look, and trees blighted with acid rain. I'm amazed that more of you aren't dead. What's the life expectancy? Not here in the ville, but outside, by your factories?"

Lord Mashashige, for the first time, was caught off-balance. "We have nothing to do with such people. But I think a man might hope to live to thirty. A woman, with all the children she must bear, a few years less."

Mildred put down her glass, making a disgusted sound. "How can...? You seem intelligent and you can sit there calmly and talk about such a dreadful situation."

"We have lost the skills. Once the day of the dark sky came to Japan, it was the beginning of the end."

"No excuse for poisoning everyone."

"There were stories from sailors that much of the land was totally destroyed and sank beneath the sea," Doc said. "Is that true?"

"Sadly, alas, yes. We had become deeply dependent on the silent power of the nukes. In the last years before the cruel winters began, we had become closer to the United States. That is why we speak your tongue. It had become a second tongue. A first tongue for business and men of power."

"California turned into the Western Islands when there was a chain reaction among reactors that triggered off the big quake fault lines," Krysty said.

Mashashige turned to face her, showing a keen interest. "It was the same with us. A 'chain reaction.' I did not know the saying, but I understand it. Like knocking over a series of mah-jongg tiles. The reactors at Mihama and Takahama triggered the chain reaction. There were eruptions and quakes and all Hokkaido vanished, followed by the smaller islands of Kyushu and Shikoku. A day later, so that story goes, there was a gigantic explosion from honored Mount Fuji. The whole of northern Honshu, which was much the biggest part of Japan, vanished in an instant."

"And tidal waves?" Jak asked.

"Oh, yes. Tsunamis, legend tells us, were a thousand feet high and swept across the steaming ruins of our land. It was narrow by the cities of Osaka and Kyoto, by the lake called Biwa ko. There it split and sank. Much of the coast of what remained was washed away, including the last big city, Hiroshima."

"You would know that name, *gaijin,*" Yashimoto barked, "too well."

Mashashige ignored his interruption. "All that remains of Japan now is an island, very mountainous and steep, less than one hundred and fifty miles long. And no more than seventy miles from north to south. I have the very great honor to be the chief shogun in this island."

Doc whistled. "That is astounding. Of course, Deathlands is a great deal smaller than the old United States was, but to nothing like that extent."

Mashashige gestured, and a girl slid forward on her knees to replenish his glass of whiskey and water. "The tragedy for us is that our population is still increasing.

"With such a low life expectancy!" J.B. exclaimed. "How come?"

"I would not speak of this before women," the lord said. "But nothing is done to stop more babies. Many die, but there are still more and more. We outgrow our space."

Hideyoshi suddenly said something in Japanese, as though he were warning Mashashige, who nodded.

"How did you find the gateway?" Ryan asked. "Been hearing stories of gangs of your people being seen in Deathlands for some months now."

Mashashige looked away for a moment, and Ryan had the sudden impression that the leader of the samurai was about to lie to him, though he couldn't have said precisely what it was that made him feel that.

"We rarely use it now. It was found by accident in the house that had once belonged to the Americans before the day of the dark sky. There was no code on how to use it, except for the number code that would bring a jumper back here."

"Did you send out raiding parties into Deathlands?" J.B. asked.

Once again there was a momentary hesitation from the warlord. "Not raiding, Mr. Dix. To explore. To see if we could learn anything from you people. Discover some way of solving our own problems."

"No success?" Ryan asked.

Hideyoshi replied, "We have a saying, *'kiken, kitsui and kitanai.'*"

"Which means what?"

"Which means that the missions were dangerous, difficult and dirty."

"And cost in lives," muttered Yashimoto. His face was flushed, and he seemed unsteady as he lolled on the couch, constantly fingering the hilt of his sword.

Mashashige this time acknowledged the comment of his second-in-command. "Yes, it has been costly in lives. There are only a dozen men of birth and honor here in my palace. And we have lost four... no, five, in the last months during jumps. Drowned, shot, stabbed, burned... Deathlands is truly a dreadful place to be inhabited."

Ryan looked around him. Though there were no windows opening from the large room onto the outside of the building, he had the feeling that the day was wearing on and that evening wasn't that far away.

Mashashige caught the restless movement. "You would like to go to your rooms and share a bath and rest?"

"Sounds good. Thanks." Ryan stood and turned toward Yashimoto. "I'm sorry about your brother getting chilled," he said. "But it was him or me. You were there. You know how it all went down."

But the samurai ignored him, studiously concentrating his attention on the pretty little girl who was serving him yet more sake.

Everyone other than the second-in-command now stood.

"I believe that you and the red-haired woman are partners together, Ryan Cawdor. Likewise, you, Mr. Dix, with the black woman who was once a doctor. Will two double rooms and one room with two single tatami—sleeping mats—be sufficient for you?"

"Sure. Can they be side by side?"

"Yes." He bowed to them.

"I will arrange for servants to show them to the visitors' chambers, Lord," Hideyoshi said.

"Anything that you require can be arranged. If the snow-haired, red-eyed youth or the old grandfather want company, I will send a pair of geisha each."

Jak was puzzled, but Doc replied for them both. "We prefer to arrange our own female company when we want it, but our thanks anyway."

The audience with the shogun was over.

Chapter Ten

The bath was like a traditional American hot tub, circular, above the ground, made from seasoned redwood and about twelve feet in diameter, with a bench seat running around the inside. There were three tubs, one for each of the double chambers and one for the room that had the single woven mats laid on the polished floor.

Ryan couldn't believe the speed and efficiency of the servants. It seemed that only a couple of minutes had passed since they left the presence of Lord Mashashige, yet the three tubs were already three-quarters filled with steaming water, carrying the delicate scent of balsam. And a pile of fluffy towels waited on a low bench seat.

Several women remained behind in each room. They weren't the pretty, painted girls in kimonos. These were of sturdier, peasant stock, wearing a looser cotton kimono of crimson and white.

Ryan and Krysty stood together and waited for the three women in their room to leave.

But nobody moved.

"What are they waiting for?" Ryan asked.

"A tip?"

"Guess not."

"Mebbe they want to take out dirty clothes and launder them for us, lover."

"Mebbe they want to scrub my back."

Krysty smiled, then shook her head. "Gaia! I think you've stepped in it, Ryan."

"What?"

"That's what they're waiting for. They're here to wash us, if we want it."

"We don't."

Krysty clapped her hands and made shooing gestures at the women, who stood their ground, blank faced. "Shove off. Go away. Vamoose. Vanish. Leave us alone."

Ryan laughed. "Like a farmer's wife trying to get some stubborn turkeys out of the corn."

"You do any better?"

"Sure." He walked to the nearest of the servants, who was also the oldest, her face wrinkled like a wintered apple. Ryan towered over her, and he could see something close to fear in her narrow, hooded eyes.

"Time you go, mama-san," he said, taking her gently by the arm and steering her toward the door of their room.

"Mama-san?" Krysty repeated. "Where in the big fire did you dig that one up?"

"Trader had some old war vids, and every now and again we'd find a machine that worked and we'd watch them. One was about the war in the Cific. Against the Japanese, as it happened." He reached the sliding panel and pulled it open with his left hand. "Out you go, mama-san,'' he said, pushing her gently outside into the passage.

"Big jerk," she said in a high-pitched voice, doubling herself over in a low bow like a folding doll so that her gray head nearly touched the floor.

"That's telling him, sister," Krysty said, giggling. "You sure have a way with a girl, lover."

Ryan turned to the other two women, advancing with hands outstretched. They both burst into fits of fluting laughter, pulling their aprons over their heads, pattering past him, one on either side, while he pretended to grab at them. They joined their older colleague in the door, where they all stood bobbing up and down, bowing to Ryan and Krysty.

"Thanks, but, no thanks," Krysty said, walking over and sliding the door panel across, shutting out the trio of servants. She waited a few moments. "Think they're still there?" she whispered. "Bet they are."

"Don't look, lover. Don't even think about looking. Let's get on with this bath."

It took them only moments to strip out of their trail-dirty clothes, leaving them in a pile by the sleeping mats. Ryan unholstered the SIG-Sauer and placed it by the side of the big tub. Krysty, still wearing her silk bikini panties, put her 640 Smith & Wesson beside it.

"Watch out for splinters, lover," she said, grinning as Ryan swung a long leg over the wooden wall and stepped cautiously into the scented water.

"Hot," he said.

"Funny. I thought that all the steam meant that it was going to be freezing cold."

"Yeah. Lotta laughs, Krysty." He slowly lowered himself to sit on the seat that ran just below the surface. "Hey, it's real good."

She slipped off her panties and joined him, gasping at the heat of the water.

"Not bad, huh?"

Krysty nodded, smiling, her vivid red hair slowly uncoiling across her shoulders as she quickly began to relax. "Not bad."

Ryan closed his eye and leaned back against the smooth, polished wood, feeling the tension ease away. It didn't seem as if they were in any danger at the heart of the fortress, as long as they had the protection of Mashashige. Just as long as his word could be trusted.

Where trust was concerned, Ryan's feeling ran with those of the Trader.

"Trust is something that you don't ever share with anyone else."

"What did you say, lover?"

"Nothing. Didn't even realize that I'd spoken out loud. Must be getting Alzie's sickness."

"Want me to scrub your back for you? There's soap on that little shelf at the side."

Ryan sniffed. "Guess so. This is nice. Haven't felt as clean as this since I don't remember when."

Krysty had slid across the tub to get the soap, her superb body glistening like a leaping salmon, agile and muscular. She came back and sat close to him.

He closed his eye again, feeling the warm suds, scented with musk, across his shoulders, her firm hands rubbing heat into the muscles, trying to avoid the criss-crossing scars that patterned his skin.

"I reckon that I could get to like Japan," he muttered. Her hands were busily soaping his chest, then lower across the flat wall of his belly.

Lower.

"Hey! Thought you said you were just going to wash my back."

"I didn't know something was going to come up," she replied, grasping him tight.

"I didn't know it was coming up, either." He leaned sideways and kissed her hard on the mouth, his tongue slipping between her parted lips.

"It's come a long way up, lover. Look. Even come peeking out of the water."

He reached out with his right hand and caressed her breasts, finger and thumb sliding from the slippery, peaked nipples, making her sigh out loud.

"Nice."

Ryan lowered his head to suck at them, tasting the musk in the soap, like an exotic perfume, while her right hand was working on him, just below the surface.

"Seems a shame to waste this," she whispered, glancing at the door. "Wish it had a lock on it."

Krysty stood and faced him, spreading her thighs and lowering herself onto him, guiding him inside with her right hand, mouth open, emerald eyes almost closed.

"Yes," she breathed.

THEY LAY SIDE BY SIDE in the quietness of the room.

Ryan had pulled on his shirt and pants, while Krysty

was almost fully dressed. There had been a certain amount of muffled noise from the room next door, where J.B. and Mildred sounded as though they, too, were having a good time and also getting clean. But the giggling had quietened over the past quarter-hour or so.

IN THE THIRD ROOM, next along the silent corridor, Doc and Jak had found it difficult to persuade the servants to leave them to get on with their baths. In the end Jak had tugged at his hair and rolled his ruby eyes at them, dropping into a simian crouch and sidling at them, knuckles trailing the floor as he poked out his long tongue.

"Well acted, young fellow," Doc applauded, ruffling the teenager's hair. "A triumph for the white plume of Navarre, is it not?"

"Is it, Doc. What's that mean?"

"It is a heraldic reference, dear lad. But too complicated for my poor foozled brain to explain to you. Let us utilize this steaming tub. Do you wish to go first?"

"Plenty of room for both, Doc."

The old man almost blushed. "I can see that, Master Lauren. But my generation was not all that used to bathing in public."

"Public? You and me?"

Doc grinned, showing his full set of amazingly perfect teeth. "I suppose that I lay myself open to the charge of becoming prudish in my dotage."

"What's prudish?"

"Not wanting to take my clothes off in front of another member of the same sex. Prudish. But not rudish or crudish. But rather nudish."

Jak was already peeling his way out of his clothes, shirt and vest dropping with a thunk due to the weight of the concealed knives. His heavy .357 Magnum pistol clattered onto the wooden floor.

"Lewdish?" Doc mumbled. "Foolish? Ghoulish? Aye, most certainly ghoulish."

There was a splash and he turned to see Jak's face, framed with wet white hair, peeking at him through the wreathing steam. "Come on, Doc. Water's fine."

"WHERE EXACTLY ARE WE in the fortress?" Krysty asked. "We went up and down so many stairs and passages that even my sense of direction got messed up."

"I think we're somewhere close to the back wall. If there was a window in that wall there, I reckon we might find ourselves looking out over the moat. Feels solid, so it's probably one of the outer fortifications."

"One of the strongest villes we've ever seen." She folded her arms behind her head and stared up at the ceiling. "Feel fairly safe for once."

"Not all that safe when there's Takei Yashimoto breathing fire and vengeance all over the place. Put us all to the sword if it wasn't for Mashashige."

"Least I can't see him being toppled."

Ryan ran his fingers through his thick curly hair, seeing if it was drying. "Not so sure. He could resist an army, unless they got heavy armor and grens, but he's got so many soldiers and servants it must be impossible to keep track of who they are. If I wanted to get at him—chill him—that's the way I'd do it. Small number of determined men.''

"You know best, lover. How long do you want to stay here? Couple of days?''

"Not too long. You don't share a house with an enemy. But I find it all fascinating." He coughed. "All apart from the dreadful pollution of the air. Makes my eye smart and my throat hurt. Guess the slant-eyes are used to it.''

"Don't let Mildred hear you use that expression. Not what she calls 'politically correct,' is it?''

"They insult us. Fireblast! Why shouldn't I insult them a little?''

Krysty laughed, but it turned into a coughing fit. "Is there any drinking water around, lover?''

"Probably poisoned with mercury or comes from some raving rad hot spot.''

He got up and padded around the room, but there was nothing to drink.

"Could you go and try get us some?'' she asked.

"Sure. Just strap on the blaster and the panga, and I'm off and running.''

"You need them?''

He shrugged. "Time you think you feel safest is the time of most danger.''

"Another Traderism?''

"No. A Ryanism." He laughed. "But I'm sure that Trader would have agreed with it.''

WITH THE REASSURING weight of his two weapons on the hips, Ryan slid the panel across and peered out into the corridor. A series of small pottery oil lamps burned brightly at intervals along the passage. He was a little surprised to find that there were no servants in sight. The palace of Mashashige was so overpopulated that it seemed odd to find a section deserted.

The short hairs began to prickle at the back of Ryan's neck, and his hand fell to the butt of his automatic. There was something wrong.

"Stay here and get hold of your blaster," he whispered. "Try and warn the others."

"What is it?"

"Don't know. Just a bad feeling. Wait here."

He didn't stop to hear any argument. He slid the panel behind him, though it wouldn't protect Krysty from an attack by an enraged mouse.

It was quiet.

Too quiet.

The SIG-Sauer was in his hand, probing at the air in front of him like the tongue of a viper.

He sniffed at the air, his forehead wrinkling as he tried to separate the alien mix of smells: the bitter, acrid flavor of the industrial pollution, the scent of flowers and the musk of the oils in the hot bath.

And something else.

It was a smell that few of the soft and effete people who lived in predark days would have recognized: fresh-spilled human blood.

Ryan considered going back for J.B., Jak and the others, but he was there, outside the rooms, on his own.

The taste of blood, hot and salty on his tongue, grew stronger as he moved a few steps toward the main part of the house.

He paused at the corner and squinted around it, every nerve combat ready, every fighting reflex on the hollow-ground razor's edge.

Two corpses lay sprawled in the casual untidiness that screamed death, the stillness that was like no other stillness in the world. Both of them were women, lying huddled together, both on their backs, the cotton shifts ridden up over their knees, showing the neat little clogs on their feet.

Both had their throats slit from ear to ear, savage cuts that had almost decapitated the servants, exposing the whiteness of splintered spinal bone. The blood was still oozing, not yet congealing, the surest sign that the murders had taken place within the past two or three minutes.

Meaning that the butcher was close by.

Ryan stepped around the corpses, careful to avoid the spreading lake of crimson, pausing to look and listen. It was almost certain that there were outside killers in the fortress.

A dead manservant lay half in a doorway a little farther around the next section of the passage, his fists clenched as though the moment of death had caught him in helpless anger.

His red-and-white cotton uniform was so sodden with blood that Ryan couldn't see at first how the man had died. Then he saw that the material was torn across the chest. The one-eyed man stooped and rolled him over, seeing a similar cut below the left shoulder blade, slightly wider. It was the entrance wound of a long, edged weapon.

Like a samurai sword.

The man's narrow eyes were open wide, as though his passing had been a matter of considerable surprise to him. Whoever was doing the chilling was good at his trade—or "their" trade, if there was more than one of them.

Somehow Ryan had the feel of a lone assassin, a single, solitary figure creeping about in the dark recesses of the fortress, perhaps wearing samurai armor, so that anyone hapless enough to meet him would take him—for those vital, fatal seconds—for a member of Mashashige's retinue.

The fourth body was a child, no more than eight years old, his little body thrown into a corner, also run clean through with a sword.

Blood still flowed, and Ryan knew that he was closing with the killer.

The walls on either side of him were oiled, silken paper, hung on bamboo slats.

The sword cut through the wall from Ryan's right and knocked the blaster from his hand in a fearsome, jarring blow.

Chapter Eleven

The attack wasn't unexpected, but it was so swift and violent that for several racing heartbeats, Ryan wasn't certain precisely what had happened. For a split second he even thought that the hacking sword had actually cut through his arm, somewhere above the wrist, and that his hand lay on the floor, still gripping the butt of the fallen SIG-Sauer.

There had been a sharp, jarring blow, the pain running to his shoulder. It had been hard enough to knock him off-balance, sending him staggering to his left, away from the plunging, whirling attack.

The man had broken easily through the flimsy wall panel, following the lead of his long blade, emerging in a crouch just ahead of Ryan.

He was short and stocky, and dressed entirely in black. A round skullcap of metal protected his head, with cheek plates on either side. A loose scarf of black silk was wrapped around his face, revealing only the eyes, which were dark, glittering and totally blank. They stared fixedly at Ryan.

The man wore some kind of light body armor below a shirt of black satin, the metal gleaming in the glow of the oil lamps. He held the sword pointed downward and stood stock-still, watching the white man.

Ryan guessed that the assassin hadn't expected to find an Occidental in the fortress and was trying to work out how best to cope with the discovery. But there was the remote possibility that this man was a follower of Takei Yashimoto and had been sent by the vengeful samurai to murder his enemies.

For a few moments the two men stood frozen, a dozen feet apart. Ryan had been working the fingers of his right hand, removing the stiffness caused by the blow to the automatic, which now lay in the corner of the passage, way beyond his reach.

"My fight is not with you, *gaijin,*" the voice whispered. "Still time go back your room. Close eyes and memory. Not your fight."

"Man nearly takes my arm off turns it into my fight. Man who slaughters unarmed women and children turns it into my fight," Ryan stated, drawing the panga.

There was a whisper of breath in the silence that could have been a laugh. "You use your clumsy great knife against my *katana*. I will cut you in half, stupid *gaijin.*"

"Talk comes cheap. Not like stabbing a little boy. Not so bastard easy."

The man still held off from the attack, unable to restrain his boasting.

"My sword is the sharpest in the world. When it was made it was laid in a flowing river. A feather was put in river and floated over edge and was cut in half."

Ryan was content to let the warrior talk. The longer he kept him there, the better the chance of help arriving. The idea of tackling the swordsman with his eighteen-inch panga wasn't one that Ryan relished.

"I can cut locust in half and half again, in middle of flight. Cut human hair in half and half and half more. Cut helmet in two pieces. Fight an army on own. Defeat greatest samurai ever born. Behead a dragon in air." He was shuffling forward an inch at a time, his eyes never leaving Ryan's face.

The great palace of Mashashige was still and silent. There was just the sound of the two men breathing.

From the way the man held the sword, it was obvious to Ryan that at some point he would have to heft it shoulder high to make the downward cut that the weight and shape of the blade dictated. And that would be the chance. He had little doubt that the samurai would be a skillful swordsman, able to use the much longer weapon against the shorter panga.

"If you have gods, *gaijin,* now is time to pray to them. Your poor blood dishonors my steel."

The men were a scant five feet apart.

Ryan's breathing was slow and steady, controlled, since he knew that the moment was close.

He concentrated on the tip of the slightly curved blade, watching for it to move.

Now.

The instant it started to lift, Ryan dived in, using the panga like a heavy cutlass, jabbing with the needle point at the samurai, who had begun a half step backward to give himself more room for the devastating downward slash. Committed to swinging the sword upward, there was no time to parry the unexpected attack from the one-eyed *gaijin*.

Ryan had deliberately aimed low, knowing that it would be more difficult to deflect his thrust. He aimed at the man's upper thigh, guessing that he wasn't likely to be wearing armor there, though his whole chest and stomach were protected.

He felt the impact run up his arm as the point drove deep through the muscles, grating on the femur. He twisted the hilt as he withdrew it, causing a massive wound in the warrior's thigh, though he just missed the big femoral artery, which would have made it into a killing blow.

The man cried out, choking off the yell, trying to back away from Ryan, stumbling clumsily, blood pouring down his leg onto the wooden floor.

He still held the sword at shoulder height, but it was suddenly a defensive weapon, as he tried to protect himself from the swift, remorseless advance of the one-eyed man.

Now the advantage lay with Ryan, up against a frightened cripple.

He moved from side to side, changing the panga from hand to hand, feinting with an empty fist, making the warrior try to parry the specious lunge.

Ryan taunted him in his distress and obvious stammering fear. "Not like chilling helpless women and children, is it, you murderin' bastard?"

The man was sweating, the perspiration soaking through the dark scarf around his nose and mouth, trying to make his way down the empty corridor, anywhere to try to get away from Ryan. Blood puddled the floor at his feet, and the one-eyed man was careful not to step into it and slip.

"Goin' to bleed to death, like a stuck pig, aren't you?"

"This is not with honor!" his enemy panted. "This is not to be done."

"Wrong, friend. It's going to be done, right to the bitter end."

Ryan saw his chance and feinted again, aiming toward the man's knees. As the samurai dropped the sword edge to counter the attack, Ryan switched the panga to his left hand and cut high instead.

The blow aimed at the angle between the neck and the left shoulder, where he could see an exposed strip of flesh below the helmet and above the armored breastplate.

He turned his wrist to use the last few inches of the blade rather than the needled point, feeling it bite home. The keen steel sliced through skin, flesh and muscle, opening a deep gash that spouted more blood.

This time he didn't step back from the attack. Now that he was in close, it was the moment to finish the job. He brought his knee up into the helpless man's groin, moving to one side as the long sword clattered to the floor, the warrior doubling over like a loving courtier. The round helmet fell off and spun to join the sword, exposing the back of the head, with a ribboned topknot of black hair.

The final blow from the panga drove downward, the hilt clutched in both hands, the point hitting the doomed man at the top of the spine, where neck became skull.

Ryan winced at the crunching sound of splintered bone. The samurai jerked backward, eyes turned up to the ceiling, the neural reaction pinching the blade between the crushed vertebrae, so that Ryan lost his grip on it.

Without missing a beat, he dodged the staggering, flailing figure, darting in and picking up the SIG-Sauer, steadying it on the dying warrior.

The panga was jerked from side to side, as though it were some sort of bizarre addition to the armor. The man was moaning, a long, single keening note, held far beyond what seemed humanly possible. But it was amazingly quiet. Considering he had two devastating wounds in thigh and neck, as well as having been kicked in the balls and the coup de grace to the cervical vertebrae, it was astounding that he wasn't screaming loud enough to bring down the paper-thin internal walls of the fortress.

Ryan watched him with an incurious gaze, knowing that death was only a matter of time.

The spinal cord was severed and crushed, and the messages from brain to limbs couldn't go on much longer.

There was a long sigh of breath, then the samurai was down on the blood-slick floor, his arms and legs kicking out like a brain-shot horse.

Ryan holstered the blaster and waited his moment to retrieve the eighteen-inch panga.

He glanced behind him, wondering whether J.B., Jak or any of the others might have followed him. He was pleased to see that their good combat sense had prevailed, and they were all staying together where they were, in the slightly more secure defensive position of their rooms.

The body was still, lying finally on its back, head jammed at an awkward angle by the protruding panga, the eyes staring blankly up at nothing.

Ryan stooped and rolled the corpse, pulling a face as he got gouts of thick blood on his hands. He tried to tug the panga free, but found it still gripped tight between the shards of bone, in the last mortal spasm. He set his foot between the dead man's shoulders and gripped the hilt with both hands, pulling it free with a loud sucking sound.

He stood looking at the blood-smeared blade, wondering if there was enough unsullied cloth on the corpse for him to be able to wipe it clean, when he heard the unmistakable sound of a pistol being cocked, close behind him.

"The only possible ending to this filthy murder is death, Ryan Cawdor."

The voice belonged to Mashashige, but when Ryan turned slowly, he saw that the New Nambu 9 mm blaster was steady in the hand of Toyotomi Hideyoshi.

The baron of the ville was still wearing the loose black cotton robe, the sword tucked casually into the sash. He was barefoot, and stood quite still and looked at Ryan, at the crimsoned steel in his hand and the butchered corpse at his feet.

Hideyoshi also wore a cotton robe, of crimson and white, with an embroidered heron across the shoulders. And like his master, he carried his sword in a sash. The corner of his mouth was curled into a cynical sneer.

"Our brother, Yashimoto, was in order in his proper anger against you, Ryan Cawdor," said the sec boss and third-in-command of the ville.

"Want to look a little farther back along the corridor?" Ryan asked.

"What would we see?" Mashashige asked softly. "More of our people thrown into death by you?"

Ryan shook his head. "You'll find at least four corpses down there. A man and two women and a little boy. All killed with a sword."

"Or with your clumsy dagger," Mashashige said. "How will we know?"

"By looking." The old familiar anger was bubbling just below the surface, partly fueled by the surplus adrenaline that raced through Ryan's veins after the mortal combat. "You can tell the difference between a narrow sword entrance wound and the kind of wound that this leaves." He flourished the panga in the shogun's face.

"To threaten Lord Mashashige is to entertain a quick bullet in the head, *gaijin,*" Hideyoshi warned. "It would please me to do this."

"Stupe bastards!" Ryan poked the body with his foot. "Just who the fuck do you think this is? Why don't you take a look at him? Not too hard, is it?"

Mashashige gestured to his number three. "Do as he says."

"Back away from me," Hideyoshi ordered, threatening Ryan with the Nambu pistol.

"He isn't dressed like any of your men," Ryan snarled. "Even I can see that."

"It is true, Lord," Hideyoshi said, stooping and keeping an eye on Ryan. He reached down and heaved the body over, grimacing as he got blood on his fingers. The corpse rolled limply onto its back, showing the dead face and dark, empty eyes.

"Ah," Mashashige said. Ryan had been watching him, and he spotted the glimmer of recognition and surprise on the warlord's face as he saw the assassin for the first time.

"Ronin," he said, sighing.

"Who's Ronin?" Ryan asked.

"'Ronin' is the name for a lordless samurai. A warrior, often a part of a gang, who owe no loyalty to any shogun. They are...renegades. Is that the correct word?"

Ryan nodded. "Yeah. Renegades, Wolfsheads, they're sometimes called in Deathlands."

"I think I recognize him, Lord," Hideyoshi said. "Is he not Morei Takarana? He was once in your lordship's service and left some years back, after trouble with one of the young serving boys from the kitchens."

Mashashige nodded slowly. "I think you are not wrong. This is unfortunate."

Ryan snorted in anger. "That the best you can say! I told you there's at least four corpses just along the corridor, and this man was responsible for them all. Could be more hidden around. Four's all I saw."

"They will be removed." Mashashige suddenly bowed very low in Ryan's direction, a gesture mirrored almost instantaneously by his sec boss. "We must offer our sincere apologies to you, Ryan Cawdor, for not believing you. It was not honorable of us to behave in that manner. You are our guest."

Ryan shrugged, stooping and wiping the blood off the steel. "Happens. If I was you, I'd be a sight more worried about how this man got into your place. And I'd be making a quick check to ensure there aren't any more around."

Hideyoshi nodded, looking at his master. "I will rouse the guards and scour out the walls."

"Fine," Ryan said. "And I'm going back to bed. Good night, all." He turned on his heel and walked away to rejoin the others and tell them what had happened.

Chapter Twelve

Takei Yashimoto greeted them the next morning in high spirits.

"One dead ronin and one fluttering its wings in the cage of Lord Mashashige," he crowed. "And all from the help of the knife-using *gaijin*."

"You mean there's a prisoner, as well?" said Ryan, who had been helping himself from a breakfast buffet set out in the dining hall. To his and the others' relief, their hosts had laid on a Western-style meal—or an approximation of what they regarded as being a Western-style meal.

The scrambled eggs were awash with vinegar, and the bacon had been pickled first. There were balls of rice and surprisingly good hash browns, along with some spiced sausage links and about four different types of fish.

Doc tried something that looked like smoked trout and spit it out on his plate, exclaiming in disgust, "I most strongly urge you, friends, not to essay any of the fish. It is a dire mix of fins, scales, bones and purest mercury. It grates with the fillings in my teeth most alarmingly."

Yashimoto was standing near Ryan. "You pick at what you eat. You know the labor and the cost of growing and harvesting this food? The price is high, *gaijin*."

"Not our problem," Jak said, pushing past the samurai to get at some sort of fine-ground rice with soya milk and a rich plum sauce.

"Tell us about the prisoner," J.B. said. "He do any chilling?"

Yashimoto shook his head, beaming at them, a stray spear of sunlight coming through the slats in the bamboo blinds and glowing across the scar on his face. "We found where the first man broke in. Perhaps there was help from within. A rope hung down into the water, and a small round boat was there made from skins, painted black. Toyotomi Hideyoshi went with three other samurai across the bridge and made a circle around and about the fortress. Through the trees. There they caught another such man. Now he waits to die."

Krysty approached the buffet to take a second helping of the rich soup called miso, which had bean curd and dried seaweed floating in it. She and Mildred had both picked it for its high nutritional value.

"He going to be executed?" she asked.

The samurai looked past her, his eyes watching dust motes in the morning sunlight. For a moment it looked as if he were going to totally ignore the woman.

"No," he finally said. "He will choose to take his own life. That way he saves his family honor from shame."

"Hara-kiri," Mildred said. "Going to chill himself with a sword?"

The warrior's face showed a passing pang of disgust. "No, foolish grandmother. Hara-kiri is vulgar and common, to be used by peasants and people of low class, outlanders and stupid old women."

"So what's the right way to describe spilling your guts on the floor?" Mildred snapped.

"Seppuku. Done not with sword but with a knife, called *wakizashi*. Followed by beheading by a friend. This conclusion is called *kaishaku*. It is a very, very honorable ceremony."

"Include us out," Ryan said.

But the second-in-command of the fortress shook his head, grinning like an ape on jolt. "That is not allowed to be possible, Cawdor-san."

"How's that?"

Yashimoto pointed a finger at him, like an angry schoolmaster. "You are all guests of honor of Lord Mashashige. He would wish all men who are honorable guests to come and show witness at the dying."

"Only men?" Krysty asked.

"Of course!"

"Well, just this once I'll go along with your male chauvinism without a protest."

"Seconded," Mildred said. "Very high on the list of things that I don't want to see."

Ryan shook his head, pouring some fresh orange juice. "I don't think any of us want to come."

He turned to Yashimoto. "Can you just give our excuses to Mashashige?"

Doc nodded. "Correct, Ryan. Tell your master that we plead a subsequent engagement."

The samurai looked puzzled. "You do not comprehend. Not a matter of choosing for you. Lord Mashashige invites, and you must all come. All four of you. It will happen as soon as the sun reaches the highest point in its journey across the celestial heavens before it begins to sink once more toward its resting in the far skies of the west."

"Noon," Ryan said.

DURING THE MORNING Doc asked for and obtained a set of mah-jongg tiles, offering to teach the others how to play that most subtle of games.

Ryan, Krysty and Mildred finally agreed to give it a go, sitting at a green-baize-covered table in a room with slitted windows along its northern flank. A trio of young geisha came in and watched, giggling immoderately at the attempts of the *gaijin* to master the complexities of the game.

After a while one of them got bored and went to sit with Jak, who was flipping idly through a pile of predark magazines, each one wrapped in clear plastic to protect its brittle rarity.

"I thought that mah-jongg was a Chinese game, Doc," Mildred said as the old man opened a beautiful inlaid box of rosewood, with patterns of mother-of-pearl on its lid. He revealed the rows of ivory-and-bamboo tiles, all of them delicately engraved with stylized designs.

"It was originally, but it spread all across the East and then to many other countries."

"Hope it's easy to learn, Doc," Ryan said. "Took me long enough to master five-card draw."

It took all of his mental powers to follow Doc's instructions. The old-timer's mind was never known for its crystal clarity, and explaining convoluted rules didn't find him at his very best.

"Now, when you have a pung of red dragons and a pair of each of the winds, then... No, I believe that the hand called Gates of Heaven is also...or is that the Wriggling Snake?"

"I've got a kong of circles, characters and bamboos, Doc," Krysty said. "Now, if I get one of each of the dragons plus a pair, is that hand called Dragonfly?"

"Yes, my dear young lady, it is. Excellent. We make progress here."

"Triple Knitting is half-limit and the Heavenly Twins are full-limit?" Mildred looked at Doc. "That right?"

"No! It most certainly is not correct." With a scant heartbeat's hesitation, he said, "Yes, it is correct. Yes, it certainly is."

"Is the Three Scholars better than the Four Blessings, Doc?" Ryan asked, puzzled.

"No. But in the Four Blessings you must beware of konging the winds."

Mildred and Krysty exchanged glances and both of them started laughing.

"One thing, Doc," Krysty spluttered, "mah-jongg sure takes your mind off any other worries."

J.B. had also been reading some of the predark periodicals, vanishing into his own world when he discovered that several of them were blaster mags.

"Interesting bit on Baby Brownings," he said, looking up at the burst of laughter. "And some superb pix of the Rossi snub-nosed revolvers."

Jak glanced across. "Pix here of famine in China. And Russkies testing bombs in Tibet. Also big issue about taking chunks national parks to build redoubts. Folks then said was raping land. And war would never happen."

"War always happen," said the young geisha who was sitting so close to Jak that she was almost in his lap, her almond eyes staring into his ruby eyes.

Ryan stood, checking his wrist chron. "You're not wrong there, miss. Ten to twelve. Best get ready to go and watch this chilling."

"But we have scarcely scratched the surface as far as the mah-jongg is concerned." Doc looked down at the scattered tiles, like spilled shards of bright porcelain, brilliant against the dull green baize.

"We can play two-handed, can't we, Doc?" Mildred asked. "While you and the others are...away for a while."

Jak stood, patting the young Japanese woman on the shoulder. "Got to go watch man rip guts out," he said.

He turned to Krysty and Mildred. "Why not play that game with Issie here? She says she knows how."

The geisha lowered herself into a submissive bow, eyes staring at the floor, shoulders hunched, hands together. Her voice suddenly rose a shrill octave. "If it would not give offence," she said. "Be glad to help."

"Fine," Krysty said. "And if one of your friends wants to make up the four?"

At that moment the lacquered silk panel slid silently back, and Toyotomi Hideyoshi stood in the doorway, in full ceremonial clothing, his dazzling robe of silk showing a snow-topped mountain with white herons flying low over the summit. He bowed to the room in general.

"Lord Mashashige wishes to welcome his honored guests from the realm of Deathlands to witness the honorable passing of the attacker of the night."

Ryan nodded to the samurai. "We wish to make it clear that we are only attending this killing because we have to. All of us would rather stay away. Your rituals of death are nothing to do with any of us."

"I note carefully in my mind what it is that you say. Now, follow me."

The whole building seemed to be in a state of high excitement as they followed the strutting figure along interminable twists and turns of corridors, up and down stairs, all designed to make an invader lose his way.

Servants popped out of doorways, some dropping to their knees as the outlanders passed by, lowering their bodies until their foreheads brushed the spotless floors.

"Quickly," Hideyoshi said. "The lord must not be kept waiting."

"Then you should have called for us a few minutes earlier," Doc stated crossly. "There should be respect due to my gray hairs."

"Respect is earned solely by rank, position and by honor. The finest house is not always that with snow upon the roof, Dr. Tanner."

HIDEYOSHI LED THEM eventually into a room that they hadn't seen before. From the magnificence of the wood carvings and the decorations, this was obviously the ceremonial hub of the entire building.

It was a hall, fully a hundred feet long and fifty feet wide, with a vaulted roof that soared above them.

The first thing that Ryan noticed was a large rectangle of pure white cotton, set perfectly in the center of the room, its corners tacked down with copper-headed nails.

About a hundred men were in the room, standing in a silent row, lining the walls beneath an array of gleaming metal lamps. The majority of them were ordinary foot soldiers, dressed in crisp uniforms of red and white. Most carried long-hafted pikes with hooked blades, though some had the 7.62 mm rifles that Ryan had seen before.

Mashashige wasn't there, though there was a raised chair close to the longer edge of the white cloth. A small group of the fortress's own samurai stood together, all in finest dress clothes and armor, all with their swords.

There was also no sign of any prisoner.

It crossed Ryan's mind that this might be a trap for their benefit, and at any moment there would be a signal and the men with pikes would rush at them. He noticed J.B.'s right hand rested on the butt of the Uzi and knew that the same thought had occurred to his oldest friend.

"Stand here with me," Hideyoshi whispered. "This is a specially honorable position, so you may all witness everything that is to happen."

"Thanks," Ryan said.

Doc placed himself to one side, with J.B. on the other. Jak, his white hair flaming like an incandescent candle, was next to the Armorer.

Ryan glanced at his chron as a blare of trumpets, followed by thunderous drums and a brazen gong, shattered the stillness in the great hall.

Two large double doors at the far end swung slowly open, and in walked Lord Mashashige. At his side, chatting to him as though they were old friends, was the ronin, dressed entirely in black—the man who was about to take his own life in front of them all.

Chapter Thirteen

The two Japanese men stood together, Mashashige slender and every inch an athlete, and his would-be assassin, who was an inch or so taller and looked to weigh a good fifty pounds more. The ronin looked calm and friendly, not at all like someone about to put himself to a hideous ending.

Mashashige clasped hands with his enemy, then went to sit on his throne, the sheath of his plain sword making a faint scraping sound on the polished floor. The ronin walked barefoot onto the rectangle of cloth and knelt, shrugging off his gown so that he was effectively naked from the waist up.

At a sign from the shogun, Takei Yashimoto strutted forward, holding a dagger on a white velvet cushion, a tassel of white silk dangling from the inlaid hilt. Ryan guessed the blade was between nine and ten inches in length.

"The *wakizashi,*" Hideyoshi whispered. "And the lord himself is to act as his . . . What is the proper word for a man who is an assistant in a duel?"

"A second?" Doc said quietly. The old man was perspiring, and his face was parchment pale. Ryan noticed that his breathing was fast and shallow.

"Yes. Is word. The lord will be second to ronin and will perform the final act."

The doomed man bowed to Yashimoto and took the dagger in both hands, laying it on the cloth in front of him, where it drew the eye like a jeweled insect.

"Now he will make short speech," Hideyoshi said.

It was done in Japanese and lasted about five minutes by Ryan's reckoning.

Hideyoshi gave a running translation, pattering it under his breath while Ryan and the others crowded close around him to hear what was being said.

"He say good to see many people here to witness his change from life to death . . . asks for prayers for ancestors . . . begs forgiveness for rising against Lord Mashashige and his house . . . regrets he will no more walk through mountains and watch eagles soar and salmon leap and smell blossom on flowering cherry. . . ." The ronin turned his eyes toward the little group of foreigners. "Now he say honored that you four here to watch him . . . don't know right word. Pay for his wrongdoing."

Finally the speech was done and the room was silent. One of the servants nearly dropped a long pike and barely caught it before it crashed to the floor.

"Now begins," Hideyoshi breathed.

It was a scene that Ryan would remember as long as he lived.

THE LAMPS THREW a sheen off the sweat that beaded the man's muscular, hairless chest and shoulders. His hair was long and sleek, tied into a tight knot at the back of the head.

Now the stillness seemed to intensify and darken, filling the hall.

The ronin leaned forward and wiped his hands on the cloth, leaving a gray smudge. He picked up the dagger, looking down at it with a blank, expressionless face, his eyes seeming to stare through the polished metal into the heart of the knife. He transferred it to his right hand and took a deep breath.

Ryan realized that he was holding his own breath, and he tried to relax. But the tension was palpable.

"Goodbye, cruel world," the man shouted, the echoes ringing off the vaulted roof.

"He's off to join the circus," J.B. said so quietly that only Ryan heard him.

Now the man sat back on his heels, tautening the skin across his belly. He reached down with his left hand and touched himself, trying to locate the precise spot to make the first cut. He found it and slashed down with the *wakizashi*, the sharp point barely brushing the skin.

A bead of crimson appeared, rolling and vanishing into the folds of black cloth across the ronin's loins. There was the faintest whisper of a sigh from the watchers, like the softest summer breeze through the tops of a sycamore.

"Now," Hideyoshi whispered.

With a grunt of effort the man thrust the blade deep into his belly, pulling it sharply across from left to right, then upward. There was a flood of crimson across the white cloth.

"May the Lord have mercy on his soul," Doc whispered, closing his pale blue eyes.

The dying man hadn't made a single sound after that sharp exhalation of breath, though the veins stood out on his forehead from the effort of suppressing his agony. Ryan figured that the silence was a part of the ritual of seppuku. It was a sign of weakness and cowardly failure if you were to scream out at the burning agony.

The man gently lowered the bloodied dagger to the sodden cloth in front of him and straightened. Mashashige shifted on his high throne, narrow fingers playing with the hilt of his own samurai sword.

"Now what?" Jak whispered.

"Watch," Hideyoshi urged, "and learn."

A thread of blood wormed from the corner of the ronin's mouth, where he'd bitten through his tongue. Now he suddenly plunged both hands into the gaping cut across his stomach and plucked out coils of his own intestines.

"Dark night!" J.B. breathed, turning away from the gory spectacle.

Loops of pink, yellow and gray, smeared with the omnipresent blood, lay in the man's lap. He sat still, looking down at them, a slightly puzzled expression on his face, as if he had no idea what they were and what they were doing there.

Moving with a leisurely grace, Mashashige rose from his chair and walked across to stand behind his dying enemy, slowly drawing his own sword.

The ronin sat still and proud, blood pouring from the hideous gash across his belly. Mashashige stood right behind him and leaned forward, whispering something in the man's ear. There was the slightest nod of the head.

It was so quick that if Ryan had blinked he would have missed the ending.

The sword rose and fell in a scything arc of glittering silver, striking the ronin at the base of the neck, below the tight bunch of hair. It sliced through like a razor cutting warm butter. There was the merest click of steel on bone as it hacked the spine apart, exiting out of the front of the man's throat, completely severing the head with that single blow.

The skull dropped forward, just missing the spilled intestines, rolling twice before ending up with the eyes staring at the ceiling. Ryan could have sworn for a few moments that the dead man's eyes continued to move, but that might have been a trick of the light.

"Amen," Doc said louder than he intended.

The corpse sat unnervingly still, its hands folded calmly in its lap. The wound to the stomach had already removed a good part of the body's supply of blood. But the beheading still produced a sizable fountain that gouted into the air, a dozen feet high, pattering down all over the white cloth. Mashashige had obviously known this would happen and had stepped smartly back as soon as he'd delivered the merciful coup de grace. Now he sheathed his sword.

With the tension gone, everyone started talking at once.

The shogun stalked out of the hall without a backward glance and without a word to anyone, vanishing through a small door at the far end, beside a tapestry of a procession of armored samurai walking through a forest of tall, feathery trees beside a limpid lake.

"Can we go now?" Doc asked, pulling out his blue kerchief and mopping sweat from his forehead. "I confess that I would not wish such an ending upon my worst enemies. Not even upon the whitecoats that blighted my life. No, not even upon them! Can we go now?"

Hideyoshi nodded slowly. His eyes sparkled, and he kept licking his lips. "It was *so* good," he said. "Oh, that was *so* good!"

"It was?" J.B. said, laconic as ever. "If that was good, then I'd sure hate to see bad."

"Such honor and dignity. The ultimate in Bushido, our code of honor. It was truly magnificent."

"I only saw a life pointlessly, pitilessly and brutally ended," Ryan said. "A man sticking a sharp knife into his stomach and spilling his guts on the floor while someone else cuts off his head. If that's your ideal of honor, then you can stuff it up your ass, Hideyoshi."

"You barbarians do not understand."

"Damn right we don't."

The sec boss of the ville looked around as the room quickly emptied of servants. A couple of old men had appeared with buckets and mops, slowly dragging a large wicker basket behind them.

"Talk is of no point. I would argue a thousand years and never convince you that our ways are the right ways. It would be like trying to talk to a stone wall."

Ryan pointed a finger at the Japanese warrior. "Couldn't agree more."

"What happens now?" Jak asked. His face was its usual dead-white hue, giving little clue to whether the teenager had been upset by the act of seppuku.

Hideyoshi took a deep breath. "One of the invading band of ronin was slain by your hand, Ryan Cawdor. Now they remove the body of the second. But there are many others. We have known of them for many long months. Finally Lord Mashashige has agreed that we will take arms against—"

"'The sea of troubles, and by opposing, end them,'" Doc said. "As the Bard puts it."

"I also know of Shakespeare, Doctor," the samurai said triumphantly. "'Sling and arrow of outrageous fortunes.'"

"More or less, my dear fellow."

"You say that you're finally moving against this gang?" Ryan asked.

"Yes. And you will all come with us."

Chapter Fourteen

Ryan kicked his heels into the flanks of the sturdy mountain pony that he had been given for the expedition, moving it on at a canter to bring himself up with the ring of senior samurai who rode around their lord.

"Mashashige!"

The shogun heard him call his name and turned in the high saddle of his own stallion, beckoning the one-eyed man to join him.

"What is it?"

"You insisted that the women ride in those carry-carriage things?"

Mashashige nodded, his face betraying no emotion. "They are called palanquins, Cawdor-san. You understand that it is only to honor you and your comrades that we allow the weak ones—these two strange women—along with us on this fighting expedition? There are no other women."

"I know that."

The column was entirely male, more than eighty armed men, all with pikes, and many with rifles and automatics. Ryan had asked Hideyoshi why, if there was so much heavy, polluting industry on what remained of the country, they hadn't got more firearms.

"Because we have too many people and too little land. Too much energy goes into keeping alive with processed food. Also, we run out soon of raw materials. Coal and iron in short supply. Ever shorter supply."

Eight samurai accompanied them, including Hideyoshi and Yashimoto. The fortress was left with a skeleton defensive complement, the drawbridge up and all shutters closed tight against any sneak attack.

Mildred and Krysty had been allowed along under strict tolerance, having to travel in the ornamented palanquins. Each was carried by six servants, the relays changing at regular intervals as they tired under the weight and the difficult terrain and the unbreathable air.

They were like large boxes on wheels, with curtains of embroidered silk, which both Krysty and Mildred had thrown back because of the oppressive heat and stuffiness. They had knotted silken cords to hang on to, trying to keep their balance in an awkward half sitting, half lying position, struggling against the ceaseless jolting.

After a couple of miles both women had called for a halt while they got out and tried to recover from bad bouts of travel sickness. Krysty had actually thrown up in an open ditch at the side of the road, her nausea not improved by seeing a bloated carcass of a dead dog, its legs missing, floating by in several inches of rancid, slime-topped scum.

After another mile Mildred had begged Ryan to go and entreat the shogun to allow them to ride a couple of the spare ponies, or to walk with the foot soldiers.

"Anything rather than travel another yard in these goddamn puke boxes."

Mashashige looked at Ryan as though he'd asked him to check the sun in its afternoon progress toward the west.

"Ride horses?"

"Yeah."

"It's difficult." Ryan had been long enough in Japan to know that this meant a denial.

"Why not?"

"Women do not ride."

"Then let them walk. They're happy to walk. J.B., Doc and Jak and me'll walk, as well. Doesn't bother us at all. Been doing it most of our lives."

The shogun shook his head slowly. "There would be a bad losing of face."

"Not for me."

"No. For me, if it was thought by the peasants that my guests had to walk in the dust."

"Then let the women take a pair of the spare ponies. Be obliged."

Mashashige sighed. "Your barbarian ways will never be understood by me, however long I try." He waved a hand in dismissal. "Let them do this." A thought struck him. "They will ride with their legs apart?"

"Only way they know," Ryan replied.

Mashashige sighed, closing his deep-set eyes for a moment as though he were suffering from an agonizing migraine. "Let it be so."

IT SEEMED that the gang of masterless samurai, known as the ronin, had been roaming the land for some time, either years or months, depending on who was telling the stories. And there was anywhere between a dozen and a hundred of them.

Yashimoto had warned Ryan, when they were safely out of the hearing of the shogun, that this expedition was fraught with danger.

"You may not return from it, *gaijin*. Any accident might happen. A false step or an unlucky blow. And then the spirit of my brother can sleep at ease."

The route would take them close to one of the sprawling conurbations that housed some of the smoke-belching factories, into the mountains and down toward the sea.

The camp of the ronin was believed to be on a headland jutting out into the ocean, something like a day and a half's steady march from Mashashige's fortress.

But like so much else in Japan, the real facts seemed shrouded in doubt and confusion.

Mashashige himself led the procession, with banner-carrying warriors on either side of him, the huge silken flags proclaiming to the world that it was the great shogun Mashashige who was passing by with his army of retainers.

There was also a marching band with brazen gongs and drums so large that two men were needed to carry them. They beat out a blaring rhythm for the whole long column, from the lord at its head to the dozen or so four-wheeled ox carts that carried provisions and extra weapons.

Ryan rode in the center, with Krysty at his side, her fiery hair catching the bright afternoon sun whenever it broke through the reddish haze of pollution.

"This air is vile," she said, wiping at her sore eyes, the bright green irises rimmed with painful crimson.

"There doesn't seem to be any quiet bits of country." Ryan stood in the narrow stirrups and scanned the area. They were climbing up a winding path that appeared to lead toward a steep hog-back ridge. "It's either barren rock, or it's filled with sprawling villes of little crowded houses and these stinking factories. And so many people."

Doc was just behind and he heard the conversation. "I lived in England for a time when I was a young man. The big cities. London, of course, and Manchester and Birmingham. They were rookeries of narrow streets and crowded back-to-back houses, with noisesome alleys running between them. I saw a dozen or more living in a single room, packed between the factories that vomited poisonous black fumes into the lowering air, day and night. Slums! Stooped, sallow figures, coughing their lungs out, and pinch-faced babies with hollow eyes and spavined ribs. It was a dreadful sight that I shall never forget." He blew his nose, wobbling dangerously in the saddle, his long legs sticking out on either side of the pony, looking in his frock coat like Abe Lincoln on a sway-backed mule.

HALFWAY UP THE MOUNTAIN they passed some kind of crude processing plant that Hideyoshi said was for alum. Low sheds stood between steaming vats of bubbling, foul-smelling liquid that was constantly stirred with long ladles suspended a few feet above the caldrons.

As the noise and color of the procession reached the place, the workers came scurrying from their dangerous positions to watch Mashashige go by.

By the time Ryan and friends reached the spiked iron gates, it looked as if the whole labor force was standing there, in an uncanny silence.

Not one of them was over ten years of age.

Ryan turned his head from side to side, hearing the sharp intake of breath from Krysty at his elbow.

The wizened faces under the layers of grimed dust might have been seventy or eighty years old. Eyes older than time itself stared blankly at the array of wealth and power moving by them. Mouths, toothless, hung open, worms of drool cutting sticky furrows through the burning white powder. Hands with the nailless fingers clenched into claws. Ribs were sunken under the thin, ragged clothes.

"Gaia, save them," Krysty whispered.

Doc kicked his heels into the flanks of his mount, pulling himself alongside Ryan. "I swear that those are the same pinched faces that I just described in the slums and back alleys of Victorian cities. If progress is the result, then those doomed, wretched children are the price."

THE HIGHER THEY CLIMBED, the cleaner the air became. Ryan turned in the saddle to look back down the trail, seeing that there was a floating carpet of reddish orange that marked the upper limits of the pollution.

J.B. was at his side, and the two old friends considered the industrialized landscape, unlike anything that either of them had ever seen anywhere in Deathlands.

"It's dying," he said.

"People are dying also. Those who live in the ville are better off, a little distance off from the worst of the lung-burning blinding fumes."

The Armorer took off his glasses and furiously polished them. "If this is the future, then I wouldn't want any part of it. You realize how much you take for granted back home. The mountains and cold, clear water and the fresh air. Take those away, and you have the dark picture of what's left of Japan."

It was an unusually long speech for the little man, showing the depths of his feelings.

Ryan nodded his agreement. "Can't find a word of argument with you, J.B.," he said. "Guess there's always something new to learn about life."

Mildred was with them. "There's times that I wish I didn't know now what I didn't know back then."

Ryan looked puzzled, thinking about what the woman had just said, working it through in his mind. "Yeah," he said finally. "I get it. You mean that things you were ignorant about when you were younger, that it was better that way."

"You got it, Ryan," she said, smiling, gazing past him. "I see that Hideyoshi's looking worried about us getting left behind. Better move it."

"THIS IS ONLY TRACK across mountain to sea," Hide-yoshi said as they stopped on a plateau, facing a steeper section of the hill that would take them up and over the ridge. The trail was only about ten feet across at its widest, barely enough for the carts to pass through.

"Looks more narrow ahead," Jak commented, shading his eyes against the setting sun.

"Wags stay here," the samurai said. "Camp here for night. Go on at dawn."

"Why not build a proper road, if there's much traffic between the sea and here?" Ryan asked.

"Quakes just knock it down again. Lucky there hasn't been one since we started. This famous part for bad ones. They happen almost every day."

Mashashige had dismounted and was walking past them, leading his own stallion, pausing as he heard what his number three was saying.

"This is a true thing," he said. "All the bravery and cunning that we show is undone by the gods that sleep beneath the mountains and far out under the waters. Near the top of the trail, it becomes very dangerous and many have died. There is a sheer... Right word? Sheer?"

"Yes," Ryan said. "That's the right word."

"Is good. Sheer drop to sharp rocks and fast river. One wrong step..." His long, narrow hands described a diving motion in the air in front of him.

BLANKETS AND SLEEPING rolls were handed out from the wags, and a number of large cooking fires were lit all around the rocky, open space.

Iron pots of rice were heated, steaming in the cold night air, along with flavorsome soups that contained shredded eggs.

"Fish," Doc said, wrinkling his nose. "More poisonous metals and chemicals wrapped in scales." He raised his voice to call out to Yashimoto, who was walking by with a couple of the other senior samurai. "Any meat cooking there?"

"Meat, foolish old *gaijin* grandmother? Meat is for warriors. For men. You may have water and cold rice."

Doc uncoiled from the ground, his knees cracking, towering over the scar-faced second-in-command. He drew the first couple of inches of the rapier that was concealed in the ebony cane. "You have got a peculiarly large mouth to counterbalance that amazingly small mind, Yashimoto," he said quietly.

The man had been strutting away, laughing, but he swung around at Doc's measured insult, hand gripping the inlaid-ivory-and-jade hilt of his sword.

"I could slay you with a single breath, but you are the guest of Lord Mashashige."

Doc smiled at him, bowing slightly. "First truthful thing you said. Your breath stinks so much of garlic and rotting fish that it could slay anyone at fifty paces. Bring the birds dead out of the branches of trees as you ride by."

"What?"

"I am sorry. I am probably speaking too fast for you. I have noticed that your grasp of American is poorer than the most foolish geisha."

Yashimoto had gone crimson with anger, the knuckles on his hand holding the sword as white as windwashed bone. Ryan had been sitting watching, and he realized that Doc had pushed the man over the brink. That no social command was going to stop Yashimoto from attacking Doc with his longer, heavier sword.

He stood, drawing the SIG-Sauer, stepping in close to the enraged samurai and holding up the automatic where he couldn't fail to see it.

"Another move and you're dead," he said quietly. "Sheathe the sword and walk away from it."

For a heart-stopping moment he thought that the man's crazed sense of lost face and dishonor was going to make him go ahead and slash at Doc, which would mean that Ryan would squeeze the trigger and blow the side of Yashimoto's head into a mist of blood and bones.

But the Japanese pasted on a smile, looking as convincing as a friendly coyote, and bowed to Ryan. "So sorry there has been trouble between us. I am sure that it will soon be over." He bowed again. "Yes, very soon over."

Chapter Fifteen

It was one of the best-defended night camps that Ryan had ever known. Even Trader at his best, with the resources of both war wags to draw on, couldn't have done any better. Takei Yashimoto was in charge, and Ryan grudgingly admitted the second-in-command of the force had done a good job.

There were three layers of sentries, the first of them nearly a half mile off toward the north, in the direction of the ocean and the supposed camp of the ronin.

The second circle of guards was between two and three hundred yards off.

And a third ring of sec warriors was within one hundred paces of the heart of the camp. Some of the samurai had their own tents, but Mashashige himself slept on the floor along with his men, wrapped in a single simple blanket. There was a black banner of silk flying at the center of the camp, with a stark symbol embroidered in white, that Hideyoshi told Ryan was simply the name and rank of the shogun Mashashige.

"I've never known a baron who was humble as he is," Ryan said. "Nothing flash about him. No pearl-handled matching Colts. No tent bigger than the others. No silver-inlaid saddle. The only thing that makes him stand out from his followers is that nothing makes him stand out."

"This is a part of the code of Bushido. Some flaunt their wealth and power. But there are men like Mashashige who choose the opposite path."

Doc had been eating from a wooden bowl of shredded beef cooked with sliced chilis and he wandered by, hearing the tail end of the conversation.

"It puts me somewhat in mind of the two great war leaders who faced each other at the famous battle of the Little Bighorn," he stated.

"That was General Custer," Hideyoshi said, beaming broadly. "We learn of him in our schools. He was the most famous loser in American history."

Doc nodded. "Can't argue with you there. Unless we take Tricky Dicky into account... But General George Armstrong Custer was the boy hero. Star-touched Autie. Tailored buckskins and fancy guns. Matched hunting dogs. Golden hair tumbling over his shoulders. Always out front, showing off his wealth and power. He was up against Crazy Horse. War leader of... I think it was the Oglala. Similar age and reputation. But Crazy Horse owned only one horse. Gave the others away. Wore the simplest clothes. Carried plain weapons. Custer believed honor came from outside. Crazy Horse thought it came from within."

"And they both died," the samurai said. "But one is remembered as a victor and the other as a man who rode arrogant and grinning to his death, sucking down his whole command with him. There is no defeat like victory, and victory can be no defeat at all. That is what we say.''

THE NIGHT PASSED pleasantly enough.

Krysty and Ryan huddled together under a large woolen blanket, warmed by the fires that were kept burning all through the hours of darkness.

They were awakened once, around midnight, by a minor quake that sent rocks clattering into the gorge ahead of them. But there were no aftershocks, and they were at little risk out there in the open.

In the fortress Ryan had come for the first time on the great preoccupations of the Japanese. A sort of vertical pinball game called *pachinko* involved dozens of tiny steel balls rolling around and around and bouncing into numbered and lettered slots. The combinations decided whether you won or lost. Most times it seemed that you lost.

It was such a craze that several of the samurai had brought along smaller, portable versions of the game, playing as the breakfast cooked, the morning air filling with the rattling and chinking of the *pachinko* balls.

Mashashige himself stopped by and sat with his foreign guests while they broke their fasts. The air was filled with the scent of fried bacon and fresh-baked bread, but the shogun simply had a bowl of hot water that contained some sliced chestnuts and shredded ginger.

He tapped J.B.'s Smith & Wesson M-4000 scattergun. "This fires the small knives. No, not knives. What is the word for the very small arrows?"

"Fléchettes," the Armorer said.

Mashashige shook his head. "No. That is not the word that I mean."

"Darts?" J.B. offered.

Mashashige nodded, his face betraying no emotion. "That is it. Is this a good gun?"

"Does a special kind of job."

"But it has little honor to it, and it is useless at a range of a hundred paces or more. Our bows can slay at a quarter mile, Mr. Dix."

"Ryan's Steyr rifle here can chill at the best part of a mile," the Armorer countered. "And this blaster can wipe men away at short range. And the Uzi could stop a cavalry charge."

"So could my archers."

"Sure. Wouldn't argue. But it would take fifty or so bowmen to have the same kind of effect that one man with an Uzi and three spare mags could have."

"We must agree to be different," the shogun said thoughtfully. "If the need arises when we reach the home of our enemy, will you use your guns on our side?"

The question was aimed at Ryan.

He hadn't actually thought that one through. The warlord had such a large force that it hadn't occurred to Ryan that a situation might arise where their firepower could be of much use to Mashashige.

"I guess that . . . we're your guests, so that puts us under an obligation to help you."

The shogun nodded and gave the one-eyed man a low bow. Then he stalked off toward the horses.

"Our baron, right or wrong," Krysty said quietly. "You sure about this, lover?"

"No. Mashashige might be a swift and evil bastard, and his enemies, these ronin, might be saints in human form. But we don't know."

"So you'll chill them if Mashashige asks you?"

Ryan nodded. "You got a better idea, Krysty? Fireblast! It's difficult enough to try and pick the difference between right and wrong back home in Deathlands. Never mind in this crazed land of slant-eyed crazies."

Mildred tapped him sharply on the arm. "Just keep a lock on your tongue, Ryan. Asked you before."

"Sure you did, and I'm sorry. But we have to watch every step in the way we deal with them here, never mind falling out among ourselves."

THE TRAIL AHEAD WOUND higher up before it leveled off, then began to drop quickly toward the distant sea. The warnings about the state of the track had been justified. It cut across the face of the mountain, where erosion and quake damage were all too obvious to them all.

The small quake of the previous night had done a great deal more damage than Ryan had believed, damage that was all too evident as he heeled his reluctant pony along, nearing the highest point of the climb.

The land dropped away almost sheer to his left, and the trail was so narrow that there was barely room for one pony at a time to pick its surefooted way along. Below Ryan was a singing chasm of sheer black stone that glistened in the early-morning mist. Spray rose out of the gorge several hundred feet below, where it was possible to glimpse a silvery ribbon of river.

"Good place for ambush," said Jak, who was riding directly behind Ryan.

"Yeah."

Mashashige had split his force, sending some of his own elite samurai ahead as scouts, following them with a third of his foot soldiers.

Krysty and Mildred had suffered the openly lustful stares of the Japanese as they rode their own ponies, perched on the saddles with the high pommels, kicking them on to keep close behind Ryan and the others.

Yashimoto and Hideyoshi were also riding just behind the outlanders, talking quietly and urgently in their own tongue. Their shogun had gone ahead with his samurai, taking up a position near the front of the long, snaking column.

"One resounding quake while we are on this section of the trail and goodbye will be all that she wrote," Doc commented. "I have seldom seen such a perilous place."

It was only with the benefit of twenty-twenty hindsight that Ryan was able to piece together what happened in the next four or five seconds.

A long way off, there was a faint sound like a bow being loosed, which was followed by a hissing sound. Then something thwacked against the flank of his pony. It immediately whinnied in pain and shock, and bucked on its hind legs, almost throwing him clear out of the saddle into the deeps of the ravine at his left.

The loose pebbles on the narrow trail gave the pony no purchase as it reared, forelegs flailing at the misty air. Ryan sawed at the reins, fighting the animal, struggling to keep it under control. He gripped its body with his knees, leaning away from the drop.

But the pony was beyond any help.

Whatever had made it buck away in the first place had hurt it, and it was now terrified of losing its balance and falling away into nothing. Its eyes rolled, red rimmed in their sockets, and spittle frothed against the steel bit.

"Jump!" someone screamed from behind Ryan.

"It's going!" someone else yelled, the high-pitched cry sounding like Jak.

Whoever it was, he was right.

Ryan sensed the balance being lost and heard the doomed animal shriek like a human in helpless despair. He kicked his way out of the stirrups, throwing himself sideways to his right, banging his shoulder on the rock face as he fell.

He rolled over, the Steyr clattering among the loose stones. He saw out of the corner of his eye the pony vanishing, falling in surprising slow motion, past the brink of the drop.

He was quickly on his feet, walking the few shaky steps to the brink of the gorge, still in time to see the animal strike the giant boulders near the bottom. Its shattered body rolled and twisted as it entered the river with a barely visible splash. The still corpse emerged and was carried swiftly away out of sight.

Krysty, Doc and Jak were all off their animals, running to him, standing to watch the last scene of the drama being played out hundreds of feet below them.

"You all right, lover?" Krysty asked, touching him lightly on the arm. "Close one."

Ryan nodded, feeling his pulse and respiration easing back toward normal. He turned from the chasm and pushed past a gaggle of chattering foot soldiers, catching the eye of Takei Yashimoto, who was staring intently at him.

"What spooked it?" J.B. asked. "Loose stones?"

Ryan shook his head. "No. Someone fired something at it. I heard it hit on the flank, behind the saddle." He stooped to look at the ground, his eye caught by something glittering in the loose red dirt.

"What is it?" Doc asked.

Ryan held out the palm of his hand, showing half a dozen small steel balls. "From that *pachinko* game they play. Must've used a catapult. Something like that."

Suddenly Mashashige appeared at his elbow, holding out his hand to take the steel balls. "Many of my men use catapults for sport. There is no possibility of finding who was responsible for this attempt at murdering. I regret this."

Ryan thought that he didn't sound as though he really regretted it all that much.

THE TRAIL WIDENED once they reached the top of the pass, enabling them to ride in a group rather than in single file. Another pony had been found for Ryan, an iron-jawed brute with a suppurating growth over one of its eyes.

J.B. had walked his animal alongside Ryan. "Reckon it was Yashimoto?" he asked.

"Probably not. We were all so close together it would've been difficult to fire a catapult at me without the risk of one of us spotting him."

"But he was behind it?"

Ryan slapped the pony across the side of the head when it turned and tried to bite him on the thigh. "Probably. If there's a firefight at this ronin camp, then it might be a good idea for one of us to try and take him out."

Krysty was alongside him and she turned, eyes wide. "Gaia! You mean chill him?"

"Sure. Best enemy's a dead one."

"You don't know it was him who tried to kill you."

"He threatened me. That's enough. You don't have to see the eye behind the gunsight to know whose finger's on the trigger. But we'll only do that if we get a clear, safe chance."

"Looks like scouts seen something ahead," Jak said. "Back in hurry."

"Ronin camp?" Mildred asked, easing herself in the saddle. "God, but I'll be pleased to get off and walk a bit."

Far below them they could see a rocky headland groping its way into the leaden ocean.

Chapter Sixteen

The camp was abandoned.

That was obvious as soon as the head of the column moved within a quarter mile of the jutting headland. A thin pillar of white smoke rose from the ashes of what had once been a big cooking fire at the center of a trampled patch of cropped turf, marked with the faded shapes where tents had stood and where a number of horses had been tethered.

Mashashige held up his hand to stop the advance as they closed to within a hundred yards, calling for Hideyoshi and Yashimoto to join him. He looked around and also beckoned for Ryan and the others to ride forward to the head of the war party.

It was an exposed section of land, with bedrock showing through the gray turf in many places, crisscrossed with the narrow tracks of wild sheep or goats.

There was nowhere for ambushers to hide in wait.

"This is known as a place of magic," the shogun said once the little group had gathered around him. "Very old and rich with spirits of ancestors."

White-topped waves were breaking high over the weed-slick rocks, kicking up a constant spray that turned into magical rainbows and then vanished.

"What kind of magic would that be?" Doc asked.

"There was once a fortress here, commanded by a great warlord called Takeda Shingen. He had appointed a young samurai as deputy shogun in his place, and this youth became fascinated with magic. He communicated with spirits of the past and ghosts from the darkness, white-faced princesses that wished to drink blood from the throat of the samurai."

Ryan flapped his hand to drive away a cloud of tiny iridescent flies that were clustering around his face. "Where was this fortress?" he asked.

"There." Mashashige pointed. "See broken walls where once was a mighty palace."

It was difficult to see much of a pattern among the tumbled boulders, though Ryan conceded that there was some possible evidence of regularity in the lines of rock.

"But he angered the great ones. He had proclaimed he would become immoral. No, that is wrong word."

"Immortal," Doc prompted.

"Thank you, Doctor. Immortal. And that nothing in the heavens or on the earth would bring low the walls of his great house. That night there came dragons with golden scales, raging with flame-filled mouths from the north. And there was fire and great destruction. By dawn not a man or woman lived, and not one stone stood upon another."

"And now it looks like all your enemies have left this place," Ryan said.

"So it would appear. But can that truly be true?"

"The smoke tells that they were here up too soon," Yashimoto said.

Mashashige kicked his heels into the flanks of his stallion. "We will go to look."

THE SHOGUN TOOK ONLY seven of his leading samurai, including both Yashimoto and Hideyoshi, along with the half-dozen curious foreigners.

There was a short spear thrust into the ground near the fire, close to a large shape hidden under a green tarpaulin, a shape that looked uncommonly like a body, with a pool of congealing blood seeping from it. The spear had a length of white linen tied to it, dabbed with Japanese symbols.

The shogun dismounted and unfolded the banner, reading it out loud. "It says 'See how we welcome Lord Mashashige, the dead pretender to an empty throne.' Then it finishes by warning me to ready myself for *shinda tsumori*. That is difficult to translate for *gaijin*. It means 'looking forward to your death.'"

"Should I look under the covering, Lord?" asked Yashimoto, also dismounting.

Mashashige nodded. "I think that I know what it is that we shall see."

The bloody cloth was heaved away, revealing the carcass of a large pig. It had been crucified with daggers, its throat slit and belly ripped open in a mockery of the seppuku ritual of suicide. As an additional insult, its genitals had been hacked off and inserted into the tusked mouth.

On its flank was another line of symbols.

"'As I am, so shall you be,'" Mashashige read. "The ronin are in a merry mood."

"The fire was lit at some time during last night, Lord," Hideyoshi said. "We didn't cross their tracks. They must have gone near the sea."

"Or taken to boats," the shogun offered.

He turned to Ryan. "You have a thought on what they have done?"

"I think they knew exactly when you were coming. This was timed too well." Ryan considered the question. "And that means that you have an informer in your ville. A spy. Probably traveling with us now. He found some way of warning them of when you'd get here so they could leave at the right moment. Been done for maximum effect. Well planned."

The three senior samurai looked at one another in silence, which was finally broken by Yashimoto. "How do we know that the spy is not one of you? You arrived here by chance, as you say. But you may be working with the *gekokujo*."

"What are they?" J.B. asked.

Mashashige answered him. "Those who would wish to overthrow the chosen leaders from beneath."

He spoke quickly to the other samurai, who nodded and bowed and scurried toward the sea, picking their way carefully over the spray-slick rocks.

"They will tell us if boats were used," the shogun said. "I believe that your thinking was correct in its details. There is a spy here with us. We must guard our backs from every shadow."

Ryan felt a tiny tremor run through the ground beneath his feet, and he looked quickly around, seeing a flock of black-headed gulls rise screaming into the air from the sea, a couple of miles off from the shore. His pony suddenly became even more restless, skittering sideways and tugging at the bridle that Ryan held in his hand.

"Quake," Yashimoto said, stamping his foot on the earth. "It would not dare to rebel against those who follow the great Lord Mashashige."

There was another movement, much stronger this time, that set pebbles rolling and made every single horse whinny in fear. Some distance away, higher up the slope, the bulk of the small army was shouting in alarm.

As Ryan looked around he saw a sight that would have been funny and remarkable, had it not also been an uneasy harbinger of danger.

Hundreds of rabbits had erupted from a massive warren that undermined the whole hillside, scampering in all directions. A second glance showed Ryan that they were all running *away* from the water, where the epicenter of the growing disturbance seemed to be located.

"Gaia! Will you look at—"

Krysty was pointing out to sea, where the calm pewter surface was ruffled, as though a localized whirlwind had sprung up, churning the ocean to a frothing maelstrom.

"It is an underwater quake," Mashashige said. "I think this might not be very pleasant. Sometimes there are tsunamis...great waves. We should retire." He raised his voice in an eerie shriek to order his war chiefs to return from their recce down on the rocky shore.

But the air was filled with noise.

It sounded to Ryan as if there were a dozen war wags at full throttle, roaring away just beneath his feet.

Now the very bedrock itself seemed to be turning to shifting liquid, sliding and moving, with long cracks running away under their feet.

"Holy shit!" Mildred shouted. "Oh, holy, holy shit!"

The sea was transformed.

Now it foamed and raged, with bubbles bursting from the deeps, kicking up a throbbing turbulence. Waves had sprung up from nowhere, raging in toward the promontory far below them, where the samurai were now fleeing for their lives.

"Let the horse go, Doc!" Ryan shouted, seeing that the old man was in serious danger of being dragged under the panicked pony's hooves.

Now the ground was rolling like the waves on the sea, with a bedlam of dust and stones. Ryan glimpsed the corpse of the butchered pig tumbling into the ashes of the fire, sending up a spray of fine gray dust.

"Higher ground!" Mashashige yelled, "or we are all to be doomed!"

"Dark night!" J.B. was still staring out at the ocean, looking past the straggling doomed figures of the leading samurai. In their turn they were gazing behind them at the fearful convulsions of the water, where the waves were raging higher and higher from the center of the quake.

Only the first ripples were breaking over the rocks, but a mile farther out the first of the tsunamis was already gathering appalling momentum.

Ryan's guess put the foam-topped tidal wave at between fifty and a hundred feet, racing shoreward, followed by several other, slightly smaller breakers.

All around him there was a barely controlled chaos.

Through the deafening cacophony he could hear orders being called out in high-pitched Japanese and glimpse the crimson-and-white soldiers running back up the hill, going for the higher ground, dropping their pikes and rifles behind them.

The few remaining samurai had abandoned their freaked-out horses and were running with the rabble, slowed by the heavy armor. Ryan noticed that none of the samurai had thrown away any of his weapons.

Hideyoshi, Yashimoto and Mashashige were all following their men, trying to strike a balance between dignity and fear, striding up the slope with an ungainly haste.

Far below them all, the other samurai had all but given up their futile efforts to escape, stopping on the slick rocks and looking hopelessly at the mighty wave that rushed upon them. Ryan wasn't absolutely sure, but he thought he had seen a slash of crimson as at least one of them was hastily committing suicide with his dagger.

"Poor bastards," Jak said.

"Should we not be making our own escape from this place?" Doc asked, a slight tremble in his voice. "Only that tsunami seems damnably high and—"

"Won't reach us," Ryan said calmly. "We're a good two hundred and fifty feet above sea level here. No way we're in any danger from it."

He almost crossed his fingers as he spoke. The tidal wave seemed to be growing larger with every few yards as it tore in toward the land. He guessed now that its roaring white crest was well over one hundred feet high and the weight of water was incalculable.

The movement of the land had eased down, though he still felt off-balance.

"Could always move a tad higher, lover?" Krysty suggested, having to shout at the top of her voice to be heard above the shrieking of the quake and the oncoming tsunami.

"Wouldn't do any harm," he conceded.

The noise had faded to a distant rumble, but the thunder of the oncoming wave was growing ever louder.

Doc was running for higher ground, elbows pumping, feet splayed out, the tails of his frock coat flaring out behind him. His mane of silver hair trailed like a bridal veil.

Jak was at his heels, followed close behind by J.B. and Mildred.

Ryan and Krysty had started walking after them, when their nerve went and they both started to spring toward the crest of the ridge. Behind them, it seemed they were being chased by a panther in a hurricane, the roaring ever closer and more frightening, as if it was aimed solely at the runners.

Ryan risked a glance behind him again, pausing in midstride, seeing that they were truly high enough to be safe, though not by as much as he'd been calmly claiming.

Even as he stopped, the tsunami reached the shore.

There was a moment when it seemed to hang, a mile high, frozen in time and space, like a mighty cliff of dark green jade, topped with snow—with the samurai, trapped forever beneath it.

If they screamed at the last moment, it was swamped by the tumult of the tsunami.

The earth shook as the wave landed, burying the promontory, surging high up over the cropped turf, almost reaching the site of the ronin camp, water roiling over the dusty land, covering everything.

The foaming combers reached within a hundred paces of where Ryan, closest of the group, stood to watch.

Then it sucked back, exposing the muddied bottom of the ocean, where hundreds of blind creatures flopped and writhed in the dense mud.

There were other, smaller tsunamis, following on the heels of that first monster wave. But none of them was more than forty or fifty feet high, still profoundly impressive, but like pygmies chasing a giant.

Krysty took Ryan's arm, staring out at the scene of Nature in its awesome pomp.

"That was something else, lover," she said.

"Yeah."

"Poor devils never had a chance."

"If we'd been farther down, nearer the sea, it would have taken us all out."

Krysty nodded. "Mashashige's lost most of his top fighting men."

"Plenty of Indians and no chiefs."

She smiled. "Nice to see you trying to run like mad and keep your cool all at the same time."

"I knew in my brain that the wave wouldn't reach us. But my heart wasn't so sure."

"The retreat's stopped up the hill. Mashashige and the other samurai are coming back."

The shogun stopped in front of the outlanders, still a little out of breath. "The ronin have gone. So we will follow them."

Ryan nodded. "Why not?"

Chapter Seventeen

"Howling Metal?" Jak had halted his pony, pointing at one of a row of abandoned, tumbledown stores in a village west along the coast from the scene of the tidal wave.

"It was name of a place selling American ceedee rock," Hideyoshi said.

It was possible to read the faded names of some of the stores, and Ryan was surprised how many were in American rather than in Japanese.

Carrot on Horseback looked as if it had once been a supertrendy boutique, with some naked dummies still leaning crookedly in the broken window. Two health shops stood side by side, one called Superfreaks and the other the No Lemon Juice Bar. There was Happy Calling, with no clue at all to what they might have once sold. The same with a store called Cuter and Cuter. Art Flower had a subtitle offering beginners' courses in origami and ikebana.

"What are they?" J.B. asked.

Mildred answered him. "The first refers to artistic paper folding and the second one's the art of flower arranging."

"I confess that I had no idea how deeply American custom and usage had infiltrated your country," Doc said to Yashimoto.

"Some say it was very bad and made us weak and feeble like old women," the samurai replied.

"Whose side were you all on in the war? Us or them?" Ryan asked, as the shogun reined in his stallion alongside them.

It was midafternoon. They had retraced their steps to rejoin the supply wags, striking westward as soon as samurai scouts brought word that they had finally picked up the trail of the fleeing ronin.

"War? I know of no war. The blossom was shaken from the cherry trees. Peaches fell from branches. The face of the sun was hidden behind frowning clouds." The man's face was a graven mask. "But I do not remember a war."

"On the side of the Russkies, I expect," J.B. said. "Way they always behaved historically."

Mashashige shook his head slowly. "There was no winner and no losers in the days of skydark. Everyone found themselves caught on wrong side of the line."

"Don't agree," Ryan replied. "There may not have been any winners, but there was a shit-load of losers. Like most of the world."

"It will not happen again." Yashimoto's face was suffused with a sudden flaring anger. "We have so many people and so little land. But you *gaijin* in Deathlands are like fat, pampered babies and we shall—"

"Enough," Mashashige said warningly. "There are words that might be spoken and some that might not."

The samurai second-in-command bowed low in the saddle. "Forgive running tongue, Lord."

RYAN OFFERED HIS SERVICES as tracker, and the shogun seemed glad to accept.

"There are so many of us in so small a space that we have little skills such as you must have in the immense wilderness of Deathlands."

"You've been there?"

Mashashige shook his head. "I greatly and very much regret that it has not been possible. You have a saying in your country, Ryan Cawdor-san, that when the rats are not present then the mice begin to play."

"Yeah, well, something like that. You mean that if you jumped into Deathlands through the mat-trans unit, then you might not be shogun when you jumped back again?"

"My powers rest on uncertain ground. There is always the snake sleeping beneath the rock."

Ryan nodded. "See the problem."

"But one day..."

Ryan had gone on ahead of the main party, taking only Jak, the two leaning from their saddles to check the trampled ground about them.

"Quite lot men and animals," the albino teenager said. "Difficult to tell packhorses."

Ryan stared down at the reddish dirt. "If I had to put a guess on the number, I'd make around twenty mounted and twice that on foot."

"Could be." Jak ran his hands through his long white hair, bringing his pale fingers away stained with the crimson dust. "This shit-awful place."

There was very little vegetation. They had already passed a swathe of pine trees, stunted and twisted, their branches grayish black and brittle with pollution.

Away to their right they could see another of the crowded conurbations, with hundreds of small huts clustered around a number of smoke-belching factories and processing plants. From the raw smell that burned the back of the throat, at least one of them was producing crude gasoline.

There was a significant number of larger properties, looking as if they dated from well before skydark, but most of them were severely run-down and in need of renovation. And nearly all of them looked to be home to dozens of families.

Ryan waited for the others to catch up.

"That looks like a picture in an old book, Doc," Ryan said, pointing to a cluster of buildings up a side trail to their left.

"Based on European design," the old man replied. "Eclectic mix of styles."

"Many houses have electrics," Hideyoshi said proudly. "We are not the barbarians."

Doc smiled. "I did not mean...but let that pass. The one at the top is based on one of the dream castles of the mad Ludwig of Bavaria, with its towers and turrets. And next to it stands a scaled-down version of a classical French château from the banks of the Loire."

"What's that one, Doc?" Mildred asked. "Looks like Macbeth lived there."

"A well-informed guess, madam."

"Why, thank you."

"A Scottish border castle in a shrunken replica. Though its battlements seem in need of repair. I think it would not withstand a siege for very long."

"The honorable ancestors who lived in these parts were very wealthy and prosperous," Yashimoto said, throwing out his chest in pride.

"All three?" J.B. asked quietly.

"Three ancestors?"

"Let is pass."

The samurai shook his head. "If we were not enemies now and enemies yet to be, then I would speak with you at much length on the subject of American humor. I do not yet understand it at all, I fear."

"What the...?" Ryan reined in his ill-tempered pony and pointed down to the right, over the crest of the hill they'd just crossed.

The large sign had been newly painted in a garish tartan script—The Clan MacHayakawa Golf Course. And, beneath it, Members Only.

"A golf course?" Mildred said. "In the midst of all this polluted desert, you got a golf course?"

"Women are not allowed," Hideyoshi stated sternly.

"Now, why could I have guessed that for myself?" She grinned. "Then again, from what I remember, there were a lot of golf courses back in the predark times, all over the damn world, that were kind of selective about who played on their fairways and greens. You weren't all that welcome on a mess of them if you were black or female.''

''Or if you were of the Hebrew persuasion,'' Doc added. ''At least, that was the case in my day.''

''You can only play here if you are at least of samurai class,'' Yashimoto said. ''I have played here many times and shot many eagles and birds.''

''I've shot plenty of blackbirds and crows in my day,'' Ryan replied.

''No, you do not understand golf speech, *gaijin*,'' the second-in-command of the Japanese ville said.

''More like you don't understand the American gift of irony,'' Ryan replied.

As they rode by, following the trail left by the retreating ronin, the scale of the golf course became clear.

On every side of them, apart from the north, where the placid sea glittered distantly, the air was thick with layers of smoke and fumes of all different colors. But they were all the colors of darkness—not cerulean or vermilion or gold or emerald, but gray, brown, muddy orange, slime green and a hideous mustardy yellow, issuing from dozens of chimneys, factories and processing plants. The squat buildings were set at the side of filthy, slow-moving rivers, so contaminated that not even the most vile mutations could live there. One of the streams was actually burning, giving off oily smoke and a foul smell like rotten fish mixed with slurry and crusted vomit.

But gleaming amid this grossly shambolic parody of twentieth-century industrialized life, there was the golf course.

It was like a glittering jewel set in a pile of rancid excrement: dark green fairways and silver sand in the bunkers, a sylvan stream running crystal-clear between the greens, with tiny scarlet flags blowing bravely.

But it was very small.

Doc scratched his forehead. "If you do not mind my asking you a question?"

"Ask away Doctor-san?" Hideyoshi said.

"What is par for the course?"

The warrior squinted up at the clouds that concealed the watery sun. "Par for the course?"

"Sure. In my day it was generally somewhere around seventy-two strokes for most of the courses. Give or take a couple of shots either way."

"Seventy-two?"

"For eighteen holes." Doc looked at the others. "Why am I finding it hard to communicate here? I'm not having one of my breakdowns of communication, am I? Not speaking in strangely biblical tongues of gibberish?"

"For once you're making real good sense, Doc," Krysty replied.

"Eighteen holes, Doctor!"

"Sure."

The samurai stared intently at him. "This is not a foreigner joke?"

"No, it is not. A golf course has eighteen holes. Nearly every golf course in the history of the world has eighteen holes." The penny dropped at the look of grievous disappointment on Hideyoshi's face. Stammering, Doc added, "Of course, not all courses are coarse... are eighteen holes of coarse golf. Of course they're not. How many does yours have, pray?''

"Four," the man muttered, eyes cast down. "Is eighteen truly the correct number for players of honor?''

Doc patted him on the back in an uncharacteristically friendly gesture, trying to cover his own embarrassment. "No, it's not that. Depends on how much land you got. Most of the old predark courses were huge, land-devouring monsters. Sure were. By the Three Kennedys! No, you got a real pretty one here. Should be damnably proud of it, Toyotomi.''

"Truly?''

"Cross my heart and... Well, just cross my heart.''

"But... eighteen holes!''

"Well, I was never that keen on hitting a bit of rubber around with a steel bar, and trying to knock it into a hole in the ground," Doc said.

"The best that I have done for the four holes is twenty-seven hits," the samurai said.

"Twenty-seven!''

"Is not good?''

"Well, I just would have expected that... The holes don't look from here to be very long.''

"Takei Yashimoto has done it in twenty-six hits.''

Doc shook his head. "One better than... Ah! I don't suppose that Lord Mashashige happens to have done it in twenty-five strokes, does he?''

"Yes, he does. But Lord Mashashige has little interest in the game.''

"And the holes are not short," Yashimoto interrupted crossly. "The first one begins in that distant corner beyond the smaller lake. Goes across to the orange flag and then back to the right until it crosses the traps of sand. The ball must then land in the circle by the two red flags. Only then can you aim for the green and the hole. It is perhaps half of a mile from flagtopin," he said, pronouncing it as if it were all one word.

Doc nodded slowly. "I think that I begin to appreciate the picture that you paint for me."

"Paint picture?" Yashimoto said. "What is talk of painting pictures? This is golfing talk?"

"Not exactly. Just that I hadn't taken on board how your course was laid out. Fine. Very clever. Space efficient. To be applauded." And he lent actions to his words by bringing the palms of his hands softly together.

The shogun had reined in his stallion, walking the animal back to where the others had all stopped. "Is there something here that is going wrong?" he asked, his voice as gentle as ever.

"No, Lord," Yashimoto replied, bowing low over his saddle bow.

"We were just admiring the golf course," J.B. said. "Pretty."

The shogun turned his head slowly and stared at the Armorer. "Your mouth does not say in the light what your mind is thinking in the darkness, John Dix."

"Mean I'm lying?"

"That would be impolite of me. But you think in your heart that this golf course is a stupid waste of time, suitable only for conceited and foolish men filled with the bubble reputation of pride. Do you not?''

J.B. hesitated a moment, then nodded. ''Guess you could say that.''

Mashashige almost smiled. ''That is what I think, but it would lose face with my followers if I did not sometimes come here and play the time-wasting game.''

Ryan cleared his throat and spit in the dust. ''Since we all feel the same, mebbe we should just get going and try and track down these ronin.''

The shogun sighed. ''Conversation with wise men whose thoughts follow the same trail is pleasant. But you are right, Cawdor-san. Let us go on.''

Chapter Eighteen

The trail had cut back toward the sea again, skirting high, rocky cliffs. The land was rugged and pleasantly void of any of the industrial complexes that ravaged so much of the residual portion of what had once been Japan.

"Good to have fresh air again, lover," Krysty said, shaking her head, letting a cool northerly blow through the tumbling spray of bright red hair.

"Make the most of it," he replied. "Looks to be more of that vile smoke ahead of us, beyond the next ridge, about six or seven miles."

"Tidal wave did no damage here." Jak walked his stocky piebald pony to the edge of the narrow path, looking down over the sea-slick boulders and foaming breakers. "Didn't come quite high enough."

"How much farther they going to run?" Mildred asked. "Riding's never been my favorite occupation. I somehow don't have the build for it. Rubs my cellulite the wrong way."

Hideyoshi seemed to be gradually coming to terms with the idea that a woman—a foreign woman—might have opinions and ideas worth considering. "The ronin can run but they cannot hide from the wrath of Lord Mashashige. His eye is sharper than an eagle's. His scent better than a wild boar. His hearing like a panther. His courage that of the fiery dragon, and his wisdom more cunning than the most cunning of foxes. Before the next day is done, we shall have ridden them down and trapped them all. And they will pay the blood price to the great Lord Mashashige.'' He smiled, the scar making it a crooked leer. ''Oh, my *gaijin* friends, so much blood will flow.''

''WHAT'S THAT?'' Ryan asked Hideyoshi, pointing to a building that stood on a tall headland that jutted out into the ocean. It was two storys high, with dozens of windows, and looked remarkably like one of the abandoned motels that were still dotted all across Deathlands.

''It was a house for staying a night. Built on American pattern.''

Ryan nodded. So his first impression had been correct. ''It in use?''

The samurai looked across at Yashimoto, who was riding a little to one side of them. ''I think it has been closed for some years, has it not?''

''I do not know. I do not travel as far as you do. My duties keep me back at the fortress more than I would like.''

''Someone's been there recently,'' Ryan said. ''Still see traces of a fire out back.''

A thin column of what looked like woodsmoke was curling up into the afternoon air, before the rising northerly breeze shredded it away.

"Tracks lead there," Jak said. "Could loop around and see if come out other side."

The column had stopped.

Mashashige beckoned for his two chief advisers to come forward to the head of the small army, indicating that the Westerners should also join him.

"We are sadly much fewer in our best samurai after the tsunami," he said. "We cannot trust our peasants to scout for us. They are lower than low."

"Want me to go ahead, mebbe with Jak and J.B. to have a look for you?" Ryan asked.

The shogun considered the offer for several seconds. "I think that it would be difficult," he replied. "My people have great *kenbei* . . ." He looked at Yashimoto.

"Hatred of Americans," his second-in-command explained. "This is very true, Lord."

"We are a society that believes in the old traditions. To go against them is to risk a loss of honor and a deep loss of face. No, I cannot accept your brave offer of help, Cawdor-san. But I thank you for it."

Ryan sniffed. "Sure. So, what do we do? Ride up and hope that the ronin has fucked off?"

"You are angry," Mashashige said. "Why?"

"Stupidity always makes me angry," Ryan snarled. "They got an ambush there and you could lose half or more of your men before you can get off a shot against them. That place looks as good a defensive position as I've seen in a month of Sundays. Could be hiding a hundred ronin."

Yashimoto laughed, throwing back his head, the pallid sunlight gleaming off the horned helmet that framed his face. "The killer of my beloved brother is frightened!" he crowed. "I catch scent of fear on him."

"Man who doesn't sometimes get frightened has got either no brain or no breath," Ryan said. "That place could be filled with your enemy."

"Then we shall slay them."

"Why choose hard when you can pick easy?" The ancient scar across Ryan's face was throbbing with fire as his anger surged.

Mashashige held up his hand. "Enough red-eyed talk. You are both right and you are both wrong. We will all ride up to the place and see if they shoot at us. If they do not, then we can bring up the rest of the sec men."

"One way of doing it," J.B. said.

"We could send in a party of foot fighters," Hide-yoshi said cautiously.

"Not honorable," the shogun replied.

"No, of course not honorable," the chief of his sec force agreed.

"Not honorable," Yashimoto echoed with rather less enthusiasm.

"Then let's get to it," J.B. said.

Ryan sighed with exasperation at the lack of combat tactics. "I guess that waiting until dark to increase your chances wouldn't be honorable, neither."

Mashashige considered the question. "It would be difficult," he said.

IN THE END they dismounted and approached the building on foot, Mashashige conceding that they would make more-difficult targets that way.

Yashimoto swaggered around, eyeing Ryan, his hand gripping the hilt of his sword.

"Tight-assed little shit, isn't he?" Mildred whispered to Krysty, watching as the stocky samurai walked away from them toward a small hill.

"Way he walks makes him seem like he's carrying a raisin between the cheeks of his butt for charity," Krysty said with a giggle, making Mildred laugh out loud. Both of them looked away as the samurai turned suspiciously at the outburst of noise.

THOUGH THE WOMEN objected strongly, Ryan insisted that they should both stay behind with the main force when the initial assault party went in.

"Why?"

"Times like this, there isn't time to start a debating group," Ryan replied.

"I think that Master Cawdor is probably correct in this," Doc said in his best orotund voice. "I sense danger in this procedure."

"And you stay, as well, Doc."

"What?"

"Deafness isn't among your weaknesses, old friend. Just me, J.B. and Jak are going in on this one. I don't like it much myself, Doc."

"The Tanners of Vermont have not been noteworthy for being backward at going forward," Doc said, drawing himself up to his full seventy-five inches, knee joints cracking like dry twigs. "In this matter I feel that the concept of our hosts regarding honor is of some relevance."

"Doc..." Ryan bit his lip. "This has a real bad feeling to me. If there's going to be some chilling, then me, J.B. and Jak are the ones with the best hope of walking from it without buying the farm."

"It is not a question of doubting courage, Master Cawdor? I would not feel happy if it were courage."

Ryan patted him on the shoulder. "When they handed out courage points, you got a whole lot more than your fair share, Doc. I swear that."

Yashimoto called over to them, "We are going now into the attack, *gaijin*. Perhaps you should all be staying here safe with women."

"Perhaps you could shove it up a dead skunk's ass," Ryan said, bowing politely to the puzzled samurai.

THE SIGN HAD FALLEN DOWN, maybe a hundred years earlier, but it looked as if it had been recently excavated and nailed back into place: Best Eastern Serendipity Overlook.

Jak jerked a thumb at it. "What's mean?"

Ryan carried the big SIG-Sauer cocked and ready in his hand as they picked their way closer to the predark motel. "Can't tell you."

He'd left the Steyr SSG-70 rifle behind. J.B. had also left the murderous Smith & Wesson M-4000 scattergun with Doc and the ladies.

They were a hundred yards from the main body of watching troops, roughly the same distance from the front of the weather-stained building. The frail pillar of smoke had vanished from the rear of the motel, and the building was still and silent. A small lizard skittered across the overgrown path, pausing for a moment to gaze at the intruders, a turquoise ruff lifting around its wattled throat.

The path toward the entrance was pocked with the marks of a number of horses. There was no doubt at all that the ronin had passed that way within the past two or three hours, but it didn't answer the important question whether they were still hiding behind the blank windows.

Just before parting, Ryan had asked Krysty whether she felt anyone close by. But the sheer numbers of Mashashige's own army blurred her mutie sense and made it impossible to focus on the motel.

Now the shogun was striding ahead of the others, still wearing his black cotton gown, one hand steadying the hilt of his long sword. Yashimoto was close at his heels, with Hideyoshi in third place. There were four more of the senior samurai who had survived the tidal wave, though Ryan didn't know any of their names, as they kept to themselves and hadn't made any real attempt to speak to the outlanders.

Ryan walked a couple of paces farther back, trying to keep a clear line of sight on the building. Jak was off to his right, his big blaster still holstered, and J.B. stalked along on his left, cradling the Uzi.

"Want us to go around back?" he called to the shogun. "Come in the other side?"

"We will all go in together. Not sneaking like thieves and spies, cowarding in bushes and trees. Together in the front door of the place."

"We'll all go together when we go," Ryan whispered. "All for one and all dead."

"This is insane, Ryan," J.B. whispered. "If they got rifles, they can take us all in a single volley."

"See the windows?"

"Sure."

"Not one of them's broken. If you were planning to ambush someone, you'd clear the glass out of the way first. Whatever the ronin got planned, I don't figure it as a shooting."

"Hope you're right, bro," the Armorer said. "Short hairs at the back of my neck don't tell me there's men with rifles all set up to take us. Then again, I could be wrong."

"More likely try and waste lots of army," Jak said. "Not just half dozen of us."

"Lure the rest in, you mean?" Ryan considered that possibility. "Could be, Jak. Could be."

Mashashige had stopped, holding up his hand, looking behind him for his foreign allies. "Now we go in," he said.

Ryan stared him in the face, sensing the unspoken challenge. "Yeah, why not?" he said.

Chapter Nineteen

As soon as they were inside the heavy glass front doors, Ryan knew that they were safe in the rambling motel. The place smelled as though it had been empty for a good hundred years, the air stale and dull.

"If they were here, they've gone," he said to Hideyoshi. "And they didn't stay long."

"Could have left a few suicide troops behind," J.B. said to Ryan. "That was the Nip way in the Second World War in the Cific. Considered it an honor to take a few Yanks with them to their happy hunting grounds. Bite on a gren."

Mashashige and his colleagues were already vanishing into the shadowy interior of the old motel. Behind Ryan, the afternoon sun was sinking lower, turning a deep red as it dropped away. It was becoming markedly colder.

"This could be good base for night," Jak suggested, hands in his pockets, narrow shoulders hunched. "How far we chase them ronin?"

Ryan shook his head, seeing a long sofa squatting in a corner and sitting cautiously on it. "Don't know, Jak. There's all this honor crap that means so much to the shogun and his merry gang. Seems that the invasion of his palace really put the rats in the corn for him."

J.B. walked around the lobby, looking at the pictures that hung on the walls. Most were stylized landscapes, some of them showing the strange foam-topped waves they'd seen before. "Strange, this place wasn't stripped," he said.

Yashimoto reentered the room, hearing the Armorer's words and laughing harshly. "This was for *gaijin.* Many were massacred here in skydark time. Bodies thrown into sea. It was revenge against Americans for many bad things. So place is now haunted by spirits of dead."

Mashashige appeared, almost invisible in the darkness. "But all that was generations ago, Takei. We are wiser now."

He turned to Ryan. "The ronin were here but they have gone."

He spoke to Hideyoshi. "Bring men and supplies. Here we will stay for the night. Any spirits left can do us no hurt."

THE WAGS CARRIED large supplies of candles and lamps, and the old Best Eastern motel was soon filled with light and noise, dismissing the shadows to the blackest corners.

Cooking fires were lit in an overgrown atrium courtyard, with caldrons of fish, vegetable soup and spiced rice soon bubbling merrily over them.

Hideyoshi was sitting with the outlanders in one of the lounges, golden light dancing off his balding pate. Like the rest of the samurai, he had peeled off his ornate, heavy armor and looked like a middle-aged storekeeper relaxing after work in a deep imitation-leather armchair.

"How many sentries you posted?" J.B. asked. "Place positioned like this should be easy to guard against a mass attack. Ocean on three sides of it."

"One samurai and ten men, changing them every two hours. Lord Mashashige fears... No, not fears. Thinks that the ronin might steal boats up the coast and try and attack us from the sea, up the cliffs."

Ryan nodded. "Could be."

He had scouted the motel, both inside and outside, and suspected that the sheer rock face down to the turbulent ocean might prove unscalable, which didn't mean that desperate men might not attempt it.

In the old war wag days with the Trader, he'd watched as some jolt-crazed stickies had come at them through banks of coiled razor wire. They literally ripped their bodies apart, leaving chunks of bloody flesh and gobbets of muscle hanging on the wire, but still fighting to reach the norms.

Most of the shogun's sizable army was camped in what had once been a ballroom or conference suite, a huge vault of a room, well over a hundred feet square, with a polished wood-block floor and heavy steel sec shutters over all of the windows, making it a good place to defend.

It had also crossed Ryan's mind that it would make one hell of a trap.

MASHASHIGE HAD ALLOCATED a large family suite for the outlanders. It was on the north side of the complex, on the second floor, with a balcony overlooking the top of the cliffs. It held two double beds and two singles.

The bowls of food served to them were good and warm and nourishing, though Ryan still found it clumsy and messy to eat with only his fingers.

There was a general air of excitement in the packed motel, as though everyone anticipated catching up with the fleeing ronin in the next day or so.

Most of the companies elected to go to bed early, with the expectation of an early start around dawn the next morning. But Ryan found sleep difficult and eased himself from the bed, trying not to disturb Krysty.

But she awakened anyway.

"Going for a leak, lover?"

"No. Just feel uneasy. Thought I might walk around. Check security."

"Not our problem."

He nodded, sitting on the bed by her, whispering to avoid waking any of the others. "Staying alive's always our problem, Krysty."

"True. Mind if I join you?"

"'Course not. Bring the blaster."

She smiled, her teeth white in the gloom. "Teaching your grandmother how to suck eggs, lover?"

He kissed her quickly and lightly on the cheek. "Sorry. I'm just taking a look off the balcony."

"Only got to pull my pants and my boots on. Be with you."

Ryan eased open the windows and breathed in the cold salt-laden air. There was a sliver of moon, half-hidden behind a ragged wall of spindrift cloud. Even from the height of the cliff top, he could hear the crashing of the breakers on the boulder-strewn shingle far below him.

He'd checked it out before dark, and he could see no possibility of a sizable group managing the climb, though a determined lone assassin might make it.

There was no sign of life outside the window. Ryan leaned across the iron railing, peering to his left, glimpsing one of the armed patrols of Mashashige's soldiers, marching steadily around an inner perimeter.

From the direction of the ballroom he caught a snatch of song, sounding harsh and ugly to his Western hearing.

Krysty was at his side, pressing against him. "No ronin?"

"Not yet."

"We going to look around inside?"

"Yeah."

"Got your blaster, lover?" she asked, teasing him. "Just wanted to make sure you hadn't forgotten."

"I haven't. Come on. And try not to trip over your own feet and wake everyone."

THE MOTEL WAS SLIDING into sleep. Even the noise from the ballroom was diminishing. They passed several internal guards and also encountered Mashashige, striding along one of the corridors past what had once been a weight room filled with rusting Nautilus equipment.

"It is quiet, friends," the shogun said.

"Hope it stays that way," Ryan replied. "Just taking a last look around."

"I will walk along with you, Cawdor-san, and with you, Krysty Wroth."

Ryan found it impossible to dislike the warlord, admiring his total cool.

They walked together in a companionable silence until they reached the ballroom doors. One of the crimson-and-white-uniformed sec men was fiddling with the outer bolts, but he bowed and walked quickly away as they approached him.

"I don't know how you recognize all your men, Lord Mashashige," Krysty said.

"I do not know them all. His face was that of a strange person to me."

"In strength there's weakness," Ryan said, holding the heavy door open for the shogun and Krysty to walk through.

There was row upon row of the troops, all sleeping on thin straw mattresses that had been carried in the wags.

"They are brave and loyal," Mashashige said.

"You pay them, or is it like family?" Ryan asked. "If you got beaten by the ronin, then would your men stay and support whoever the leader of the ronin is?"

"You mean my younger brother, Ryuku?"

"Brother?"

Krysty stared at the shogun. "All of this is a matter between you and your brother?"

"He has tried for some years to defeat me. But he becomes more bold and tries to slay me in my own home. That is not to be forgiven by me."

Ryan whistled softly between his teeth. "I never knew that we were involved in brotherly hate."

The shogun came close to smiling. "Do you know anything of brothers, Cawdor-san?"

Ryan touched the eye patch. "Brother did this to me," he said. "Oh, yeah, I know all there is to know about how brothers can treat each other."

Mashashige gestured at the room filled with men. "It is great stupid thinking from Ryuku. He has less than half the number of warriors, though we have been sorely wounded by the tsunami slaying some of our best samurai. Such men are not easily replaced by me."

The moonlight was filtered through the steel shutters over all the windows. Here and there men were snoring. A few were awake, propped up on their elbows to watch their lord and the *gaijin*. The main door of the ballroom closed softly.

Ryan heard the faint sound of a bolt sliding across and a lock clicking into action.

"What?" He turned.

Mashashige also heard it and swung around, his sword miraculously appearing in his right hand. "We have been locked in," he said quietly.

"Man who was messing with the bolts when we came in," Krysty stated. "Got a bad feeling from him."

"You were right." The shogun looked around the room. "Does this mean they hope to hold us trapped here while traitors open the gates to my brother and the ronin who wait?" He shook his head. "No, they would not pass the guards without a warning."

Ryan was like a caged panther constantly moving, head darting from side to side, trying to see what the threat could be and how it would be delivered.

Other than the main door and the windows, the only other way in or out of the ballroom would be through the rectangular air vents in the ceiling. But they weren't big enough for access.

One of the sec men in the far corner of the huge room, directly below one of the vents, suddenly began to cough.

Ryan spun, seeing that two more of the sec soldiers, close in the corner, had also awakened, stricken with coughing and sneezing fits. He looked up at the big air vents, a sudden dreadful suspicion filling his mind.

Krysty did the same, grabbing him by the arm as still more of the army jerked from sleep, spluttering, choking and rubbing at their eyes.

It was Mashashige who voiced the danger, seeing a faint white mist billowing down from the ceiling. "It is an attack with gas," he said with an almost insane calm. "The ronin have trapped us like foxes in their den and will kill us with poison gas."

Chapter Twenty

The doors were reinforced with sec steel, and Ryan saw immediately that there was no way he could shoot out the locks. It would take four ounces of ex-plas or a couple of implode grens to break them down.

"Windows," Krysty said.

"Shutters are sec steel, as well."

Now it seemed as if everyone in the room was waking to a choking fog of swirling poisonous gas. Near the entrance doors, Ryan, Krysty and the shogun were farthest from the attack, which had started in a distant corner.

Ryan caught the first sniff of it and immediately found his eye watering, the back of his throat prickling as though someone had sprayed pepper in his face.

Krysty had pulled out a kerchief and pressed it against her nose and mouth, standing still with her eyes shut. "Gaia! What is it?"

Mashashige replied, "Sarin gas, I think. There was a supply left after terrorist actions in last predark months. It kills."

Ryan wondered whether the gas was heavier or lighter than air. But he decided immediately that it didn't matter, since the panicking men were running around and stirring it up all around the ballroom.

"We cannot block the vents," Mashashige said. "There is not a hope. I regret that you will die with me in a fight not of your making."

"No rad-blasted fight, is it?" Ryan coughed so hard it felt as though he was going to bring up his guts, sickened by the realization that time was racing away and the last train to the coast was already pulling out of the station.

With everyone on board.

There was a little light filtering in through narrow strips of wired glass set in the entrance doors. Only about three inches wide, they offered no chance of escape.

But Ryan stumbled toward them, holding the SIG-Sauer in front of him, dragging Krysty with him. Mashashige followed them, ignoring the mayhem behind as men fell down, bleeding from the eyes, noses and mouths, hands clawing at their own faces to try to relieve the agonizing effects of the gas.

"Can't get through there," Krysty panted.

Ryan pressed the muzzle of the heavy blaster against the nearest panel and fired three shots, shattering the glass, letting in a tiny amount of fresh air. He did the same on the second and third of the three strips, pressing the barrel out into the cool air of the hallway and firing off the rest of the mag.

He was glad that the built-in baffle silencer had finally given up the ghost some months earlier, allowing the full-throated roar of the blaster to echo out into the rest of the Best Eastern Serendipity Overlook.

"Someone will hear and come," Mashashige said, coughing, his voice muffled by the wide sash that he'd wrapped around his narrow, angular face.

Behind them there was a scene of nightmare horror.

Ryan glanced over his shoulder, wiping his streaming eye, seeing that the gas was still vomiting from the vents, swirling around, flooding the lungs of every man there.

"This," Krysty panted, pressing the short-barreled double-action Smith & Wesson 640 into Ryan's hand. "Use it as . . . it as well. . . ."

He pushed it through the broken glass, the muzzle snagging a moment on the torn reinforcing wire. He pumped the trigger with five spaced shots, the boom of the .38s seeming deafening in the confined space.

"Push face against holes," he panted to Krysty. "Get bit of clean air."

"And you, lover."

"Not room."

Ryan could feel the gas burning deep in his chest. His tongue felt swollen and tender, his lips as though someone had peeled them and rubbed them with sliced jalapeños. His right eye was watering, hot liquid gushing down his cheek. The raw socket of the missing left eye was brimming with fiery salt.

Breathing was becoming more and more difficult, and he could already sense that he was losing control over his mind. The swirling feeling was like the worst jump ever made, but with the additional burden of the choking gas.

"Do it," he panted, grabbing at her, his fingers locking in her tight-curled hair. He forced her in front of him, onto her knees, pressing her face toward the shattered glass in the locked sec doors.

He felt her struggle against him, but only weakly, like a drowning puppy.

The noise from behind Ryan was coming in waves, louder and quieter. Several men had pushed against him, trying to get at the doors, but he'd fended them off, beating at them with the butt of the empty SIG-Sauer. Mashashige was at his side, sword drawn, using it in great scything sweeps to hold back his own men and keep the doors free.

The shogun was barking at them in short, coughing bursts of Japanese, but they were all around him, like weeping, rabid dogs, lurching and coughing, strings of bloody phlegm dangling from mouths and noses, eyes protruding like the stops on a mission-hall harmonium.

Ryan felt Krysty move against his hand, her fingers pinching his leg. He bent to hear what she was trying to say.

"Mildred..."

Now the air was filled with a helpless, hopeless screaming, like lost souls in the deepest circle of purgatory. Ryan opened and closed his good eye, unable to tell any difference. There was so much pain that he was blinded by it, fighting for breath, losing his hold on Krysty.

There was a freezing agony suddenly, from somewhere in front of him. A cold wind from the dark side of Hades, searing his tender skin.

Hands reached for him, pulling at him. Ryan made a last attempt to drive away these new demons, clubbing at them, but the darkness gathered around his legs and swept up his body like a rising black tide.

And he was sinking into it, admitting to himself that the waters around him had grown and grown.

And grown.

RYAN OPENED his eye, rolled on his side and threw up, the blood-flecked puke splattering on the dusty wooden floor. The pain was excruciating and he coughed, feeling it rending deep in his chest.

"Want some water, lover?"

He'd closed his eye with the sharpness of the agony, but now he cautiously opened it again. His field of vision was filled with what looked like a veil of living fire. He blinked to try to clear his sight, feeling a flood of salt tears coursing down his stubbled cheeks.

The vivid scarlet banner that waved in front of him was the hair of Krysty Wroth. She sat in a folding chair at the side of his bed.

"Water?" he muttered.

"Yeah. Helps. We can bathe your eye later and rinse out your mouth."

"Yeah." He was aware that while he'd been unconscious someone had crept by and filled his throat with red-hot coils of barbed razor-wire, and that the inside of his mouth and his tongue lacked any skin. He licked at his lips, finding them blistered and tender.

"Sit up." She put her arm around him, eased him into an upright position and held a glass of water to his mouth for him to sip at.

He swallowed a couple of mouthfuls, gagging at the discomfort, trying to push the glass away.

"Slow and easy, lover," she whispered.

Gradually the memory of the last moments before diving into the dark lake came back to him.

"You're all right?" he whispered.

"Yeah."

"The shogun . . . What's his name?"

"Mashashige?"

"Yeah. He make it?"

"In the next room. Real sick like you, but Mildred says he'll pull through all right."

"Mildred opened the doors for us?"

Krysty nodded, giving him another sip of water. "Heard the shooting and came running. Got here just in time for you and me and Mashashige."

Ryan caught the subtext in her careful choice of words. "The others?"

She took the half-empty glass from him and rested it carefully on a small table by the head of the bed. "Not many made it."

"The sarin gas chilled them?"

Krysty nodded. "J.B. says there's no doubt that's what it was. Sarin. Says the Nazis developed it, and then it got used a lot by terrorist groups in the States and in parts of the Far East. Lethal stuff. Cheap and easy to make as soon as you got the right chemical mix."

"How many dead?"

"Not sure. By the time the doors were opened, most of those who'd been on the far side of the ballroom had already received a fatal dose. Drowned in frothing fluid that filled their lungs. Bastard way to go."

Ryan sniffed. "Tell me about it, lover. So, the death toll was high?"

"Hundred dead, or so badly tainted by the gas that Mildred says they won't see out the next twenty-four hours. Only about a dozen are going to make it."

"Fireblast! Bad as that?"

Krysty looked at him, and he saw that her vivid emerald eyes were streaked with red, the lids swollen and sore. "Almost a perfect trap."

"Near enough."

"Yashimoto wants to chase after the ronin. Hideyoshi is all for caution. Points out that the ronin most likely outnumber us now. He thinks we should try and get back safe to the ville, soon as possible."

"Sounds right to me," Ryan said, moving to a more comfortable position on the bed.

"But neither of them'll want to move a muscle until Mashashige recovers."

"What's our total force now?" He reached up and wiped his eye with the sleeve of his shirt.

"The six of us, Mashashige, Yashimoto and Hideyoshi, and four or five of the top samurai. Half a dozen men who were with the wags. Very few survivors from the ballroom."

"Men on sentry watch."

She nodded. "Seems they saw someone snaking out of the motel, presumably after he'd set the gas going. He slipped over the edge of the cliff, and they lost sight of him. Samurai with them claims the ronin must've been chilled, but there's no proof."

Ryan swung his legs over the side of the bed, groaning at the pain, holding up his hand to stop Krysty from helping him. "No, I'm all right. I'll be all right. Doesn't much matter whether the man triggered the gas is alive or dead. Like to think the son of a bitching bastard bought it, but it doesn't matter much one way or the other."

"They say they'll have to dump the corpses into the sea. No way we can bury them or take them back to the fortress."

"True. Water's so contaminated it won't make much difference to it."

Despite his protests, Krysty put her arm around him to steady him as he stood. "Mildred said that the more water you drank, the quicker you'd feel better. And take slow, deep breaths. Get rid of all the sarin inside you."

Ryan sighed. "Hope she's right."

AS IN ALL MATTERS MEDICAL, Dr. Mildred Wyeth had the ace on the line.

By noon, after drinking about five pints of water, Ryan was feeling more himself. The swelling had gone down from his mouth and tongue, and he had washed out his eye several times, until it ceased weeping. The pain in his chest was still there when he took a particularly deep breath, but that, too, seemed to be easing with every hour that passed.

He found Mildred out on the field behind the motel, where corpses lay in serried ranks, with a dismally small number of survivors receiving her attention.

He walked across to where she was crouched over one of the sec men in his bright red-and-white uniform. But this man's clothes were stained with blood, vomit and excrement. Ryan had already learned that a significant number of those most seriously afflicted by the murderous gas had lost control of both bladder and bowels.

He touched her gently on the shoulder. "Just to say thanks for doing the business, Mildred," he said.

"Wish I could 'do the business' for a few of these poor bastards."

It was a heavenly morning, with a bright sun peering over the mountains to the east of the motel, sparkling off the calm ocean.

And they stood surrounded by the stillness of death, broken only by the coughing and weeping of some of the living.

"Need to get them home, soon as possible," Mildred said. "Quicker we do that, the better their chances of pulling through successfully."

"Mashashige got anything to say on that?" Ryan asked.

"Not a lot. I thought that John Dix was a man of few words, but he's positively garrulous compared with the shogun."

"Doc says he's spoken to Mashashige, and we're pulling out of here just before dusk. Move at night. Reduces the risk of the ronin coming at us. Be sitting targets for them at the moment."

"Think they'll attack again?" Mildred asked, wiping her hands on a piece of bloody cotton waste and throwing it down to the sodden dirt.

"Don't see why not." Ryan thought about the tactical aspect of what had happened. Of what might happen. "They had to have a contingency plan in case the gassing didn't work. Outnumbered, they must have withdrawn a good distance. Leave scouts close by to recce on us."

"So?"

"So they'll know by now how successful they were. But they know we'll be on triple-red alert. Won't come at us now, out here in the open. No, if I was the leader of these ronin, I'd wait. Try and circle around. And then mebbe stage an ambush some time tomorrow. That's my guess."

Like most of Ryan's combat guesses, it turned out to be correct.

Chapter Twenty-One

They set off as Mashashige had wanted, leaving the site of the slaughter as the sun disappeared behind a dusty bank of cloud, away to the west.

The wags were loaded with the sick and the dying.

"I doubt more than a dozen of those who were trapped in the ballroom during the worst of the sarin attack are going to make it back home," she said, which left the shogun with a total force of less than twenty-five, not counting Ryan and the others.

The rocky coastline was littered with the drifting corpses of the dead sec men, mostly floating facedown beneath the cliff from which they'd been tumbled.

Ryan had been watching the grim procedure, seeing the way an occasional V-shaped fin appeared in the calm water. More and more of the sharks scented the feast and arrived to dine, turning the ocean into a pink, frothing maelstrom.

But there were so many bodies that even the hungry predators eventually went away, leaving most of the dead sec men to bob and rock around the weed-slick boulders.

Jak had suggested that the reason the sharks seemed to be less than enthusiastic to finish the feasting might have been because the corpses were contaminated by the gas.

THEY TRAVELED ON through the hours of darkness, under a sailing moon that gave them enough light to see the trail. The narrow and dangerous part of the track, where Ryan had nearly plunged to his death, was impassable for the wags, which had come around by a longer path. Now they had to return to the fortress by that alternative route.

Ryan led the group of six friends, riding ahead of the wags, behind Mashashige, Yashimoto and Hideyoshi. The second-in-command, Takei Yashimoto, had renewed his threat against the *gaijin*, picking a moment when his lord had ridden on to the front, joining the scouts for a while.

"I think that your life is now numbered in days," he said darkly.

Ryan's thoughts had been miles away, many mornings and a thousand miles back. He wondered about the last glimpse that he'd had of Trader, facing odds on a bleak and lonely beach, wondering if the old man had finally taken the high trail into the mountains, or whether they'd meet one day, somewhere further down the line. It was hard to think of Trader as finally dead.

"What?" he said to the samurai.

"What happened back there in motel was your fault. I have told Lord Mashashige that I believe you are bad luck to us. Probably working with ronin traitors."

"And what did the shogun say?"

"He said yes to me."

Ryan smiled. "Truly?"

"Of course."

"He believes that we are helping the traitors? Even though Krysty and I came close to being chilled by the gas? And the few men who were saved were saved only by me and by Mildred Wyeth? Mashashige still thinks us evil?"

Yashimoto's badly scarred face broke into a broad smile. "Yes, he does, *gaijin*."

"I'll go and ask him myself."

The smile disappeared like good health in a rad hot spot. "Ask him?"

"Sure. I'll just kick on and ride alongside and say that Yashimoto tells me you think we're all traitors. See what he says then."

"No. That is not good idea."

"Why not?"

"He will think you mad."

"Mebbe he'll think you mad, Yashimoto," Ryan said, grinning wolfishly.

The samurai shook his head, his armor and helmet glinting in the last shards of moonlight. Dawn was close around the corner, and they weren't all that far from home.

"Do not say this thing."

"Because it's a damn lie?"

Yashimoto pointed a finger at Ryan. "You and I are linked together. I cast the stone in the mirror, and the face in the shards of glass is yours. I light the incense, and the eye in the smoke is yours. I spill blood, and the pattern spells your name. The protection of Lord

Mashashige will not run forever. His great eagle's shadow will not cover you, and you will run clothesless in the snow like a trembled hare."

"You want to sort this, we can get down and do it right now," Ryan said. "Knives or blasters or hand-to-hand. I don't give a flying shit how and when."

"Lord Mashashige would not allow me to fight. In any case I would lose honor in slaying a *gaijin* such as you are, an untouchable village scum peasant filth lower than dog."

Ryan nodded. "Sure. And on top of all that, the real reason you won't fight me is because you're chicken-shit frightened. You know I'd chill you. Any of us could chill you. Doc or Jak or Mildred. Any of us. Braggart blowhard coward is what you are, Yashimoto. When we get back to the fortress, then I might just tell you that out loud, in public. See how you like them eggs."

THE SHOGUN CONSULTED with his leading warriors, involving the outlanders in the tactical discussion.

"It is soon dawn. Do we go on or stay until dark again? I know from Dr. Wyeth—" he nodded to Mildred "—that speed will save lives. But to travel out in open daylight might also lose lives. If ronin come after us."

"They will," Ryan said.

"How you do know that?" Yashimoto asked suspiciously. "You know their plans?"

Ryan ignored the question. "There's been dust blowing from the trail to the north of us. Over the steep pass where our wags can't go. I'd bet a peanut to a candy bar that it's the enemy. Means they're likely to get ahead of us in an hour or so, whatever you do."

"You say we should go or stay?" Mashashige asked. "I do not understand."

"We go on in daylight, they'll likely coldcock us. More chance for us in darkness. Cuts the odds advantage that they got over us. Sneaks their edge."

But all of the samurai were for going on in daylight. Both Yashimoto and Hideyoshi pushing hard, the senior warriors falling back on the old standby of honor.

"We lose face to ronin if we hide our heads like *obasan* scared of mouse in kitchen."

Krysty nudged Mildred. "Wish they'd use grandfathers instead of grandmothers as term of abuse."

"Still better to be a little humble and a lot alive than a very proud corpse," Ryan offered.

"To live without honor is the same as not living at all," Yashimoto snarled.

"You listen to your dog?" Ryan asked.

The shogun shook a finger at him, like an old-fashioned schoolteacher reproving an overfamiliar pupil. "Insulting someone can be like a sharp sword that twists in the hand and cuts the owner," he said.

"So you'll go in daylight?" Ryan asked.

Mashashige nodded slowly. "We will be home the quicker and, I think, none the less safe."

"Sure hope you're right," Ryan said.

THE WAGS CRAWLED along through the dawning, stopping only once at first light for Mildred to go through them and check quickly on the living and the not-living.

The latter were put into one wag, for safe burial with honors when they returned to the palace.

Six of the sickest had died during the latter part of the night.

It was around nine-thirty in the morning by Ryan's wrist chron. They had moved down to a lower level during the hours of darkness, passing the factories with their blazing hearths, ovens and smelters.

Shadowy figures scurried through the pools of golden-and-silver light, among the raw fires and wreaths of bitter, choking smoke, looking, as Doc commented, "like something glimpsed in one of Doré's illustrations of immortal Dante's Hades."

Now they were passing through a vestigial forest, alongside one of the sulfurous streams that ran, arid and lifeless, across the blighted landscape.

When the shooting began.

GREAT CLODS OF DIRT erupted from the slope behind the lead wag, and long splinters of white wood were stripped from the conifers. The sound of the blaster followed hot on the heels of the shells, a steady rumbling, like distant thunder across a mountain range.

Everyone on horseback swung from the saddle and dropped to the ground.

"What the fuck is it?" Ryan yelled. "Sounds like bastard artillery."

The invisible gunners weren't that good with their powerful weapon, failing to range it in, even with a prolonged burst of firing.

"Something big and strong," the Armorer shouted. "Sounds like one of them revolver cannons, an Oerlikon-Contraves 35000."

There was a pause in the shooting.

Mashashige was up on his feet, sword drawn, eyes searching the woodland on the far side of the shallow valley, trying to locate the enemy.

"Get himself blown apart doing that," Jak said, lying facedown a few paces to the left of Ryan.

The ponies had been freaked by the noise and the sudden disappearance of their riders, and had galloped off into the woods on the left of the trail.

The gun opened up again, this time with a much shorter burst, two or three shells striking the second of the wags, literally blowing it apart in a giant explosion of canvas, wood and torn flesh.

"Got us cold," Ryan said. "Anyone see where they got the blaster located?"

Krysty nodded. "Yeah. See that bald rock, yonder, splashed with white? Go about twenty yards left and there's a hollow. Gun's in there."

Ryan looked where she pointed. "Yeah. Got it." He looked around the area. "If I got a little higher up on our side, I could see them. Hit them with the Steyr. Slow them some."

J.B. rattled off his knowledge of the hidden piece of light artillery. "Built just before skydark. Fires thousand rounds a minute. Thirty-five mm ammo. All sorts. Antiaircraft, armor-piercing, full and subcaliber. Linkless feed. Real major triple-power. If they got enough ammo, they can wipe us all out here. Too heavy to move easy and quick.''

A third burst of shells whistled through the torn air, exploding to the left, far back on the trees.

"Not the finest marksmen in the world, are they?" Doc commented.

"Don't need to be with a gun like that," Ryan said. "Like J.B. says, if they got enough ammo..." He let the sentence trail away into the morning air.

Mashashige had also spotted the concealed blaster, and was pointing to its position, calling out to his samurai to charge it.

Ryan crawled across the clearing, wincing as another volley rattled overhead, the 35 mm shells bursting just above the lead wag.

"What you planning?" he shouted to the shogun.

"They hold the highest ground," Mashashige replied. "We must go and stop them from shooting at us."

"Just walk up there, nice as pie, and ask them to stop? That the idea?"

"We are men of honor. Though they are ronin, they are not without honor."

The air vibrated around them as another five seconds of shells crashed into the ground about thirty yards in front of them.

Everyone, including the shogun, dropped to the earth, hands over heads.

"Let me and my people handle it," Ryan said, feeling his ears ringing from the concussion of the explosions. "We can probably take them out."

"With your rifle?" Yashimoto asked. "It will be another page in the book of betraying."

"You might die," Mashashige said.

"Life is not worth a feather," Hideyoshi said with a laugh, slapping Ryan on the shoulder as they scrambled to their feet.

"One way of looking at it."

He turned to Mashashige. "Try and get your men and the wounded back into the trees. Give them some cover from the Oerlikon gun."

The shogun hesitated a moment, then nodded. "May all your gods go with you, Cawdor-san."

"Yeah. Yeah, thanks."

Chapter Twenty-Two

The plan was simple.

"I go up behind us and find a sighting place. Let the gunners have it. Once I start shooting, the rest of you go down into the valley fast as you can. Up into the forest the far side. And try and get close enough to the Oerlikon to take out anyone left with it. Destroy it and then straight back here."

"Want me to try with the revolver?" Mildred asked. "Range could be too long."

Ryan nodded. "I reckon so. Getting on for six, seven hundred yards. Should be easy meat for Steyr. Anyone got any questions?" There was a short pause. "No? Then, let's get on with it. Good luck, everyone. Do it to them before they do it to you. See if we can level up the odds some."

IT SEEMED THAT THE ENEMY wasn't all that experienced in using the heavy armament.

The shooting came in irregular bursts, and each time they were obviously having trouble aiming the Oerlikon. The 35 mm shells scythed overhead or sent up great bursts of dirt and splintered stone from well in front of the trapped expedition.

Ryan ran as fast as he could, ducking instinctively each time he heard the crackle of the revolver cannon, twisting and turning between the trees, working his way uphill. He glanced behind him to see when he could get in a clear shot across the valley.

Behind him J.B. let Jak take the lead, the rest of them strung out behind him as the white-haired teenager zigged and zagged between the trees, taking the narrow stream in a running jump. Doc was the only one who found the leap difficult, but he made it with a little help from his friends.

Krysty and J.B. were there to steady him, preventing him from falling back into the monstrously polluted, stinking watercourse.

"My good, good comrades... My thanks. I would not have cherished tumbling into that brimming cesspit." A dried leaf stuck to his lapel, and he plucked it off, allowing it to drift into the stream.

There was a puff of dirty yellow smoke and flame as the leaf ignited on contact with the water. Or what had once, possibly, been water.

"Gaia!" Krysty exclaimed. "I thought you might have got a soaking if you'd fallen in. I didn't expect you to run the risk of spontaneous ignition."

Doc smiled a little shakily. "Nobody expects the Spanish Inquisition," he said mysteriously.

Mildred laughed.

RYAN FOUND what he was looking for.

A broken pine, forked where it had been struck by lightning, provided a shooting platform about thirty feet in the air. It was easily accessible by the tumbled top half, which provided a simple ladder for him to climb.

Ryan shinnied up, the rifle bouncing on his back. He saw the muzzle-flash from the Oerlikon and flattened against the trunk of the pine as the half-dozen rounds whistled by, forty yards or so to his left, blowing a hundred-foot pine completely out of the ground.

He steadied himself in the fork and brought the Steyr SSG-70 to his shoulder. The bolt-action rifle fired a full-metal jacket 7.62 mm round, with ten in the clip. In the morning sunlight, there was little use for the night-scope, but the laser image enhancer was vital.

His initial guess at the range to the Oerlikon wasn't far off. It looked like about six hundred and fifty paces across the wooded valley to the long-barreled gun.

Ryan put his right eye to the sight and squinted. A vague thought crossed his mind that it was lucky that it had been his left eye cut out by his brother. It was almost impossible, even for the best of marksmen, to fire a standard bolt-action rifle left-handed and left-eyed.

He eased off the safety and took up the first pressure on the trigger, bringing the sight around to cover the Oerlikon emplacement.

There was a group of at least fifteen or twenty men around the light artillery piece, several of them shifting it by hand, while a man in a horned helmet strutted around giving orders. It struck Ryan that this might be Mashashige's renegade brother, Ryuku.

In which case, it would be a good idea to try to take him out early on.

The gun pit was the scene of frenzied activity. Before opening fire, Ryan used the laser sight to range around the wooded ground between himself and the ronin. He tried to spot some sign of Krysty and the others to see how far they'd gotten across the dead ground toward the enemy.

At first there seemed to be nothing moving among the deep shadows of the forest. Then he saw a flicker of light, a glimmer of white where there had been only blackness. Ryan focused on it, seeing that there was a splash of brilliant crimson close behind the magnesium flare that he knew was Jak Lauren. Krysty was right on his heels.

They were closer to the ronin than he'd expected, less than a hundred yards and moving cautiously upward.

"Time to get started on the chilling," he whispered to himself.

He set the sight and calculated drift and windage, then took up the pressure on the trigger again, the walnut stock firm against his shoulder.

Ryan braced himself and squeezed the trigger, feeling the familiar jolting impact run through him, the muzzle jerking upward.

He worked the bolt to lever another round under the hammer, the ejected spent cartridge tinkling against a jagged branch of the shattered tree, glinting in the morning sunlight as it fell to the soft carpet of leaf mold.

He peered again through the sight, seeing to his chagrin that the samurai who had appeared to be in charge of the ronin was unwounded. At a quick first glance, it looked as if he'd completely missed.

Then he saw a man just to the left of his target clutch at his chest and fold onto the ground.

At nearly a half mile across the valley, it wasn't possible to hear any shouts or screams, but he could watch the silent movie scrolling on.

Instant panic erupted among the gun's crew as they realized that they were under fire themselves.

Ryan had to keep shooting, before they realized where the bullets were coming from and took cover. He didn't just want to stop them shooting the long-barreled Oerlikon. It was important to kill as many of the gang of ronin as possible.

He aimed and fired three more spaced shots, seeing three men drop. The samurai had been quickest to react, pointing toward the invisible shootist with a drawn sword, hiding himself behind the body of the revolver cannon.

"Fireblast!" Ryan breathed, annoyed with himself for allowing the man to escape him. The wind had to be a little stronger in the valley than he'd allowed for. But to anyone else, it would have been remarkable shooting to put down four men with four bullets at that range.

"RYAN," J.B. said, as soon as he heard the cracking echo of the hunting rifle bounce across the valley. "Wonder if he can see us?"

"Still in cover." Jak looked ahead of them, up the slope. "Another couple minutes and can be among them."

They heard the booms of three more of the 7.62 mm rounds, snapping through the air not far above their heads, producing screams of pain and shock.

"Doing good," Mildred said, the ZKR 551 target pistol gripped in her right hand.

"Long as he doesn't shoot any of us by mistake." Krysty brushed back her hair from her eyes. "Wind's freshening, bringing the stink of pollution more strongly."

Doc discreetly cleared his throat. "Should we not be talking less and moving more?"

J.B. gave the old man the thumbs-up sign. "You're right, friend," he said. "Let's go do it."

RYAN FIRED TWO MORE SHOTS, but the gun emplacement was almost deserted now.

As far as he could see through the laser enhancer, four dead men lay sprawled around the silent Oerlikon, and one wounded man, who looked to be gut shot, rolled back and forth, his mouth open in a scream of agony.

"Time to move," Ryan said, starting to climb down from the tree.

THE SCREAMING WAS ENDLESS, a long, thin, high, hopeless note that rasped at the nerves.

"Bullet in the belly," J.B. said, taking the lead from Jak as they climbed within a few yards of the concealed gun emplacement.

"Ryan's stopped shooting." Mildred glanced over her shoulder, across the valley. "That mean he's chilled them all?" She angrily answered her own question. "'Course not, stupid bitch! He took out as many as he could. Rest are hiding."

"Or coming this way at a run," Krysty said. "Best all get ready. Expect the unexpected. Isn't that what Trader used to say, John?"

The Armorer frowned. "No. Can't say I ever heard him say that."

"Someone coming," Jak hissed.

RYAN FOUND Mashashige waiting for him, framed between Hideyoshi and Yashimoto.

The shogun called out as soon as he saw him. "The long gun has fallen into silence. This is your doing, Cawdor-san?"

"Yeah. Tried to get the samurai leading them."

"My brother, Ryuku?"

"Mebbe. Horned helmet. But I missed him. Got about four or five of the men with the Oerlikon."

Mashashige nodded. "Now we can follow your companions and hope to harm the ronin."

Ryan grinned. "Hell, why not?"

THE ACCURACY OF RYAN'S sniping had freaked out the ronin who'd been grouped around the gun. They had known that Mashashige and the outlanders with him were the better part of a half mile away from them, giving them the good sport of safely using the Oerlikon they'd found in a hidden military base a few weeks earlier. They'd saved it for just such an opportunity.

And then the gods turned their backs on them. Bullets struck from nowhere.

Five men were dead.

It seemed that every time the marksman fired his rifle from the distant trees, one of them fell dead or dying. There was no way that any ordinary human could shoot with such accuracy. It had to mean that Mashashige had enlisted some sort of supernatural help in his fight against them.

One of the fleeing ronin cried out that it was a punishment for using the dishonorable tactic of poison gas. It had turned the gods against them.

Krysty and the others, separated from the gun pit by only a thin screen of pines and some berried bushes, heard the harsh shouting. A commanding voice seemed to be trying to restore order and overcome the panic.

They could hear men running all around them, horses neighing and whips cracking in the panic of terror.

One of the ronin suddenly appeared through the brush, arms pumping, eyes wide and staring. He hardly seemed to notice the foreigners, carrying on as though he intended running straight past them.

J.B. shot him through the head with a single round from the Uzi, tumbling him over in the loose earth among the trees, his body rolling limply against the trunk of a slender, blighted, leprous conifer.

Another Japanese appeared, struggling to skid to a halt as he heard the vicious crack of the 9 mm machine pistol. He reached for the Nambu blaster holstered at his waist, but he was way too slow and way too late.

A second round from the Uzi took him between chest and throat, knocking him over in a welter of blood, his hands clasping the neat entrance wound, crimson gushing between them.

He tried to speak but failed.

And died.

"Let's go get the Oerlikon," J.B. said. "Shoot anything that moves."

But the clearing was empty. The only thing living was a fat little man, who was trying to push back loops of blood-slick yellow intestines that had slithered out of a gaping exit wound in his stomach.

He had stopped screaming and was muttering to himself in a quiet, preoccupied undertone, oblivious to the appearance of five of the hated round-eyes.

"Nearly done," Jak said, pausing to stoop and slit the dying man's throat with one of his throwing knives.

J.B. had moved, quick and catlike, to the far side of the clearing, where a narrow trail wound down the far side of a hogback ridge. "Off and running," he said.

"All of them?" Mildred asked.

The Armorer shook his head. "Can't be sure. Likely a few have taken off in other directions. Panic's real good way of losing your sense of direction." He grinned at Mildred. "Fact is, love, it's a good way of losing all your senses."

"How we wreck gun?" Jak had wiped his knife clean and sheathed it. He stared with his bloodred eyes at the immensely long barrel of the revolver cannon. "Never seen nothing like it. Not never."

"Easy," J.B. said. "Get plenty of mud. Enough around. Good and thick and rich in stones. And fill the damn blaster with it. Much as you can. Pack it in hard."

"Allow me to help," Doc said. "I can't wait to see the effect of John Barrymore's plan. Unless I miss my guess, it will be brutish and spectacular."

THOUGH HE WAS as fit as most men in Deathlands, probably fitter, Ryan was hard put to keep up with the slight figure of the barefoot Mashashige, as the elusive shogun darted toward the scene of the fighting.

The two men quickly outdistanced the other samurai, leaving the foot soldiers struggling in their wake as they leapt the polluted stream and started to climb the far side of the shallow valley toward the Oerlikon.

"The gun has stopped for good," the shogun said over his shoulder, seeming not the least out of breath. "You and your friends have done us well and proudly."

"Let's hope so," Ryan panted.

WHILE THE OTHERS WORKED quickly, jamming mud into the barrel of the revolver cannon, J.B. rigged up a long lanyard to the firing mechanism, uncoiling it to a safe distance behind the huge blaster.

None of the ronin remained in the area to bother them, though they'd heard a few of them slipping and sliding through the pines toward the stream that bisected the valley, sounding as if they were heading toward Ryan and the surviving Japanese.

"Sure that the shogun won't want to keep the Oerlikon for himself?" Mildred asked.

J.B. shook his head. He pushed back the fedora, wiped sweat from his forehead, then took off his glasses to give them an extra polish. "Thing this big takes some moving. The ronin have taken most of their transport. Mashashige doesn't have the manpower to shift this baby."

"You ready?" Jak was grinning, wiping mud off his hands onto his pants.

"Pretty well. Everyone get out of the way, around the back, far as you all can, and keep alert. Or better, move on down the hill, among the trees. I don't know exactly what'll happen when I fire it, with the blocked barrel, but it should be good and triple big. Spectacular!"

THE STEYR ACROSS RYAN'S shoulder was bruising his back as he jogged up the hill, now several yards behind the shogun, his heavy combat boots slithering in the damp dirt.

One of the ordinary fighting men who was part of the ronin's gang had appeared, sprinting for his life, down the narrow path toward them. He saw Mashashige standing foursquare in front of him and gave a small cry of dismay, hands coming together in prayer, starting to gabble for mercy or for forgiveness. Ryan wasn't sure which.

Either way, the shogun totally ignored him, using the point of the sword rather than the edge, lunging into the man's stomach. There was a savage twist of the wrist as the blade was withdrawn, opening a great sliced gash in the flesh, just above the dark blue cotton sash around his midriff.

The man fell and rolled on his back, eyes staring at the waving branches of the trees, losing focus as they moved toward Ryan. The mouth opened, speaking to the foreigner in a normal conversational tone. "I also wished to look through my wealthy uncle's microscope," he said.

Life deserted the eyes and he was dead.

"Horsemen!" Ryan called, pointing with the barrel of the SIG-Sauer.

There were three of them, all in samurai armor, all on small hill ponies. They lay low over the necks, spurring on, not hesitating at the sight of the shogun and the foreigner standing together, blocking the center of the path.

They were coming fast from uphill, all waving swords, faces contorted with hatred under the polished cheek plates of their ornamented helmets, tugging at the reins to make their mounts turn and twist.

"Mine!" Ryan yelled, expecting Mashashige to step aside to give him a clear shot at bringing down all three riders with the SIG-Sauer.

But the shogun stood statue still, the sword out in front of him, point to the earth, seeming totally oblivious to the triple death that galloped toward him.

Ryan had no chance at getting in a kill shot at all three of the enemy samurai.

He did his best, picking off the leader with a shot through the chest, the full-metal jacket bursting easily through the medieval armor, kicking the man back off his pony to clatter into the trees.

A snap shot at the second man missed completely as Mashashige shuffled a couple of paces to his left, forcing a split-second alteration of Ryan's aim.

There was just time for a third shot. The shogun was totally in the way, readying himself for a swing at the second mounted warrior, leaving Ryan a chance at the last man in the line. He was surprisingly tall, and his helmet was decorated with a silver life-size skull.

Ryan snatched at the shot, seeing the spurt of blood from the man's right shoulder, the wound making him drop his sword and also lose control of his pony. It veered from the explosions of the automatic pistol, nearly tipping the rider from the high-pommeled saddle.

It gave Ryan the bonus chance of a fourth shot, as horse and warrior careened past him. The bullet hit through the side of the throat, under the rim of the brightly enameled helmet, ripping an exit hole the size of a man's fist under the left ear. A torrent of arterial blood streamed out behind the samurai like a torn veil of crimson silk.

Two out of three wasn't bad shooting in the cribbed conditions of the twisting trail, the trio of samurai yelping as they rode at the two men on foot.

Two out of three still left one of the whooping warriors, a skinny man, wearing an embroidered green satin kimono over his traditional armor, his long sword poised above his head to cut down at Mashashige.

Ryan was already moving quickly to the side, trying to put one of the pines between him and the charging man, finding it impossible to imagine that even the shogun could defeat an armor and mounted attacker.

The sword hissed so fast that Ryan barely caught the flicker of sunlight off the polished blade. But Mashashige hadn't tried to aim at the samurai, picking instead on his horse.

The heavy sword cut clean through the pony's right foreleg, just above the fetlock. It was like a big war wag losing all the wheels on one side at once.

The pony went down like a ton of bricks, whinnying in shock as its leg went from under it. There wasn't time for pain. The amputation was too neat and instant for that.

The rider was tipped over the animal's head, his sword flying from his hand, burying itself deep in the trunk of a withered alder, thirty paces across the narrow clearing.

He went down rolling in a clatter of armor, ending up motionless near the screaming pony.

"Neat," Ryan said.

"Not honorable," Mashashige replied. "But honor is a movable feast, as you say. Needs must drive when devil at gate. Please shoot horse and put it from misery."

"Don't think that samurai's dead," Ryan said. The helmet had come off the man's head, and he was lying on his side, groaning softly, mouth working with pain.

"His name is Mashashita," the shogun stated. "Once I would have called him a friend. But he chose to run with the wolves and lick the ass of my renegading brother."

"You going to chill him?"

Mashashige shook his head. He looked past Ryan, down among the trees, where Hideyoshi was leading a group of the sec men, Yashimoto a little farther behind. "No. We shall take him prisoner back to our fortress."

Both men looked around as they heard movement up the slope, seeing Jak leading Doc over the steep, slippery part of the trail, followed by Mildred and Krysty.

Jak called out, "Take cover. J.B.'s about to fire big gun!"

Chapter Twenty-Three

Everyone waited in the silence.

Ryan had a moment to place a bullet through the skull of the dying horse, putting it out of its shocked agony. And Hideyoshi grabbed at the stunned figure of the ronin, Mashashita, snapping out orders for him to be bound.

The other two ponies had galloped off, and both the men that Ryan had shot were now lying still.

"How's he done the cannon?"

Krysty answered Ryan's question, showing her filthy hands. "Shoved mud down it."

At that moment they all heard the voice of the Armorer, shouting as loudly as he could, "Stand away! Five and four and three and two and one and—"

The "zero" vanished in the roar of the explosion.

It was a strange sound, partly muffled and partly shriekingly loud. There was the screech of tortured metal, and fragments of steel sliced through the treetops above the waiting group.

"Goodbye to their big blaster," Ryan said quietly as the echoes bounced back and forth across the valley, a cloud of pale gray smoke drifting down from the top of the ridge a hundred yards or so away.

"I would see what happened," said Mashashige.

J.B. STOOD PROUDLY by an enormous crater, at least fifteen feet wide, containing a few recognizable pieces of torn metal. The shattered end of the long barrel was there, and part of the breech block, driven into the trunk of a big redwood. Stinking smoke billowed from the muddy pit.

"All the ammo went at the same time," the Armorer said. "Good job I had plenty of cord to fire it. Any closer and I could have gone up with it."

The explosion had torn branches from many of the pines that stood around the gun emplacement, and leaves and needles were scattered everywhere.

Doc stepped cautiously to the edge of the crater and stared into it, then turned to Mildred at his side. "I have a question for you."

"What?"

"It is somewhat Zen. A question of a metaphysical sort, Dr. Wyeth."

"Don't try and blind me with your big words. Just ask me the question, Doc."

"What is a hole?"

"What?"

Mashashige stood close by, with Hideyoshi and Yashimoto, his face showing his interest in the discussion between the two outlanders.

"What precisely is a hole?" He gestured at the muddied pit with the ferrule of his swordstick. "Tell me how you define it, if you would be so kind."

"A hole is a hole...is a bastard hole. I don't get what you mean!"

Doc pointed to the middle of the crater. "Is the missing part in the center the hole? Or—" he gestured to the perimeter of the crumbling pit "—is it the hard stuff around the outer edge that is the hole?"

"For Christ's sake, Doc!"

"I'm serious, madam!"

The shogun tapped Doc on the arm. "I find your question most fascinating. Would you do me the honor of walking with me back to the castle and we might discuss such problems. Such as the sound of one hand clapping. And if a tree tumbles in a forest, with nobody to hear it, does it actually make any sound? So many interesting topics."

Doc bowed. "My dear Lord Mashashige, I would deem it an honor to take part in such a discourse. Let us leave these crude peasants—" he directed a withering glance at Mildred "—and talk of shoes and sealing wax and whether pigs have wings."

He led the way back down the hill, arm linked with the shogun's.

THE TRIP BACK had been uneventful, though three more of the men poisoned by the sarin gas had died within the past two hours. There had been no further attacks from the ronin.

The prisoner, Mashashita, trudged along at the tail of one of the surviving wags, his hands bound behind him.

Yashimoto had been slapping him across the face, spitting at him, until Mashashige stopped him, demanding that the landless samurai be treated with more respect.

"But he is a traitor, wishing to cut the ground below our feet, Lord."

"He is still a samurai and should be respected. I will fight against him myself after we have tried him."

THE REST OF THE DAY was R & R.

Doc went off to bed, claiming that he needed to do some thinking with his eyes shut.

Jak was approached by the pretty young geisha, Issie, who persuaded him to play *pachinko* with her on one of the rows of beautiful antique machines in one of the first-floor rooms. Ryan and Krysty watched them for a few minutes, smiling at the enthusiasm of the Japanese girl, who squealed and clapped her hands and gave Jak a hug each time one of the assortment of tiny steel balls bounced into a winning slot.

Takei Yashimoto also passed by, pausing to try to outstare Ryan.

"Not surprised to see you're interested in *pachinko*," the one-eyed man commented.

"How is that? It is a game meant only for young and foolish and weak people. Not for honorable warriors who follow the code of Bushido."

"There's that word *honorable* again, Krysty," Ryan said. "As in saying that it's honorable to take some of those innocent little steel balls and fire them from a catapult to try and murder an enemy that you're scared of."

He hoped that the warrior might rise to his bait and give him an excuse to challenge him to an out-and-out fight. But the scarred Yashimoto snorted and turned away.

J.B. AND MILDRED HAD GONE for a walk among the ceremonial gardens that lay in the large courtyard at the center of the ville, though they weren't gardens like anything the Armorer had seen before. They were very spare and seemingly barren, mainly carefully raked patterns of gravel, kept immaculately smooth, with some larger, rounded stones set at careful intervals. There were only two or three plants, a brilliant red acer and a weeping cypress with a small cropped willow. At the center of the garden, a tiny fountain dribbled water through a series of iron bowls stained with ancient verdigris.

"Kind of restful," J.B. admitted.

Mildred smiled at him and kissed him gently on the lips. "Makes me feel rested, too. In fact I wouldn't mind too much if we emulated Doc and went for a short rest."

The Armorer considered it, looking past her at the steep roof of the main house. She could see the fountain reflected in his spectacles.

"Yeah," he said.

"Don't be too enthusiastic, love," she said tartly. "I can always go and watch the water dripping."

"Sorry." He squeezed her hand. "Just thinking how well built this place is. To have survived a hundred years of quakes. Knew what they were doing."

RYAN HAD BEEN TOLD that the captured ronin was being examined and tried in front of a panel of the surviving samurai, headed by Mashashige.

"Wonder what the punishment is going to be?"

"I heard him say that he would fight the prisoner himself if he was found guilty," Krysty said. "I can't imagine that there'll be much doubt about that. Not with a hundred or more dead servants floating in the sea back there." She shook her head. "Their attitude to death and dying is strange. Most villes that'd lost three-quarters of their fighting men would be in a state of total shock and anger. They just seem to feel philosophical about it. It's happened. So we might as well get on with living. Don't understand it."

As they strolled together through the quiet corridors of the fortress, they saw a pile of magazines set on a lacquered bamboo table in a room that looked out over the courtyard and formal garden. They spotted Mildred and J.B. walking past the window, hand in hand. Ryan was about to call out to them, but Krysty hushed him.

"Leave the lovers alone," she said.

"Yeah. Guess you're right."

She walked to the table and picked up one of the magazines, finding that it was a hand-printed comic in bright colors. She flipped through the pages.

"Gaia!"

"What is it?"

"Look at these mags."

"What about them?" He picked one up and started to look at it. "Fireblast!"

"Strong meat, huh?"

He didn't answer, his eye held by the amazingly pornographic and startlingly violent sexual images portrayed in the pages of the comic.

Though he couldn't read the Japanese lettering that was splashed across the side of every page, it wasn't difficult to follow the story.

A woman pirate queen seemed to have taken a ship prisoner and was having all the captives taken to her cabin for the most hideously inventive bouts of sexual torture.

Krysty's was an alternate version of a similar story. It seemed like a Japanese general from the Second World War had taken a truckload of American women—nurses by their uniforms—prisoner, and was submitting them to an almost identical hell to that shown in the magazine Ryan held.

"I've seen porn before," Ryan said. "Mostly I don't mind it, long as there's not kiddies or animals in it. What's the old phrase they used to say before skydark?"

"Consenting adults?"

He nodded. "I don't mind, long as it's consenting adults. But this is real triple-sicko stuff."

One of the victims was bloodily bound with barbed wire, and his hands had been severed at the wrists. He was stretched out on a rack in front of the pirate queen, who was forcing him to pleasure her with his tongue. One of her minions was straddling the mutilated prisoner while pouring hot candle wax over his chest. In the background there were some even more unspeakable tortures going on, cunningly and graphically drawn and colored.

The principal color on the pages of the comics was a brilliant crimson.

Ryan dropped the comic on the pile. "I think Mildred mentioned these things," he said. "They got a special name. Manga. I think that was it."

Krysty nodded. "Rings a bell with me." She threw the magazine she'd been looking at back onto the table. "I think I've seen enough to get the picture."

THE TRIAL HADN'T TAKEN very long.

No more than an hour had passed since the prisoner, Mashashita, had been taken into the secret court, still wearing his bloodied, muddied green kimono.

Ryan and Krysty saw Jak coming toward them, with Issie tottering along after him on her tiny bound feet, hands clasped together in the sleeves of her beautiful gown, her eyes fixed adoringly on the teenager.

"Hey. Heard trial over," Jak called.

"Who told you?" Ryan asked.

"Yashimoto. Sort nasty grin when told. Said to tell all that punishment was soon. We was to watch."

"When?" Krysty queried.

Jak turned to Issie and repeated the question. The geisha giggled and unfolded a fan, covering her face, whispering something that Jak had to ask her to repeat before he was sure that he'd understood her.

"Tonight. Courtyard in center. Lord Mashashige will do it. Punishing."

"How? Said he'd fight Mashashita."

Jak looked again at Issie, who was still giggling. Now she folded the fan and brought it down against the side of her slender swan's neck with a savage, unmistakable cutting blow.

Chapter Twenty-Four

"How come he's not allowed to commit suicide?" J.B. asked, sipping at a porcelain beaker of sake.

Hideyoshi had been sent by Lord Mashashige to make sure that the outlanders joined all the surviving members of his household to see the execution—or fight. Nobody seemed totally clear which it was to be.

"Call all hands to witness punishment," Doc said. "Flogging around the fleet."

"Not flogging, Doctor," the samurai said.

"Merely a figure of speech, my dear fellow," Doc replied amiably, a tumbler of the weak local beer in his hand. "Old Western custom."

"Like tarring and feathering? I have read that is old Western custom."

Doc was puzzled for a few minutes, working out what it was that the samurai had said. Finally he realized. "Yes. Or rather, no. Or on third thought, perhaps it is better just to let the matter lie where it is."

RYAN AND J.B. HAD SPOKEN to Mashashige about the danger of a direct and rapid attack by the ronin.

"They know how very weak you are with such devastating losses from the sarin gas," Ryan warned. "You must use every available man for defense duty."

The shogun had listened politely, head slightly on one side. He nodded occasionally, listening as both men made their tactical points.

"We could take out a small raiding party of three or four of your best warriors and a dozen of the surviving sec men," J.B. offered. "Try and locate the camp of the ronin and take a few of them out. Balance up the odds."

"It is a kind offer, thoughtfully made, Dix-san. But we must not hurry into something that is unwise."

"Not unwise to get your licks in first," Ryan argued. "Firstest with mostest."

"Nathan Bedford Forrest say that." Mashashige gave them one of the first full, ear-to-ear smiles. "I have studied the war and its men. Marching through Georgia. Shiloh. So many battles and such honor."

"And it's right. Get in a preemptive strike against the ronin. Be offensive, not defensive."

The shogun's smile disappeared like the dew from a summer meadow as he looked at Ryan. "The code of *kokoro* combines heart and soul and mind. We will fight from our home."

"But you have more chance of winning if you accept our advice," J.B. said. "Killing's a craft like any other. And we're good at it."

"Hai, hai, wakarimashita, wakarimashita." He spoke crossly. "Yes, I understand what you are saying. It is not a very bad plan. But it will not happen."

"Cut down your enemy."

"Yes, Cawdor-san. When you watch after the trial, you will, I think, see me cut an enemy down."

IT WAS TO TAKE PLACE in one of the number of court-
yards that were set in the middle of the fortress, among
the endless maze of corridors with their fragile rice-
paper walls and sliding panels and shutters.

A skeleton guard was placed on the outer walls,
watching from the turrets and battlements among the
peaked roofs. Everyone else in the palace lined the
courtyard.

Everyone male.

Issie and her fellow geisha were forbidden, as were all
of the female servants. It was one of the first things that
Krysty had noticed. Neither Mashashige nor any of the
senior samurai seemed to have wives or families.

Hideyoshi had tried to explain. "Women are weak
and cracked vessels. Useless to men of action and honorable fighting. If we seek release, then we can find it
with each other or with boys. That way we do not dilute... Is right word? Dilute? We do not dilute our seed
and waste it on women."

Krysty had nodded, knowing that there were times
when it might be worth arguing.

And times when it was obviously going to be a total
waste of time.

KRYSTY AND MILDRED WERE the only women in the
courtyard. At a rough guess, Ryan figured that the
shogun still had something close to one hundred men to
call on, probably still enough to hold off the ronin.

The sec men had on their finest crimson-and-white
uniforms. Many were carrying rifles and pistols, which
was unusual in itself, since the blasters weren't sup-

posed to be honorable weapons. The samurai all wore gorgeous kimonos, embroidered with foxes, herons, dragons and cherry blossom. Carrying their sheathed ceremonial swords, they strutted to their places at the front of the long line of spectators.

The captured ronin, Mashashita, stood alone at one end of the open room, wearing his green kimono, carrying an unsheathed sword, the point resting in the raked gravel in front of him.

He didn't seem to have been harmed in any way. As Ryan looked at him, the lordless samurai flexed his shoulders and grinned nervously at the Westerners.

Lord Mashashige made his entrance quietly, slipping into the open space through one of the concealed panels. It was late afternoon, and the sun was almost gone. The wind had veered and seemed to be blowing some specially virulent polluted air their way. Even the sec men were sneezing and coughing and wiping their prickling eyes.

Doc was flourishing his blue kerchief, blowing his nose loudly. He sounded like a broaching narwhal, drawing every eye to him. Mashashita laughed out loud, with a touch of hysteria cracking in his voice.

But the shogun didn't laugh. He was bareheaded, dressed entirely in plain sable cotton, with his feet bare. His sword was unsheathed, tucked into his black sash.

He took his place at the far end of the open space, bowing first to his opponent, then to Ryan and his friends, finally to his own people.

Yashimoto took a long step forward, clearing his throat. "To all present, greetings. Lord Mashashige has challenged the felon and traitorous dog Mashashita to fight a duel to determine which has the right in the matter of honor.''

It was a long sentence, and he ran out of breath before completing it, doubling over in a coughing fit that turned his face puce and made his eyes water. Everyone waited for him to continue his speech.

''It has been declared by Lord Shogun Mashashige that should he be the loser in this fight, the ronin samurai, the landless and lordless Mashashita, shall be allowed to walk free without any hindering and gives his solemn oath that no revenge shall be carried out against him by any man of Lord Mashashige.'' He turned to face Ryan and his friends. ''This is also bounding on the *gaijin* who are the honored guests here.''

Ryan nodded to show that he understood, whispering to the others, ''Shogun loses and the ronin walks. Nobody is to try and stop him.''

''Stupes,'' Jak hissed under his breath.

Yashimoto had nearly finished. ''There is no quarter given, but the laws of Bushido will operate. This fight is to the dying.''

He turned to the ronin. ''Now you may speak.''

The skinny outlaw had a high-pitched voice, pushed higher by his obvious and sudden nervousness at the imminent fight.

''I thank the warrior Yashimoto for his speaking and I thank Shogun Mashashige for giving me this chance of fight. It is just.'' He coughed and fell silent. It looked as if he'd finished, and there was a general clearing of throats and shuffling of feet from the audience.

"When they getting on with it?" J.B. whispered. "Too much jaw, and not enough war."

But the ronin hadn't finished. He stopped and scattered white granules from an earthenware pot at his feet, bowing to the four quarters of the courtyard.

"Salt," Hideyoshi explained. "As they sprinkle in a *basho* in sumo wrestling."

"I give my soul to the honor of my ancestors and my poor body to my sword," the ronin cried, his voice soaring ever higher. There was a large storm crow, perched on the peak of the roof, preening its iridescent feathers. It suddenly flew away into the evening sky, cawing furiously at being disturbed by the shout of the samurai.

Mashashige took a couple of slow steps forward, his bare feet crunching on the layered gravel, the point of the sword held down and out, in front of him. Almost like a metal detector, it swung back and forth over the ground.

His opponent began to move.

Both men shuffling toward each other, through the group of silent watchers, moving in a gentle counterclockwise circle, eyes locked to each other. Ryan noticed that the shogun was breathing slowly and steadily, while the ronin was snatching at every breath, as if he were frightened that someone was going to steal it away from him.

"I fear that we are about to witness bloody murder being done," Doc said quietly.

"How long do these duels usually take?" Ryan asked Hideyoshi, who was standing next to the companions, holding his breath, eyes narrowed with excitement.

"A little time until the swords are raised. Then life is worth no more than a feather. It will not take more than the blinking of an eye."

The men had approached each other, moving the length of the courtyard, leaving a trail in the fine gravel as though a pair of large snails had passed by.

Mildred coughed, struggling to bring up phlegm trapped in her throat, but not succeeding.

Now the shogun was less than a dozen feet from the convicted prisoner.

"Soon," Hideyoshi muttered. "Very soon now it will be all done and over."

The ronin swallowed so hard that every one of the watchers heard him.

As though they had been given a secret signal, both the shogun and the ronin suddenly half lifted the blades to the level of their waists.

"Now," Jak said.

There was a dazzling flicker of movement as both men stepped in closer, like two puppets controlled by the same length of silken cord.

Ryan thought he heard a breath of steel against honed steel, then there was a strange, harsh, clunking sound, reminding him oddly of a butcher's cleaver coming down from a height to slice through a haunch of buffalo meat.

For a moment he couldn't make out what had happened. The two samurai still stood toe-to-toe, face-to-face, chest-to-chest, neither of them moving.

Then . . .

"Jesus Christ!" Mildred breathed.

"Dark night," J.B. said.

"God save the mark," Doc mumbled as he turned his face away.

Mashashige's speed with his sword was unbelievable. He had lifted the blade and brought it down with a devastating force before the ronin could begin to parry the cut.

It struck Mashashita at the side of the throat, on the left side, hacking through the collarbone and the top ribs, emerging well below the right arm, cutting the body into two.

Though Mashashita's feet were firmly planted in the gravel, the head and part of the chest and the entire right arm, fingers still grasping the sword, were falling to the floor. Blood gouted in a solid sheet of crimson from the amputated trunk, flooding into the courtyard.

The shogun stepped away, watching as the knees of his dead enemy folded and the body lay in its two disparate parts in the sodden gravel.

He turned toward Ryan, blood dripping down the length of the long sword. "I said that I would cut my enemy down, did I not, Cawdor-san?"

Ryan nodded in the silence. "Sure did. Yeah, you sure did."

KRYSTY LAY ON HER BACK, one arm across Ryan's chest, her breathing slowing back to normal after their long, gentle lovemaking.

"Never known so much death, lover."

Ryan reached and held her hand in his. "Life's worth no more than a feather. That's what they say. And they live up to that, as well."

"Think we should leave the ville and get back and jump out of here?"

He shook his head. "Not yet. I still don't know what Mashashige's plan is for the gateway and for Death-lands. Need to stay and try and find that out."

"How long?"

"Another couple of days or so. I know there's something they're not telling us. Something that's staying hidden. I reckon we should try and find it out."

Chapter Twenty-Five

"I am enlisting more men. That is the right word? Or should it be 'conscripting'?"

Ryan considered the shogun's question. "I reckon either word'll do."

"It is not hard to get men to come and fight for me. But time is taken in training them how to become skilled at it. The outside world is overflowing with people. It is by far our greatest problem, Cawdor-san."

"Sure. We've seen that. And the awful factories and processing plants that you need to provide food. Seems like every damn thing is polluted here."

"In Deathlands is different?"

"Sure. There's the blighted hearts of the ruined cities, where only ghoulies walk. And plenty of rad hot spots still left. But mostly it's God's good land."

"Which god?"

Ryan grinned at the shogun. "Who knows? Years I've lived and I've never seen too much evidence of any particularly benevolent god."

"Nor me. But I would not admit that to my people. It would not be proper."

"You see any hope for the situation here?"

"For me against the ronin?"

Ryan shook his head. "Not just that. If you can get more men and train them quick and right... No, I mean any hope for the terrible pollution you suffer from."

The shogun looked away for a moment, and when he answered, Ryan could almost see the impenetrable mask that had slipped into place over his features.

"I have thoughts on this matter, but it is difficult...."

AS HE WALKED ALONE through a silent wing of the ville, Ryan found himself wondering more and more about what was going on here in the last quake-riven section of old Japan.

His throat was sore, and his good eye was prickling from the intolerable levels of filth in the atmosphere. And it was like this all the time, not just because of some freak of wind and weather. All the time.

The shogun had mentioned going for a hunt, as the sun had broken through and what wind there was blew the worst of the polluted smog away from the fortress. It had been more or less settled for the afternoon.

As he walked, he suddenly heard a voice, talking in what sounded like an artificially bright voice. Like an adult talking to a backward child.

"You have been naughty. Very, very naughty, and Uncle must make you stop."

The voice sounded like the second-in-command of the ville, Takei Yashimoto, but Ryan knew that the samurai wasn't married and had no children. In fact, during their stay at the palace of the shogun, he hadn't once seen Yashimoto even speak to a female servant or geisha or any of the resident concubines.

He moved closer, his hand dropping to the cold butt of the SIG-Sauer.

"Now, that won't do, Petal. And Daddy will have to take down your panties and give you a spanking." The voice was still weirdly high and bright, and it sounded as if Yashimoto was breathing faster and faster as he spoke.

Ryan found himself deliberately walking catfooted and quiet, moving silently through the sun-splashed corridors like a hunting panther.

"Take off your panties and spank your ass with my bare hand. Make your bottom and your thighs get red and sore and tender, and then Uncle will have to stop his dear Petal crying. Stop her by kissing her better!"

The breathing had gathered momentum, finishing with an explosive sigh, followed by a deep stillness.

Ryan flattened himself against the wall and peeked through a narrow gap in the rice-paper sliding panel, into a small room that contained a black table that bore a maroon vase holding a single white carnation.

A long sofa was covered with a dazzling array of satin scatter cushions.

It *was* Yashimoto.

Ryan half drew his blaster, finger sliding onto the trigger. He was on the verge of bursting into the room and stopping the samurai at his vile game.

Yashimoto was holding a little girl, aged ten or eleven, across his lap. His left hand was holding a pair of pink lacy panties to his face, and his eyes were closed in ecstasy. His right hand still gripped himself through the folds of his disarrayed kimono. The child hung facedown, buttocks and sex exposed, motionless in the warrior's grip.

He was still breathing very heavily, and there was the mute, visible evidence of how he'd pleasured himself, polluting the polished floor.

Realization came to Ryan just as he was about to step into the room.

The child was a doll, made of some kind of flesh-colored plastic, incredibly lifelike in every biological detail.

As Ryan looked, the samurai began to fondle it with his right hand, turning it over so that the pert little face smiled coyly up at him.

"You make Uncle so wicked that he has to do wicked things to his little Petal...."

At that moment Yashimoto had to have sensed that he was being watched, and his eyes suddenly opened, the scar on his face beginning to twitch, livid against his suddenly pale skin. He spotted Ryan's face, framed in the doorway, watching him at his little game.

"What...?" he stammered, dropping the panties from his left hand, letting the realistic little girl doll fall onto the floor between his legs.

Ryan grinned wolfishly. "Sorry. Didn't mean to spoil your very honorable fun."

He moved back down the corridor, quickly, glancing twice over his shoulder to make sure that the enraged and humiliated samurai wasn't coming after him.

It helped to deepen and enrich their feud.

THE HUNT WAS POSTPONED to the next morning.

No reason or explanation was given, the message being passed along to the outlanders by Toyotomi Hideyoshi.

"Why?" Ryan asked.

The samurai shrugged, his face as blank as a sheet of parchment. "It would be difficult to say."

"Nothing to do with the ronin?"

"Not precisely."

"The weather?"

"Not that."

"The shogun just decided to change his mind?"

Hideyoshi considered that question, eventually deciding that it was a safe one. "Yes," he said.

"We hunt tomorrow?"

The warrior nodded at Ryan. "If Lord Mashashige wills it, then must it be."

DOC HAD DISCOVERED a *karaoke* machine, standing polished and gleaming in one of the largest rooms. He had immediately gone and called for the others to come and see it, collecting Hideyoshi on the way.

Jak arrived with Issie in tow.

"They had one of these most brilliant inventions in the rec room of the whitecoats' lab on Operation Chronos. I had the greatest of pleasure with it. Have you seen one of them before, any of you?" He gestured proudly to it, thumbs stuck in the buttonholes of his vest.

"Read about them," Krysty said.

"I remember them." Mildred cleared her throat into a kerchief. "God, this air! Yeah, they're the invention of the devil, Doc. Many a good bar and restaurant's been ruined by having one of those stuck in a corner."

"What does do?" Jak asked.

"It is powered by waterwheel," Hideyoshi replied. "Switch on and gives a choice of many singings. Classic American rock, as well as traditional Nippon songs. Words come on screen in front so you can sing to endorsement tape."

"Backing tape?" Mildred said, puzzled.

"Is such laughter," Issie squeaked, clapping her hands, her varnished nails glinting in the afternoon sunlight.

"Sounds good," Krysty said.

"Not for me." Ryan looked suspiciously at the silent machine. "Me and singing have never been the best of traveling companions. Know what I mean?"

"Do you wish to try, Cawdor-san?" the samurai asked, looking doubtfully at the geisha. "How does it start?"

"Press switch on back, and writing of song names comes on the window."

"Ah, yes." He still looked bewildered. "Perhaps you start machine?"

She bowed low, voice fluting up the scale like a little child. "Will be honored, Lord."

The machine crackled into life, lights flashing across the front, some of them staying on and most of them going out again. White lettering flickered into sight on the large dark screen, offering about a hundred songs.

Roughly half of them were Japanese and the rest American.

"Who go first?" Issie asked. "Jakki? You sing special for me?"

"Don't know them."

Everyone, even Ryan, crowded around this rare artifact from the predark days. Mildred read out some of the songs, nodding her head appreciatively. "Some good old rock and roll. 'Lonesome Tonight.' 'Bye Bye Love.' 'Everyday.' 'For All We Know.' Real golden oldie. Rave from grave. Zoom from tomb. 'Bat Out of Hell.' That was the truly amazing Meatloaf. 'Daydream Believer.' God, that was a hit for the Monkees. Written by one of my all-time favorites, John Stewart. Some stuff I haven't heard of."

"How does work?" Jak asked.

Doc had assumed the role of master of ceremonies. "You pick out a song, and I will program the machine to play the backing for it. And the words come up on the screen, there." He pointed with the ferrule of his swordstick. "And you sing along to the music. Elementary, my dear Lauren."

Mildred indicated number forty-seven. "'Amazing Grace.' You know that one, Jak?"

"I know it, too, Jakki," Issie said with a giggle. "You and me sing together."

"Suffering succotash! All right."

Doc flourished his index finger over the green button, ready to trigger the machine. Issie took one of a pair of microphones for herself and handed another one to Jak.

"Ready, steady and go, Jakki, go," she crowed.

Doc pressed the button.

Immediately there was a loud crackling from the *karaoke* machine, and an insistent hip-hop backbeat started up, heavy on the drums, with an amplified bass throbbing in the foreground. It was only just possible to hear any resemblance to the old frontier hymn, 'Amazing Grace.'

Everyone was taken by surprise, except Issie, who began to sing along with the bouncing ball in her high-pitched, little voice. Confused, Jak finally joined in on the third line, already half a line behind the geisha girl. They eventually got together as the song drew toward its close.

There was a round of applause when they finished, and the girl drew Jak to her and kissed him, long and slow, on the mouth. Hideyoshi tutted with disapproval at such forward behavior.

Krysty was persuaded to go next and gave an enchanting performance of 'We've Only Just Begun,' the old Carpenters hit from forty years before skydark.

"Would anyone mind if I was to take the next spot?" Doc asked eagerly.

"What're you going to give us?" Mildred asked. "'Silver Threads among the Gold'?"

"No. In my time at the tail end of the nineties—the 1990s—I developed a fondness for the harmonious singing of a pair of brothers. Donald and Philip Everly. Voices like angels. I see that there is one of their best songs, 'All I Have to Do Is Dream,' here on the machine. Could you perhaps start that for me, my dear Issie?''

A shimmering chord of unearthly beauty led into the slow ballad.

Considering that Doc and singing went together like cheese and chalk, the old-timer didn't make a bad fist of the lovely song, eventually finishing at more or less the same time as the *karaoke* backing.

There was more applause.

Ryan looked around and saw that Yashimoto had come in, accompanying Lord Mashashige, who had a slender middle-aged woman on his arm, a lady that Ryan believed might be an older sister of the shogun.

''You want to join in?'' Doc called, flourishing the microphone at the samurai.

''It would be difficult, Dr. Tanner,'' the shogun replied, ''but we enjoyed your song. Is Cawdor-san or Dix-san going to entertain us?''

J.B. pushed his battered fedora to the back of his head, pursing his mouth. ''Kinder for all if I pass on that one. Thanks, anyway.''

Ryan grinned. ''There's things I'm good at. Things I'm not. Put singing into the latter box.''

''I'll have a go,'' Mildred said, joining Doc and peering at the list of possible titles.

The woman with Mashashige hissed something to him and pulled at his arm. But the shogun frowned and whispered something back, his whole body showing his sudden anger.

''There's a problem here?'' Mildred asked. ''Don't want to upset anyone.''

Mashashige shook his head. "My sister forgets herself. Forgets you are the guests of the lord shogun and must be treated with all respect."

Mildred sniffed. "If you're sure. Then I'll give a shot at some heavy metal. 'Lightning on the Highway.' Let's go."

The machine hissed and crackled into life again.

There was a howl of guitar feedback that made everyone jump, then a driving beat with a saxophone wailing away in the background to the hard-driving tune.

Mildred started to softly clap her hands together, eyes closed, head shaking from side to side, her beaded plaits tinkling against one another.

Krysty picked up the beat, starting to clap along with her friend, followed by Issie and Jak. Ryan, Doc and J.B. also lent their support to Mildred, who was beginning to cook.

"Bitch is back!" she yelled during the long instrumental break.

The rhythm was strange, hobbling, but Mildred followed the bouncing ball with no trouble, shaking her hips as she waited for the last verse to come along.

The woman stamped across the stage from side to side, head rolling, dropping to her knees as the tune eventually faded away into silence. She put the microphone on top of the *karaoke* machine and grinned a little embarrassedly at her applauding audience.

Everyone clapped, except for the pinch-faced sister of the shogun, who brushed away Mashashige's restraining hand and hobbled toward the sweating black woman on her bound, crippled feet. She held her hands like claws, muttering under her breath.

"No!" the shogun called sharply. "You will regret any bad action here."

But his sister had reached Mildred, standing for a moment and glaring at her through hooded, malevolent eyes. Then spit full in her face.

Chapter Twenty-Six

Ryan had never seen Mildred Wyeth in such a towering rage.

They had persuaded her to return with them to their rooms in the heart of the ville, where she sat on the edge of her mattress, tight-lipped, sighing and shaking her head in disbelief. "He can't do it."

"He can," J.B. said, squatting next to her, trying to hold her hand. But Mildred pulled away from him.

"Leave me be, John," she said warningly, her voice tight and angry.

Ryan stood by the barred window, looking out across the moat. He turned to speak to Mildred, then caught a glance from Krysty and closed his mouth again.

Doc tried. "It is appalling, Dr. Wyeth. Truly disgraceful, but it is their way. When in Rome..."

"Now, how did I guess you were going to trot out that old cliché, Doc?"

"It was bad, what she done." Jak was absently polishing the leaf-shaped blade of one of his throwing knives on his jacket, sitting cross-legged on the floor.

"It was spit! Saliva, for Christ's sake. It wasn't concentrated nitric acid."

"But it shamed Mashashige and made the whole damn palace lose face."

Mildred turned to him. "Sure, Ryan. Look, get this straight. I'm not a stupe person. I'm not having a breakdown. Like they say, I don't have acute psychosis. I have a cute face. Right? I understand the way wheels turn here in this shitty, rotten place. Shogun says jump and all his people ask how high."

"Mebbe if we let a little time pass, then we can go to Mashashige and ask him for... What's the word, Doc?"

"Clemency, Ryan."

"Yeah. Mebbe he'll let his sister off from having to chill herself."

"Just don't bet the mortgage on it, bro." Mildred stood and paced the room, her boots clacking on the polished wooden floor. "And there's no time, anyway."

"I can go and ask him," Krysty offered. "Gaia! The man's not an animal."

"No. Just a gut-proud samurai who thinks he's lost face because his sister spit in the eyes of an American nigger bitch! That's all, isn't it?"

The outburst left them all silent.

Doc coughed to clear his throat. "Just for once I find myself totally on the side of Dr. Wyeth. It seems intolerable that this suicide should be forced on the wretched woman."

Ryan punched his right fist into his left palm. "Fireblast! This is a bastard waste of time. We all feel the same. But what are we going to do about it? Doc? It seems intolerable, you said. How do you propose we save her life? Stage a rescue and a firefight? This is their world and their rules."

"Wish never saw *karaoke* machine," Jak muttered. "Issie's dead upset."

"We all are." The Armorer was walking slowly up and down the floor. "What Ryan says is right. I don't see what we can do to stop it happening."

"He says I have to be there to watch the insult cleansed in blood." Mildred was on the edge of tears.

"Mebbe he'll reconsider." Ryan put his arm around the woman's shoulders, feeling her body as tense as spun crystal, flinching at his touch.

"Fuck and damnation!" She eased away. "If he's going to make her chill herself, then I'll be there. I want to look in the cold-heart shogun bastard's eyes when it goes down. Nobody has to come with me who doesn't want to."

THEY STOOD IN A SOLEMN, straight line, Ryan at the center, with Krysty on one side of him, Mildred on the other. J.B. was next to her, his hand clasped in hers, with Jak at the end. Doc had nearly withdrawn himself from witnessing the killing, but had decided to go with them at the last moment, and now stood next to Krysty, feet together, fingers aligned with the sides of his pants, the silver lion's-head hilt of the swordstick gripped in his right hand.

It was to be a private function, in one of the maze of ornamental rooms that lay to the side of the main courtyard. Unlike the previous ritual suicide and the brief and bloody fight with the ronin, this was only to be witnessed by the outlanders and by Mashashige, Yashimoto and Hideyoshi.

There were also three elderly female servants, two of them weeping openly, ready to help their mistress from this world into the next.

A swathe of white linen cloth covered the central section of the room.

Mashashige looked across at the foreigners. "We are all ready now," he said.

Mildred took a step forward, her whole body as tense as a drawn longbow. "I have a request, Lord Mashashige. Please, will you grant it to me?"

"If it is within my powers."

"I am the person insulted by your sister. Allow me to be the one to spare her this."

"No." He held up a small black fan in his left hand. "The ink is spilled, as you say."

Mildred went down onto her knees, head bowed. "I am begging you."

"You might beg a river not to flow. A petal of cherry blossom not to fall. A wave to return to the ocean and not break upon the beach. All things in the world of Shinto are set and settled. The woman's doom is fixed like iron. She chose death when she insulted you."

"Nothing I can say?" She got to her feet.

"Nothing. Your heart is too soft. We have found this to be a weakness in Deathlands. It will be the undoing of your people, I think."

Mildred nodded, her face like marble, her eyes like jet. She turned away from the shogun to rejoin her friends. J.B. put out his hand, and she gripped it.

A door opened and in walked the sister of Masha-shige. She wore a long robe of glittering white silks, in-terwoven with threads of pure gold.

"What kind of material's that?" Krysty whispered, awestruck. "It's beautiful."

Doc was the only to know the answer. "The lady in the lake in Arthur. Her arm as it emerged from the dark waters of the mere and gripped Excalibur was clad all in white samite. Haven't seen any in close to two hun-dred years. Seriously wealthy women in Boston might wear it to their exclusive parties, back when I was a brash young whippersnapper."

The woman shuffled forward, dropping a deep bow to her brother, who returned it. She moved to the cen-ter of the rectangle of material in the middle of the room and knelt gracefully on it, her head turning toward Mildred, her face a cosmetic mask with a rosebud smile painted on.

When she spoke, her voice was so high and thin that it was barely audible, like the whispering of a bird's wing against a pane of glass.

"So sorry for bad manner. Please forgive."

Mildred looked past her, directly to the shogun. "What the fuck difference does it make whether I for-give her or not? You're still going to make her top her-self."

"She will pass on to next world with easier heart," Mashashige replied.

"For Christ's sake."

"Do it, Mildred," Ryan said quietly. "It might make the passing a tad better."

The black woman nodded, biting back tears. "I forgive you," she said.

The shogun bowed to her and to his sister. "Now we can begin the ending," he said quietly.

"This is called *jigai*," said Hideyoshi, who had moved to stand alongside the outlanders. "It is the woman's version of seppuku. She will use that weapon you see being held in hands of woman servant." It was halfway between a short spear and a daggerlike sword, with a honed edge that glittered coldly. "Called *naginata*. Weapon for woman."

"She going to spill her guts out, like a samurai?" J.B. asked.

"No. Different for women. You will see."

Mashashige's sister had now laid herself down, feet pointing away from the watchers, while one of the weeping servants tied her feet and legs together with a length of silken cord, knotting it carefully around the knees.

"Why that?" Jak asked.

Krysty answered him. "To maintain the propriety, I guess," she said. "So that we don't get to see her bare legs while she's involved in the dying process."

Hideyoshi nodded at her words. "You are correct," he whispered.

Mashashige stepped forward and knelt on the unruffled white cloth by his sister. He leaned over her and said something to her in Japanese. Amazingly she smiled up at him as she pattered a fluting reply.

The shogun straightened and bowed again to his sister, handing her the *naginata,* moving back to join Yashimoto.

"Into thy hands..." Mildred breathed.

The servants had stepped away from their mistress, standing in a line by the door.

She gripped the leather-bound hilt of the weapon and brought it up toward her face. She closed her eyes and touched herself softly on the side of the throat, below the right ear, as though she was judging the correct place.

With an audible sigh, the woman thrust the point of the weapon into her neck, where she'd been touching, drawing it swiftly and firmly from right to left.

Her eyes came wide open, as though she'd been given a massive electrical shock.

The artery was severed immediately, and blood jetted out, gushing across the room under great pressure, splattering over the edge of the cloth, dappling the white paper wall within a couple of feet of Mashashige.

Moving with great control, the dying woman carefully laid the crimsoned blade at her side, then lay back, closing her eyes again.

The only sound was the pattering of blood, like light summer rain on a conservatory roof. The pulse faded as life closed down, the blood pumping more slowly, like a fountain that had just been turned off.

Until it was barely a trickle, and still nobody in the large room moved or spoke. All three women servants were crying now, tears tumbling down their wrinkled cheeks and plashing onto the wooden floor.

At the very last, with all the neural lines going down, the body began to twitch, the tiny bound feet drumming out a staccato beat, the hands opening and closing as though the woman were trying to reach out for help.

Finally it grew still.

Mildred looked Mashashige in the eye. "I just hope you and your bloody honor are satisfied, you brain-sick son of a bitch!" She spun on her heel and almost ran from the room, barely avoiding the edge of the spreading lake of crimson, jostling the servants aside as she pulled open the door.

THE MESSAGE WAS SENT via a young manservant in immaculate crimson and white. Bowing so low his forehead almost touched his skinny knees, he pattered off the words with eyes half-closed concentrating on remembering them precisely. "Lord Mashashige begs to inform his honored guests that there will be hunting tomorrow, and he hopes all will be present."

Ryan had just removed the patch from his left eye, sprinkling fresh filtered water in the prickling socket. The sight unnerved the young man, who took a stumbling step backward.

"Tell him we'll be glad to join him," Ryan said. "And tell him thanks."

Chapter Twenty-Seven

"You have all this land just for hunting?" Ryan couldn't conceal his amazement.

"It is only a few thousand acres." Mashashige had become defensive.

"But you keep telling us how bad your problems are of overcrowding."

"True."

"And everything's all crowded together. All the filthy air and pollution. Yet you have miles and miles of untouched parkland and woodland."

The shogun nodded. "This land is my land."

"'From the redwood forests to the Gulf Stream waters,'" Doc quoted.

"Why not let some of the peasants who live in your slums into this territory?"

The shogun shook his head, showing surprising emotion at the pressure from his guest. "This is not our way. My family has always held this land. We had more, but bad quakes have sent much into the sea."

Krysty pointed an accusing finger at him. "You seem a good man, Mashashige. Got some problems from the way you have to live. But it feels like your heart's in the right place. You care some about your people."

"I do. I do care."

"Then open up this park."

There was coil upon coil of razor wire all around the perimeter of the hunting land, which lay to the east of the fortress. There were white porcelain conductors every fifty yards, and death's-head signs warning of high-voltage electric current powering through the lethal fence.

Mashashige stamped his bare foot in the dust. "I care much and I have plans that will give my people more land than they dream of in their...in their dreams."

"How?" Ryan asked, sensing that the shogun was about to spill some interesting beans.

But Hideyoshi touched his master on the arm, whispering something out of the corner of his mouth.

The shogun regained control of himself, biting his lip, nodding to his third-in-command. "Thanks to you," he said quietly, "I had operated my mouth without first engaging the gears of my mind. Stupe of me."

"Go on," Ryan prompted, though he knew the moment had passed. "How you going to help your people get more land? Wouldn't be by using the gateways, would it?"

"Of course it would not." The mask was back in place again. "Now, let us get to hunting."

THE HUNT WAS TO BE carried out on foot.

Ryan and all his companions had risen shortly after dawn and breakfasted on coffee sub and sugary doughnuts, served with bowls of cream laced with nutmeg and cinnamon.

"What kind animals we going to hunt?" Jak asked.

Yashimoto was sitting farther down the long table with three or four of the other samurai. He looked up at the albino teenager's question.

"Since skydark there have not been many creatures left living alive here," he replied. "We have farms in factories for chickens and cattle. Very intensive. Some fish in sea, but some have growths and cancers and warts and cysts and weeping ulcers all over their flesh."

"We had noticed that all was not well with the denizens of Neptune's deeps," Doc said.

"So, if there's this shortage of animals, what are we going to be hunting?" J.B. asked.

Yashimoto laughed. "It will not be a hunt like you have ever seen."

IN ADDITION TO the samurai and the shogun, they were accompanied by eighteen of the older surviving sec men, all carrying both rifles and pistols.

The outlanders had their weapons with them, including the Armorer's scattergun and Ryan's Steyr rifle.

Mashashige was, as usual, barefoot and clad in the simple black kimono, carrying just the unornamented sword. His samurai had mostly elected to wear their full armor. It was a scorchingly hot day, and they had all chosen to leave their helmets behind.

Hideyoshi was wearing a red-and-white baseball cap tipped back on his head, which he handled as though it were a religious relic. It carried the slogan "San Francisco 49ers—Superbowl Champions 2000."

They entered the hunting domain through a tall gate of barbed wire, guarded by half a dozen sec men. As soon as the hunting party was inside, the gate clanged shut.

"This is called Jurassic Park," Mashashige said.

"Why?" Ryan asked.

The shogun hesitated. "I do not know, Cawdor-san. I think it was once a famous place in old America." He looked at the rest of the foreigners. "Does any person know?"

Mildred put up a hand. "Movie," she said.

"BE A HELP if we had some idea what kind of prey we're after," Ryan said.

Hideyoshi smiled his crooked smile. "You will see what you will see."

"But are we looking in the trees or in the streams or the valleys? Big or little?"

The samurai patted him on the arm. "Yes to every of those. Up and down and around about."

"We seek it here, we seek it there," Doc intoned. "We seek our quarry everywhere. Is it in Heaven or is it in Hell, that demned elusive..." His eyes narrowed and he scratched his head. "I fear that I have forgotten what it was that was so demned elusive."

"We staying together for this hunt?" Ryan asked. "Or do we get to split up?"

"Together," Hideyoshi replied. "Or there could be much danger from beasts."

"You mean beasts like Yashimoto over there?" Ryan grinned at the samurai. "Just joking. Of course."

Again the scarred smile. "I understand, Cawdor-san. Understand joke. Of course."

THE BRIGHT SUN was glinting off something running across the far hillside, dipping down into the valley ahead of them. "Looks like rail lines," J.B. said.

A quarter-hour later, having still seen no sign of any kind of wildlife, they reached the remains of a set of double rails, finding them buckled and twisted by one of the frequent quakes that had ravaged old Japan.

"Look there," Jak said, pointing with a long white finger. "Locomotive, halfway in tunnel."

"Handsome." Ryan leaned on the butt of the rifle and admired the train. It was covered in patches of rust, its silver flanks marked by a hundred years of rain and bad weather. The front was round and tapered, like a missile.

"If I remember, they were called bullet trains," Doc said. "They were the fastest locomotives in the world. Around two hundred miles an hour, I believe."

"Two hundred!" Ryan exclaimed. "Come off it, Doc. Nothing but planes could go that fast."

"Not so. Racing motorcars went faster than that."

Ryan laughed. "Times that your brain gets more addled than month-old milk, Doc."

"No, I do assure you, my dear fellow. Bullet trains. Two hundred miles an hour."

Ryan glanced at the Armorer, who pushed back his fedora and tapped his forehead.

Mildred saw the gesture and snapped at the two old friends. "Because you got areas of ignorance bigger than a rutting hog, it doesn't mean that you can disbelieve things you know nothing about. And because Doc can be a doddering old fart some of the time, that doesn't mean he's not also right some of the time. Japanese bullet trains, like that one rotting away there, went two hundred miles an hour. All right?''

Ryan shuffled his feet. "Sure, sure, if you say so, Mildred. Sure.''

"Not because I say so. Or because Doc says so. Just because it was so, Ryan!''

Doc saluted her with his swordstick. "We thank you for your kindness and courtesy, my dear Dr. Wyeth. Uncommon, but none the less welcome.''

A MUTIE HERON, with enormous pink wings eighteen or twenty feet across, flapped toward them over a grove of thornbushes. Ryan cocked the rifle and brought it up to his shoulder, but Mashashige called out a warning to him.

"This is not to be hunted, *gaijin*.''

Ryan eased down the hammer and slung the Steyr over his shoulder. "Then what do we shoot?''

Yashimoto waved a finger at Ryan. "Patience is a virtue linked with honor. I am not surprised that you lack the one as you also lack the other.''

Hideyoshi gestured ahead of them with his sword. "Beyond temple you see. There hunting will begin.''

"You guarantee that?''

"Of course, Cawdor-san.''

THEY PASSED the tumbled stones of the ruined temple, containing a small bronze statue of a cloven-footed faun clutching a set of pipes. Like the relic of the train, a century of extremes of weather had taken its toll, and it was stained green, one arm split open by the frosts.

"Now we see animals to hunt," Hideyoshi said, reaching out for one of the 7.62 mm NATO blasters, a 20-round mag and a bipod for prone shooting.

"How can he be so sure?" Krysty whispered.

"You feel anything?" Ryan asked.

She sniffed, wiping her nose on her sleeve. "Air quality's a bit better up here. A bit. Feel anything? Not really. Nothing out of the ordinary."

"There!" Hideyoshi called. "They come."

Ryan had heard a strange clicking noise, like bolts being opened or locks clicking back, and he saw a couple of the sec men scurrying away to the right, a hundred yards ahead of them, trying to keep low under the cover of the bushes.

And he saw their prey.

In Deathlands you always watched out for creatures that had been mutated by generations of radiation sickness. That meant changes in appearance, sometimes subtle and sometimes totally gross. Also, it often meant changes in size, which generally seemed to mean muties were bigger and more dangerous.

The animals that scampered from the long grass looked like wild boars, but they were less than ten inches in height, with tiny curling tusks and button-bright little eyes, their hooves twinkling across the dry earth.

"Shoot them!" Mashashige called, waving his long sword above his head.

There was a crackle of fire, and the ground erupted into fountains of dust and torn turf, all around the herd of tiny wild pigs. Several were hit, blown apart by the powerful ammunition of the sec men.

Ryan had unslung his Steyr again, but he held his fire, unwilling to take part in a massacre. None of the outlanders shot at the miniature boars.

The standard of marksmanship of the Japanese was amazingly poor, considering the ever-shortening range and the large number of little animals. There were still about a dozen of them alive, squeaking excitedly, dodging and weaving through the hail of lead. The nearest of them was closing fast, less than thirty yards from Ryan.

"Take part in sport, *gaijin!*" Yashimoto yelled, his face flushed, a thread of spittle dribbling from his distorted mouth.

"Unsporting," Doc grunted.

There was another round of shooting, but the creatures were now so close that the bullets were more of a threat to the huntsmen. The nearest of them was crying out like a baby, a long weal from a bullet graze seeping blood through its delicate golden fur.

It headed straight for Ryan.

Yashimoto swung the rifle around, dangerously close to the one-eyed man, who responded calmly by leveling the SIG-Sauer at the head of the samurai.

"No careless mistakes," Ryan grated, and Yashimoto looked away, dropping the muzzle of the blaster.

The terrified little boar reached Ryan and rubbed itself against his leg, cowering and trembling. He stooped and patted it, his fingers brushing the wickedly curved tusks.

It wasn't that much of a surprise to find that they were made of pliable plastic, stapled to the sides of the wretched animal's skull.

The odd business of the sound of bolts and the lurking sec men all made sense now.

"They were trapped," Ryan said, straightening and looking at Mashashige. "Poor little bastards that you caught or bred and tried to make them look dangerous. About as dangerous as a field mouse! Then your men let them go so you could blast them to hell and back and call it sport!"

"We have no natural animals here," the shogun said. "It was best we can do."

"Well, it was a long way shy of being good enough," Ryan said, kneeling to pat the little animal. Several of the surviving mutie creatures had flocked to the foreigners, rubbing against their legs, making a strange, contented purring noise.

"If you move out of way, we can finish the hunting," Hideyoshi said.

Mildred had her hand on the butt of the ZKR 551, her gaze narrowed with anger. "First man touches the trigger of his blaster gets a .38 smack through the middle of his forehead," she warned, her voice as cold as pack-ice.

"They are born to die," the shogun said, shaking his head in bewilderment. "Their lives are not worth a grain of dust. Better they die as they are meant to."

"Like I said, first man harms one of them gets to be lying on his back looking at the sky."

As she spoke, Mildred gazed around, realizing that the bright sun had vanished, as though a black cloud had passed over its face.

Ryan also looked up, followed by all of the others, at the unnatural darkness that had come sweeping in over the hunting park.

"Fireblast!" he whispered.

It was like watching a giant's fist, clenched and angry, sweeping its way across the summery sky. The sun had vanished, and an unnatural stillness had fallen over the land. Not a breath of wind touched the feathery top branches of the trees.

Yet the cloud was swooping fast toward them, seeming to possess a seething, malignant life of its own.

The little piglets cowered and whimpered, bellies against the dirt.

"The plague of death," Mashashige whispered, his face ashen. "Plague of death."

Chapter Twenty-Eight

"What?" Jak said. "Not storm?"

It was J.B. among the outlanders who spotted first what the cloud was.

"It's insects," he guessed. "Locusts."

Hideyoshi nodded mutely, turning toward the shogun as if he were waiting for some mystical instruction that would take away the advancing horror.

"Will not..." Swallowing hard, Mashashige tried again. "Will not harm us. Cover face and mouth. They may land. They may pass by us."

The cloud looked to be about a mile or more in diameter, roughly circular.

"Seen them in west Texas," Jak said. "Stripped crops in minutes. Starved villes."

"I remember seeing predark vids of plagues of locusts out in the East and the Middle East," Mildred said, looking apprehensively at the gathering cloud. "Must be millions upon millions of them in that swarm. Sure they aren't special mutie locusts with a taste for meat?"

Ryan grinned at her. "If they are, then it's time to start the prayers. Not even your blaster's going to do much to save us from that many."

"Couldn't we hide?" Krysty asked. "Do a runner for that old wrecked train?"

Hideyoshi heard her and his eyes widened, and he called to Mashashige, "The fire-haired *gaijin* suggests we flee to the bullet train, Lord."

The shogun didn't waste a minute. "It might be safer. Each man for himself."

He turned and led the way, holding the long sword in his right hand, his bare feet kicking up puffs of dust as he ran back, past the slaughtered corpses of the little animals, toward the distant glint of the locomotive.

Everyone followed him, though several of the accompanying sec men kept looking back over their shoulders at the advancing cloud of insects.

"Goin' to be close, lover," Krysty panted, running stride for stride with Ryan, her hair flowing behind her like a bridal veil of living flame.

Jak was right on their heels, J.B. and Mildred few yards behind him. As usual, when foot speed was called for, Doc was trailing back in sixth place.

But he was still beating all but one of the sec men and both Hideyoshi and Yashimoto.

They were a quarter-mile from the moldering remains of the bullet train. Risking a glance behind him, Ryan's guestimate put the cloud of locusts at less than a mile away.

He'd seen something similar, years ago, out on the Idaho panhandle, when he was riding with Trader. Everyone had piled into the war wags, closing all the vents, but some of the locusts still managed to get inside the vehicles. When they'd finally passed on, and everyone had emerged into the blessed fresh air, it was to find that the green oasis where they'd parked had been stripped utterly bare, with hardly a single leaf remaining for a couple of hundred yards around.

The rusting metal of the train was only a hundred paces off, but the closest insects were already pattering to earth around Ryan, settling on the twigs and branches of the bushes. The sky had grown darker so that there were no shadows.

And the air was filled with an ominous fluttering, humming sound, like the sinister, rhythmic dopplering of chopper blades in old movies.

Mashashige was still in the lead, his slight figure seeming to flow effortlessly over the ground. Jak was close second, with the rest of the runners strung out over a hundred yards or more of the narrow trail.

As he got closer to the train, Ryan was able to see the extent of the damage. Other than the stained panels, several of the windows were broken, and it was now obvious that it had been derailed, probably during a skydark quake. It was high off the ground, but the corroded remains of several emergency ladders gave easy access to the interior.

The shogun was there, clambering up one of the ladders into the cab of the locomotive, reaching back immediately to offer a hand to the albino teenager. Ryan's back was sore from the pounding of the Steyr, and he slowed a little to allow Krysty to climb to safety.

Now, the locusts were falling from the sky all around him, several of them landing on his back and in his hair.

But Ryan ignored them, concentrating on getting aboard the old train, then helping the rest of the group.

The noise of the insects was astounding, drowning out the yells of the sec men, who were laboring in their armor. Most had dropped their blasters, but they still struggled toward safety through the cloud of locusts. There were so many pulped bodies on the track, that it had become slippery and dangerous.

Now that he had a moment, Ryan saw that the insects were like large grasshoppers or cicadas, pale green, about three to four inches in length.

"Gaia!" Krysty panted. "Living-nightmare time."

It was becoming difficult to see the rest of the party as they struggled toward the bullet train.

J.B. and Mildred had made it, and Doc was just being helped up one of the ladders, his grizzled hair dotted with a dozen of the locusts.

"By the Three Kennedys! This is exceeding high on the list of the most disgusting experiences of my long and eventful life," he panted.

Yashimoto appeared from the fog of insects, hesitating as he saw that the hand offered to him belonged to Ryan Cawdor. But he finally seized it and was hauled aboard, Hideyoshi right behind him.

The sec men were lumbering out of the seething cloud, several of them on the ragged edge of hysteria, brushing frantically to remove the locusts from their clothes and hair.

Ryan moved forward into the nose cone of the bullet train, peering out through the smeared armaglass, seeing the land around disappearing under wave upon wave of the voracious insects. He heard a loud cracking and saw a thick branch of a sycamore snap off under the weight of thousands of locusts.

Krysty was at his elbow. "It's dreadful," she said, having to raise her voice to be heard above the constant pittering of the tiny bodies striking the metal shell of the locomotive.

"Least they aren't killers," Ryan said.

"Speak too soon." Mashashige pointed to where one of his sec men had ignored the warning and had stopped about fifty paces off, barely visible, looking as if he'd become terminally disoriented. He stood still, arms flailing at the air, eyes staring wildly, mouth open in a scream of panic and terror.

"I'll help him," Jak shouted, but Ryan reached out and gripped the teenager by the arm.

"No. Doomed. Stay here, Jak, or you'll go under with him. Too late."

The wretched guard was on his knees, his face masked with the locusts, dozens of them forcing their way into his open mouth, crawling up his nose, suffocating him. As the rest watched in horror, he slipped down and rolled on his back, where his whole twitching body became carpeted with insects.

Hundreds of the locusts were finding their way inside the wrecked train, but they were only a tiny drop in the vast ocean of hopping, vibrating creatures.

J.B. had taken off his fedora, flapping at the insects, brushing them from his clothes. He removed his glasses and wiped them on a white kerchief.

"How long they going to stay here?" Mildred asked.

Mashashige had recovered his composure. "Normally it only takes an hour or so to strip all vegetation from a region. Once they have fed, then they will move on again."

Outside there was the occasional noise of breaking branches as the shrubs and trees collapsed under the unimaginable weight of the swarm.

The train was coated with the insects, all of the windows covered in a shifting layer of gray green.

"Makes my skin crawl," Mildred said, shuddering. "Like being inside a huge creature."

"It was a good idea to run here," Hideyoshi said to Krysty. "We saw what happened to a man caught in the out-of-doors open. It might have been more dying."

IT WAS AN HOUR and thirty-five minutes by Ryan's wrist chron, before the uncountable swarm of locusts completed its feeding and took to the air again, circling and rising, gathering together, blotting out the sun again before moving off in a southwesterly direction.

The shogun led the way out of the security of the bullet train, climbing down into a changed landscape.

Thousands of the insects had died during their brief stay, their brittle corpses blanketing the earth, crunching underfoot as everyone moved among them.

The body of the sec man, his mouth still jammed with dead locusts, lay where it had fallen.

For a quarter-mile around, the vegetation had been stripped, leaving only bare, broken branches and peeled stumps of trees.

Nothing else remained.

Nobody spoke for a minute or more, everyone wandering around, staring at the devastation.

Jak suddenly looked around. He knelt and laid the palm of his hand flat on the barren earth. "Quake," he said.

Everyone froze. Mashashige stared at the white-haired boy. "I feel nothing," he said.

"Nor do me," Yashimoto agreed. "Perhaps it is the trembling of fear."

"No." Krysty was standing still, her emerald eyes tight shut. "I can feel it, too."

Then Ryan knew that he could detect the faint tremor. It had been there for several seconds, but it just hadn't forced itself into his consciousness. "Me, too," he said.

It wasn't a bad one, the familiar roaring, just below the surface of the earth, like a full-throttle wag.

A deep rattling rose from the stranded bullet train, just behind them, one of the stressed windows shattering into starring splinters of glass.

The land itself moved gently, back and forth, dust flying everywhere, damaged trees toppling over.

There was the sound of tortured metal, and the bullet train shifted a couple of feet sideways, settling deeper on the left, more of the remaining windows smashing.

Several of the sec men flung themselves onto the ground, hanging on as if they were participating in some sort of nightmare funfair ride.

Ryan kept his balance easily, riding the shifting dirt like the waves on a schooner. The noise began to diminish after a half minute, the dust settling, the world quickly returning to what passed for normal.

"It is over," Mashashige pronounced. "Collect that body and we will return to the fortress."

NOT LONG AFTER they had passed through the high wire fences and gates to the hunting zone, the ronin attacked again.

But it was a poor, halfhearted effort, a sporadic burst of firing, at maximum range. The shooting came from the farther side of a wide-bottomed, shallow valley, the puffs of smoke visible among the dark green trees.

There was time to dive for cover, and nobody was hit.

Ryan had a look through the scope of the Steyr, using the laser image enhancer. But the range was too great, the would-be assassins too well hidden in the woods.

"Should we go after them?" J.B. asked.

"They'd just slip away into the back country," Ryan replied. "Soon realize they're wasting ammo at this distance. Best keep our heads down."

Yashimoto realized that the bullets that hissed among the leaves were spent rounds, offering very little danger. He stood, waving his drawn sword, screaming out boastful threats in a mixture of Japanese and American, echoing across the valley.

"Dung-eating corn rats! Belly-crawling *gekokujo!* Cowardly *metsuke!* Yakuza scum who would fuck your own *obasan.* Which of you will come and fight against Takei Yashimoto, man to man, hand to hand, throat to throat, sword to sword?"

One of the spent rounds pinged off the blade of the sword in his hand, almost knocking it from his grasp, making him aware that he was still in some danger. With a final flourish, the samurai made a hasty retreat among the trees.

As Ryan had predicted, the ronin realized that they were wasting precious ammo, and the shooting faded away into silence. One by one the Japanese and the outlanders stood, brushing dried leaves and dust from their clothes.

"They finished?" Krysty asked.

"For the time being." Ryan picked a few twigs from her hair. "But I'd be surprised if that was the last we ever heard from them. Don't strike me like men who are going to just leave and ride around the problem."

Mashashige heard him and nodded. "It is truly said, Cawdor-san. But we will return to our humble home. Collect and train more men. And so it will go on."

RYAN COULDN'T UNDERSTAND why such an efficient man as the shogun was so casual about the threat from the landless samurai, the ronin.

Hideyoshi had sent out messengers proclaiming that Lord Mashashige was keenly interested in recruiting new sec men for his palace, and at least two hundred of them had arrived, some traveling fifty or sixty miles on foot in less than forty-eight hours.

J.B. had watched them as they milled around in the outer courtyard, waiting to be called and given a basic fitness test. "Ten percent of them looked to be over sixty, and another twenty percent looked way below sixteen. About a third of the remainder were visibly unwell. Most had respiratory illnesses, coughing and fighting for breath, even from doing a basic series of three or four short wind sprints. Shogun'll be lucky to eventually find himself twenty good men. And that still leaves him way short against his losses to the sarin gas.''

Chapter Twenty-Nine

Ryan called a council for that evening.

Supper had been the usual filling mix of Oriental and American food, served by silent servants and shared with the surviving samurai. The shogun sat at the head of the table, eating sparingly at a weak soup with bean sprouts and water chestnuts, washed down with a small bowl of fragrant, bitter tea.

Doc had chosen a fiery sauce of mixed chilies with spit-roasted prawns and fried rice, with more of the ubiquitous water chestnuts. He held a slice up in his chopsticks.

"Sniff the wonderful aroma of ginger from the rice," he said. "Do you wish to know a peculiarly interesting fact about water chestnuts?"

"Dazzle us, Doc," Mildred said, through a mouthful of cheeseburger and fries smothered in a piquant tomato sauce, accompanied by a reasonable impersonation of the best-known cola in the world.

"The water chestnut is unique, I believe, among vegetables, in that it doesn't matter how you cook it, the texture will always remain the same. Fry it or poach it or broil it or bake it. Doesn't make a jot or tittle of difference. Still have the same light, crunchy texture."

Mildred wiped ketchup from her chin with a linen napkin. "Well, if that don't beat all, Doc. Where do you get all this wealth of useless information from? You must have been a leading trivia-meister at Harvard."

"Knowledge is power, Dr. Wyeth."

"Well, you could have fooled me, Dr. Tanner. You never struck me as brimming with power."

"Shows how little you know, madam."

THEY WERE ALL in the large room shared by Ryan and Krysty, Mildred muttering crossly to herself as she tried to remove a ketchup stain from her shirt.

Ryan clapped his hands. "All right, friends. Thought it was time we made some sort of decision."

"Stay or go?" Krysty asked.

He nodded. "Obviously we're moving on sometime. Don't plan spending the rest of my life in this polluted shit-hole. Question of when we go."

"Soon," said Jak, who was standing by the window, taking advantage of what little breeze was blowing, easing the swamping humidity that had squatted down over the palace in the past couple of hours.

Doc grinned at the teenager. "Glad to hear that youth and beauty think along the same lines. This rotten air is playing Old Nick with my breathing. Tubes rattle at night like the *Mary Gloster* sinking in the Mindanao Trench."

"Still wonder just what old Mashashige's up to." J.B. was furiously polishing his glasses. "Solved the mystery of how they plan to use the gateways?"

Ryan looked at his old friend. "Got the ace on the line there, bro. My worry, too."

"Think they plan to take people back here as slaves?" Mildred suggested. "From Deathlands?"

Ryan shook his head at that. "No. If anything, they got too many people here and a sickly land. My personal reckoning is the opposite. Suppose we stay here another couple of days. All try to find out what we can. Jak, you might be able to ask little Issie about it."

"Can try. Don't want betray her."

"You wouldn't be. There've been clues. But we need to be sure. If we got the chance to pick up a few grens, they might come in useful."

"Take out the gateway after we've jumped?" Krysty asked. "Dangerous?"

"Mebbe. But it's better to have the weapons and not use them than to need them and not have them."

"Another Traderism, lover?"

"Sure."

There was a gentle knock on the door, and Jak opened it, smiling and bringing in Issie.

"Lord Shogun Mashashige invites his guests to witness play by visiting Kabuki troupe of actors," she said in her whispering child's voice.

"Theater?" Krysty said. "Could be interesting. Will we go, Ryan?"

"Why not?"

He turned to Issie. "When is it?"

She performed a little mime of a clock hand revolving through three hundred and sixty degrees. "One hour."

She glanced at Jak. "You come now. Others can come later."

"Go with her," Ryan urged. "Get what you can while you can, Jak."

"At your heels you'll soon hear time's winged chariot drawing near," Doc intoned. "And yonder all before you lie deserts of vast eternity. In other words gather those damn rosebuds while you can, laddie."

Jak patted the old man on the arm. "Time's don't know what fuck talking about, Doc."

Ryan gestured to him to leave. "Be down soon, Jak," he said. "Real soon."

Issie snatched at Jak's arm and shepherded him out, sliding the paneled door shut behind them.

"Think she heard?" J.B. asked.

"Doubt it." Ryan looked at the others. "Not sure she's got more than two brain cells to rub together."

"Pretty little girl," Doc said.

"Oh, yeah. Pretty enough. All right, let's go see this play. And keep eyes and ears extraopen."

A STAGE HAD BEEN SET at one end of the larger rooms in the heart of the ville. It was like a raised dais, with a double row of cushions set on the floor in front of it.

Doc groaned when he saw the cushions. "Oh, my aching knees and back." He sighed. "The good Lord did not intend me to sit cross-legged like some contemplative ape. He would have supplied me with more supple and mobile joints if that had been his declared intention."

At that moment Mashashige came in, accompanied by Yashimoto and Hideyoshi, with a few of the senior warriors. Jak and Issie were part of his company.

The shogun bowed to Ryan and the rest of the outlanders. "You are welcome to the play," he said.

"I've never seen a . . . what's it called?"

"Kabuki," the shogun said. "It is a very old and formal kind of theater. This is a time to relax. We have many men come to join us from the places around. They will soon be trained as sec men. Then we can think of marching to remove the threat of my brother Ryuku, and his ronin forever. But we must make the new men welcome. There will be a *basho* tomorrow morning." He saw incomprehension on the faces of the foreigners. "Sumo wrestling," he explained.

"And there will be flying of kites," Hideyoshi said, beaming. "These are not toys, but big enough to lift a man. Their cords have small knives attached to cut strings of enemy kites. It is battle, just like life."

"Battling kites!" Mildred laughed. "I've heard of dueling banjos, but not fighting kites."

"This play last long?" the Armorer asked. "Not all that keen on long plays."

"Is sumo wrestling with men about four hundred pounds, wearing diapers?" Jak asked. "Saw old mag with pix. Looked kind of hot pipe to see."

"It will be excellent entertainment," the samurai promised. "A visiting troupe of sumo. That will be tomorrow. But now—" he turned to the noise of gongs, flutes and drums "—it will be the Kabuki play."

RYAN FOUND IT incredibly difficult to follow.

It was all in Japanese, which didn't help matters at all, though Hideyoshi did his best to give them a running whispered commentary on the dialogue and the action. Not that there seemed to be very much action.

The actors were all men, even those who were playing the parts of princesses, courtesans, geisha and wandering female spirits.

They wore heavy makeup that transformed their faces into masks of startling beauty or boggling horror. Eyes and mouths were emphasized, and the actions were all very melodramatic and stylized, relying a great deal on mime.

Their long dresses were magnificently embroidered with floral patterns, and the ornate material hissed as the actors moved slowly about the stage.

The men gesticulated furiously, their voices raised for much of the talking, while those who played the women simpered and drooped submissively, their voices thin and fluting.

The story was complicated.

It seemed that a lord had gone away to war and had left his favorite wife behind in the care of his most trusted nobleman. But the couple had fallen hopelessly in love, and the wife had chosen to throw herself from the castle's battlements rather than betray her husband. The stricken samurai lover wandered the world, seeking his own death. But he was so brave and uncaring that he always won his fights.

The wife visited him as a ghost, wandering in slow motion across the stage, calling out to him that she had loved him but she had loved honor more.

The husband and lover met on a battlefield, set on a darkling plain, where mists blew and ghostly corpses writhed and staggered across the stage. They fought each other in a stylized duel and struck simultaneous mortal blows, dying together amid much mutual forgiveness, watched by the white-faced ghost of the princess, who moved and stood silently between the two bodies, looking from one to another.

And there, in that frozen tableau, the play finally came to its end.

There was a ripple of polite applause, and the elegant leader of the actors, who had played the beautiful princess, came to the front of the stage, bowing so low that his black wig brushed against his knees.

He spoke in stilted English. "Thank you for honor of appreciation. We do short play in honor of foreigners, written partly by great warlord Mashashige."

The curtains were drawn across the stage, and there was a short delay.

Doc leaned across to Ryan. "What do you think of this Kabuki, my dear fellow?"

"Found it bit like trying to track an Apache walking over a mountain."

"How's that?"

"Difficult to follow."

Doc smiled, showing his perfect set of teeth. "Dashed pretty little filly, the ghostly princess. If I hadn't known that it was a chap, I might have made a bit of a fool myself over her. Him, I mean."

Mildred heard him and grinned. "Not too difficult for you to make a bit of a fool of yourself, Doc. God gave you a running start at it."

"Why..."

But the curtain drew back, cutting him off in his righteous anger.

The stage had been split into two equal parts, with a strip of rippled blue silk laid between them.

"It is the ocean," Hideyoshi said, "dividing the two countries."

A white-bearded actor sat alone on one side, dressed in a blue frock coat covered in spangled stars and maroon stripes, wearing a top hat and carrying a long musket.

"Looks like Uncle Sam," Krysty said.

Hideyoshi nodded in approbation. "That is well seen. He is the spirit of Deathlands."

The other side of the stage was packed with all the other members of the company. They were dressed in a variety of fashions and seemed to be playing families, with some capering like children and others imitating women, working at laundry and on what looked to be factory production lines.

Most of them had white faces with red-rimmed eyes and weeping sores painted on their cheeks. All of them suffered from dreadful coughs and running noses. They all mimed extreme exhaustion, and when they sat to eat, it was obvious that there wasn't enough to go around.

"I believe I am getting the picture," Doc said quietly. "Sort of a parable, isn't it?"

"That left-hand side of the stage is supposed to be here, isn't it?" Ryan asked. "I guess that it's supposed to represent what's left of Japan."

Mashashige nodded, turning from his cushion in the front row. "It is how we see the world."

"We have all the land and few people," Ryan said. "You have the other side of the jack."

"Watch," the shogun urged.

One of the peasants, who had donned armor to make himself look like a samurai, had stumbled upon some sort of cave, which he entered. There was a flash of orange flame and a puff of smoke. The stage went dark for a moment, and when the light came back, the man had shifted to the Deathlands side of the stage.

"Jump from a gateway," Ryan said.

More flashes, and more of the actors crossed from one side of the stage to the other, circling around a frantically terrified Uncle Sam, who had fallen to his knees, trembling like an aspen in a typhoon, hands clasped together.

"Get the picture?" J.B. whispered.

"Yeah, I see." Ryan watched, fascinated at the way that the shogun seemed happy to reveal his plans to them in this obvious allegory.

He was going to use the gateway to ship his fighting men, then some of the grossly surplus population, back into Deathlands to take what they wanted.

Living space.

Chapter Thirty

The following day was dull and oppressive, without a breath of wind to stir the trees around the ville. It seemed to be trapping the layers of pollution that hung over the peaked roofs like an orange fog, catching at the back of the nose and the throat, making the eyes burn and water.

Hideyoshi looked in at breakfast to tell them the kite-flying exhibition had been abandoned because of the inclement weather.

"But the *basho* for the sumo wrestlers will go ahead as planned."

"What time?" Ryan asked, his mouth full of scrambled eggs and undercooked hash browns.

"An hour or so. Do not hurry your food. That is bad for the soul of the inner man. Take time to chew and digest all properly. That way there will be balance within the body."

He stalked out, the tip of his sword's sheath scraping on the wooden floor.

Only the outlanders were left, sitting together at the long table, with silent servants standing against the high walls of the dining room.

Ryan lowered his voice. "First chance we've had to talk about it," he said.

"Their plan to move in on Deathlands?" J.B. asked. "Gotta stop them."

"Agreed." Jak was munching a huge honey-filled doughnut, ignoring the stickiness that trickled over his chin.

"Need the grens," Ryan said. "They keep weapons in that... What they call it?"

"The *yagura*," Mildred answered. "The corner tower where they store ammo, arrows and stuff."

"That's it." He looked at the Armorer. "Before they have this wrestling contest, you and Jak try and get along there. Shouldn't be a problem. They're amazingly trusting. Let us go where we want. These new men he's letting in as sec men worry me... bound to be one or two ronin spies among them. They get at any plas-ex or grens, and it'll be goodbye time for Mashashige and his merry men. Just get three or four grens, J.B., and make them timers. Then, when we find the right moment, we'll head for the gateway and blow it on the way out."

"Sure." J.B. wiped his mouth on a napkin. "Get that honey off your chin, Jak, and we'll go to it."

"GAIA! THAT'S triple spectacular," Krysty said admiringly, stopping at the entrance to the room where the competition was to be held.

Seats were arrayed in a large circle, with a couple of aisles between them. At the center of the room was a raised platform, covered in what looked like very fine sand. It was contained within a loop of thick rope that was coiled several inches high, making the arena into a sort of pit.

Bright satin ribbons were tied to posts at each corner of the *basho* area.

Hideyoshi had seen the outlanders come in and scurried to greet them, rubbing his hands together with excitement. "This is such a thrilling thing for us all. After the bitter sadness of the dying, we have this visit today from some of the top *rikishi* in all of the country."

"Are the *rikishi* the wrestlers?" Mildred asked.

The samurai hardly seemed to notice that he was actually having a discussion with a woman.

"Yes. One is called Konishiki, after one of greatest sumo fighters. And he came from a foreign country. One of the greatest *yokozuna* of all times."

"That means a champion?" Mildred asked.

"Yes. The original Konishiki was a fine champion. Very big, big man."

Mildred scratched the side of her nose. "I believe I've heard of him. Was he one of the real top fighters around just before skydark?"

Hideyoshi nodded. "Yes, he was."

"I saw him fighting on teevee," she said.

The samurai gasped, eyes wider than pinwheels. "You saw the great Konishiki himself? No. That cannot be, Dr. Wyeth. He passed to the land of spirits during the long winters. That was fully every bit of eighty years ago. How could you have seen him fight?"

Mildred swallowed, seeing the trap that yawned in front of her. It was better to explain nothing than to try and fail to explain everything, Trader used to say. She knew that because John Dix had told her.

"I once was in a ville where the baron had a nuke generator and he had a working vid machine. Konishiki came from the island of Hawaii, didn't he?"

"Yes," he replied, his voice still heavy with suspicion.

Inspiration sharpened her already excellent memory. "And his real name was Salevaa Atisnoe."

Hideyoshi gaped again. "That is, I believe, true. But the stories were vague and difficult to believe in. You saw him on a vid! How was he?"

"Magical. He had the grace of an eagle and the speed of a striking cobra and the power of...of...of something immensely powerful."

"I so envy you, dear lady." He forgot himself so much that he actually clasped Mildred by the hands.

Behind them Yashimoto had entered the room with the shogun. As soon as he was aware of their presence, Hideyoshi was overcome with embarrassment and let go of Mildred's hands as though they'd become red-hot.

"Where is the small one with poor sight and the cripple with hair like snow and eyes like rubies?" the second-in-command of the ville asked, sneering.

"The white-haired cripple could probably beat the best of your sumo wrestlers in a hand-to-hand," Ryan snapped angrily. "And they'll both be along soon."

"That frail child beat Konishiki!" Yashimoto grinned. "Stupe *gaijin*. The age of miracles is long past. As easy for a mouse to defeat a lion."

Doc changed the subject. "Why are the ribbons different colors at the corners of the *basho?*" he asked. "Do I detect some sort of symbolism?"

"They are the pointed parts of the compass," Mashashige replied. "And also the seasons of the year. Black is the north and winter. Red is summer and the south. Green is spring and the east, while the west is white and is the fall."

Krysty had started to walk down toward the *basho* arena, staring up at the fluttering ribbons. She was about to climb the shallow flight of steps that led onto the actual fighting surface, when Hideyoshi stopped her with a shout.

"No!"

"No, what?"

"No, it is not allowed. The surface of the basho has been purified and sanctified by salt by the visiting priests. If a woman sets foot there, then it is defouled."

"Defiled," she corrected. "Though I guess that 'defouled' is nearly as good a word. You think I might suddenly have my period all over the religious salt?"

Al three of the Japanese men took a step backward in perfect synchronicity. Yashimoto actually started to draw his sword, then thought better of it and resheathed it.

"That is not the way a guest talks," Mashashige said very quietly.

Krysty nodded. "Guess that's right. And I apologize for it, Shogun."

"Apology accepted."

"And I'll be very careful not to go and step all over your nice clean *basho*."

RYAN AND COMPANY WERE given seats in the front row, in places of honor, close to the shogun and his aides. It was only when the fighting began that the seats of honor were also the seats of danger.

The sumo wrestlers were all enormously large people, almost like muties. The smallest was about five feet ten inches tall and tipped the scales at just over three hundred pounds. He was known by his fighting nickname, "Little Tiger."

But some of the bigger men at the *basho* dwarfed him. The legendary Konishiki was a good six and a half feet tall and weighed four hundred and seventeen pounds.

Each bout followed the same ritual.

The two huge men, swaddled like hogs in diapers, waddled up onto the dais, bowing to the corners and scattering handfuls of salt on the surface of the *basho*, while a small, wizened priest with a sort of fan carried out a short Shinto service.

Then the wrestlers would squat on their own side of the roped arena, looking, as Ryan remarked, like linemen in football just prior to the snap.

But there were innumerable false starts, where one or the other would stand up and strut around, trying to psych out his opponent. Konishiki was particularly good at this aspect of sumo.

"Wouldn't fancy meeting him in a dark, narrow alley," Ryan whispered to Jak.

The teenager was watching the fights with intense professional skill. "Reckon good little one could still beat them," he said. "Weight against them."

"You reckon?" Ryan said thoughtfully.

"Sure."

"Like to try it?"

Jak shrugged, his long white hair moving about his narrow skull like sea spray. "Wouldn't mind."

"See what I can do." Ryan sat back, smiling to himself. It might be another blow in his feud against Yashimoto. But the moment had to be right.

Eventually both the fighters would decide that the time had come and they would charge together, slapping, pawing and pulling, trying to grab each other by the cloth bindings around their thighs and loins. The object of the match was to either throw your opponent from the *basho,* over the layer of rope, or push or pull him out or throw him off his feet so that he fell in the middle of the *basho.*

Generally speaking, the bouts were decided within about ten seconds, more often than not by one of the fighters staggering out from the ring.

That was when the honorable front-row seats could become positively dangerous, with several hundred pounds of out-of-control wrestler landing in your lap.

Konishiki's opponent in the final bout contrived to hurtle from the raised platform, straight at Ryan, who had been anticipating something of the sort and was able to get out of the way before being injured by the huge man.

The incident raised much laughter from the watching Japanese, led by Yashimoto.

Ryan resumed his seat as Konishiki was still walking arrogantly around the ring, slapping his chest, calling out what seemed to be some sort of challenge in his native tongue.

"You were nearly caught out there, *gaijin*," Yashimoto mocked. "Our men are too big and strong, and all you can do is try and skip from their path."

"I got a man could beat that lump of overblown lard," Ryan called.

"Yourself?" Mashashige asked, instantly fascinated by the idea of a contest between one of the top visiting sumo and one of his guests.

"No. Not me.

"Me," Jak said, taking his cue, standing and shrugging off his jacket. "I'll beat him." He pointed at the puzzled Konishiki.

"You will die," Yashimoto said, forcing out the words between tears of merriment.

"We all will . . . one day," the albino replied.

IT TOOK more than an hour of argument and bickering before the bout was finally agreed.

The owner of the traveling sumo circus was extremely reluctant to allow her most valued wrestler, Konishiki, to compete against someone who stood only five feet five inches tall and would hardly have shifted the scales much above one hundred pounds.

"The *gaijin* will die and he is guest of honored shogun, Lord Mashashige," said the manager, a chubby woman with pebble glasses. "It will be a bad joke and cause loss of face to my fighters."

"We set aside all responsibility," Ryan insisted. "Jak will fight on your rules and terms. No weapons. Winner throws loser out of the *basho* or topples him on his back. That it?"

"That is it," the woman agreed.

The shogun had taken her to one side and engaged in a long whispered conversation. Shortly after, Yashimoto had approached her, and there had been the chink of jack changing hands.

And it was agreed.

But with reservations.

Konishiki had strode down to confront Jak. The wrestler was wearing a flowing robe, with foxes embroidered all over it in gold-and-silver threads. He had pointed a strong, stubby finger at the young man.

"You know might die?" he asked.

Jak nodded. "Sure. Be good clean fight. Best man win." And he shook hands, his own white fingers disappearing inside the hamlike hand of the sumo star.

IT PROVED IMPOSSIBLE to find a sumo costume anywhere near small enough for Jak. One had to be improvised by the sewing women of the ville, from a length of stout white linen. It was then wrapped around Jak's waist and knotted in the approved manner.

"Looks like a chicken against a rhinoceros," Doc muttered, as everyone took their seats again. "Not quite a balanced fight."

"But who would you put your money on, Doc?" Mildred asked. "My jack goes on the chicken."

He smiled at her. "I rather think that I must perforce agree with you, ma'am."

Ryan had taken the chance to snatch a few quick words with Jak before the commencement of the bout.

"Gotta keep clear of him."

The youth had grinned, red eyes flashing with excitement. "Sure, sure. No worry, Ryan. Looking forward."

"If it looks like he might be trying to crush you or do serious injury, then I'll..."

Jak had held up a hand. "No. No need. Just watch and enjoy, Ryan."

Now the proceedings were ready.

The priest had pattered out the ritual, and both men had scattered salt to the corners of the *basho* area.

Ryan weighed up the protagonists, trying to figure whether he'd made a serious mistake in pitching Jak in against the vast bulk of Konishiki.

The sumo giant wasn't just fat. There was layer upon layer of hard muscle, and he had already shown evidence of his speed and agility in the earlier fights. Jak was as lean as whipcord, his body deathly white, hair knotted back with a length of red ribbon that had come from little Issie.

The geisha was sitting in the third row, a handkerchief crumpled in her hand, held against her painted rosebud mouth, her whole body tense with worry for Jak.

Now Konishiki dropped into his three-point kneeling position, matched by Jak, whose eyes never left his gigantic opponent.

Three times they did this, and twice the sumo wrestler broke and stood, slapping at himself, his fringed belt swinging as he walked around. The third time, not to be outfaced, Jak rose and copied him, getting a muffled giggle of laughter from some of the audience.

The fourth time was for real.

Konishiki was faster than any person that size had the right to be. He moved up and across the *basho,* which seemed to have shrunk to the size of a tablecloth, grabbing at Jak to smother and destroy him. The big man was already grinning with anticipation of his easy victory.

Only Jak wasn't there to be smothered and destroyed.

He'd dived onto the floor, rolling to the side of the advancing Konishiki, coming up into a crouch as the wrestler started to turn to face him. He hurled himself at the back of the man's huge legs, catching him off-balance, making him stagger to one side, his bulk and momentum carrying him toward the raised rope that marked the edge of the arena.

Yashimoto was on his feet, fingers digging into his own cheeks, as he saw the colossus stumble.

Jak was up again, as nimble as a monkey, vaulting onto Konishiki's back, his hands covering the startled man's eyes, blinding the giant.

The sumo star reached up to pluck him off and dash him to the floor, breaking every bone in the lad's body, but once again Jak wasn't there.

He had hopped off behind Konishiki, pushing him with his shoulder in the small of his back, hastening his rumbling charge toward the edge of the *basho*. Finally he stooped to catch at Konishiki's left foot, heaving it off the ground for a vital couple of seconds.

Like a maddened bull, the monstrous figure roared out in blind rage, swinging a clubbing forearm to try to strike Jak to the sand. But he was too slow, too off-balance. Pivoting on one leg, he reached the rope and caught his right foot on it.

Jak let go of his other foot at the crucial moment, letting gravity do the rest.

Hopelessly out of control, Konishiki gave a last despairing cry before tumbling facedown, over the rope and out of the arena, nearly crushing Yashimoto as he fell.

There was the unmistakable snap of bone as he dropped, his leg crooked under him, the knee joint popping open.

The sumo giant gave a thin scream and fainted.

J.B. stood and grinned. "And that, friends, concludes the entertainment for the day."

Chapter Thirty-One

They had watched the disconsolate troupe leaving the main gates of the ville, one of the wags carrying the crippled figure of Konishiki, sumo star of the morning.

Mashashige had been forced to make a huge payment to the woman manager for the damage done to her prime attraction.

The defeat by the skinny little *gaijin* had cast a pall of depression over the whole fortress, and the outlanders were left to their own devices.

The shogun had offered his stiff, formal congratulations to Jak, as had Hideyoshi. Yashimoto and the rest of the senior samurai had stalked off like wounded peacocks, without saying a word to anyone.

"Need a hot bath?" J.B. asked.

Jak shook his head. "Didn't even break a sweat. Knew it'd be easy."

J.B. AND JAK HAD MANAGED to get into the armory in the corner tower. Guessing that many of the sec men would be wanting to watch the sumo champions, they had picked their moment, talking their way inside.

Each of them had stolen three grens. Four were implodes, with the distinctive scarlet-and-blue bands around their tops, and two were burners.

"When do we go use them?" J.B. asked. "How about this evening?"

Ryan nodded. "Why not? Anyone have any doubts about taking this course of action?"

Jak cleared his throat. "How about Issie?"

"How about her? You thinking about bringing the girl with you, Jak?"

"Yeah, Ryan. And not girl. Issie's a woman."

"Well said," Mildred stated. "Really about time you stopped coming the old male chauvinist, Ryan."

He grinned a little sheepishly. "Sorry. But she seems to be a child."

"She wants to come with us. Knows plan to leave soon. Sees hope getting away from shit air and water and stuff. Anyone object her coming?"

There was a general shaking of heads.

Ryan looked at the teenager. "You think she'll be able to keep up with us in Deathlands, Jak?"

"Why not?"

"You haven't talked about the idea of destroying the gateway? It'll mean she can never get back."

"I know. She doesn't want return."

"Sure?"

Jak nodded. "Sure."

YASHIMOTO AND HIDEYOSHI both failed to put in an appearance at the lunch table, doubtless licking the wounds to their pride in their own quarters.

But the shogun was as calm and imperturbable as ever.

"The score lies with Deathlands against the warrior gods of Nippon," he said quietly while sipping at his usual bowl of clear soup with a few shredded vegetables floating in it.

"It is the side that wins the war, not just individual battles, who is the victor over all," Doc said, seeking to pour oil upon the troubled waters.

"This is truly said. The scars caused by the Americans during the ending of the Second World War are so deep they can never be quite overlooked."

J.B. ran his tongue along the blade of his knife to remove the last smears of egg. "You mean when we dropped the big one?"

The baron of the ville nodded, his dark eyes fixed on the Armorer's face. "The big one? That is your name for the atomic bomb. I had heard it called 'Fat Boy.'"

"Did job," Jak said. "You started it with sneaky attack on ships."

"Pearl Harbor," Mildred agreed. "Frankly I feel like most Americans. That what happened was terrible, but you deserved it all."

"It was the generals who fought the war. Wanted honor of victory for the emperor. But it was the ordinary soldiers and the people in the cities of Hiroshima and Nagasaki who paid the final toll."

Krysty drained her coffee mug. "I don't know much about these things," she said. "Uncle Tyas McCann back in the ville of Harmony told me some of it."

Mashashige nodded. "History is written by the winners, so they say. The beautiful city of Nagasaki had something over two hundred thousand citizens. The bomb is dropped." He clapped his hands once to symbolize the action. "In a single beat of the heart, over seventy thousand are dead. Snuffed out like candles in the wind. The same number are so badly injured that most of them will die. Over half the city is destroyed in a single flash of fire, the wretched peoples without homes."

"The deaths were immeasurably higher in skydark," Ryan said quietly. "Tens of millions. Every city in the land destroyed. The world ended, turned upside down."

The shogun shifted his gaze to Ryan. "True, Cawdor-san. But that was rightly the ending of the world. What happened in Hiroshima and Nagasaki was without... What is the word for something not happening before?"

"Precedent," Doc offered. "You mean that those bombings were without precedent?"

"Quite so." The shogun stood. "We have a very rare old black-and-white film of survivor of Hiroshima talking of what happened. It would interest you?"

"Yeah," Ryan said. "I guess it would."

HISTORY WASN'T ONE of Ryan's strongest subjects.

He knew a fair bit of what had happened in Deathlands in his own lifetime, and some of life in the old United States during the last three or four years before the enemy missiles blackened the skies all around the planet and civilization caught the last train west.

The period of the dozen years or so after skydark, during the horrendous times of the long nuke winters, was a dark age in every sense of the words. There were very few records of any kind, and it was an era of death and decay.

The Second World War in the middle of the previous, twentieth century, was a topic of some interest. A surprising number of the books and mags and vids that survived from predark days seemed to touch on the war, showing how it had to have still preoccupied everyone at the end of the millenium.

But now they were to have a unique opportunity, offered by the shogun.

They followed Mashashige through the maze of twisting passages at the heart of the sprawling ville, while he snapped out orders to a pair of sec men on duty by the double doors into the dining room, sending them scurrying to make preparations for the showing of the old film.

"I don't know that I want to see this," Mildred whispered to J.B.

"Why?"

"Seen documentaries about the bombing. Oppenheimer puking out his crap about becoming the destroyer of worlds. Flattened buildings. The sick and the dying. Experts with rows of gold braid all over their uniforms like flashy wreaths for the corpses. Explaining how it had been. How it had to be. I'm not saying they were wrong. I'm saying I got real gut-tired of it all."

"This'll be from their side. Their Hiroshima."

"Yeah, *mon amour*," she said bitterly, and, to the Armorer, quite inexplicably.

THEY SAT IN TWO ROWS on stiff-backed chairs in a darkened room. Mashashige sat with them, the only Japanese in the room other than the bearded young man who was operating the ancient cinema projector.

A white screen had been unfolded and placed at one end of the chamber.

"We are ready," the shogun called.

There was the clattering of machinery, and after a hesitation, a beam of sharp silver light lanced across the room, illuminating the screen with a dazzling rectangle.

"The sound is poor," Mashashige said, "but there are words below the pictures."

"Subtitles," Mildred stated. "That's what they're called. Subtitles."

"I am grateful to you for this interesting information," the shogun said with a low bow.

The film began.

It was immediately obvious that there was a chunk missing from the beginning, as it started in the middle of an interview with a middle-aged woman.

The face was seamed with shock, the voice harsh, stammering, obviously still devastated by an event that had happened several months earlier. She was talking about the country's surrender, the subtitles giving a cold, dispassionate rendering of her emotional words.

"It was all for nothing. They say we had lost the war. We should have stopped fighting sooner. The emperor was held hostage by the generals and had no power. I heard him speak about our stopping fighting and I cried. But crying makes my eyes hurt too much. The tears are like acid."

There was no visible interviewer, just the occasional off-screen question that prompted the woman onto a different aspect of her experience.

"The sun seemed to burst. A light so bright I couldn't see for minutes afterward and thought I had gone blind. A heat like a giant's oven door had been swung open. The fire flashed across the city like daggers of burning death. All my clothes were scorched from my body, and then the shock wave struck me like the fist of a strong man. I was hurled against the burning wall of a shack that disintegrated with the blast."

The voice, in Japanese, asked her about her injuries. Turning her face away from the camera, she dropped her plain kimono off her shoulders, baring her back, down to the shadowy cleft of her narrow buttocks.

"Holy shit!" Jak breathed, sitting in the seat next to Ryan.

Ryan had seen men—and women—flogged in some of the frontier pestholes, but the woman's back was unimaginably worse than anything he'd ever seen. There were great coils of scar tissue, swollen and livid, as though she had been sprayed with some sticky acid that had made her flesh bubble into grotesque shapes. Some of the scarred lines ran down her arms, disappearing under the thin material of her gown. It was a miracle that she had survived.

"Look at sores around her mouth," Mildred whispered to Krysty. "And her nails. An advanced stage of rad cancer. Couldn't have been long."

After the silent display, the woman was asked to describe what she had seen as she wandered the ruined, burning city.

She slowly and painfully hitched the kimono back into place before answering, turning again to stare deep into the blank eye of the camera.

"You will be surprised, but I was not then in great pain. My whole body felt numb. There was little life in the city. Many dead. As I moved along, the skin was peeling from my body, and it fell about my feet and tripped me so I pulled it loose where I could reach. I saw places on my arm where bone showed white through blackened flesh."

Doc stood and pushed his way along the row, mumbling apologies. "Sorry, sorry, but I have seen enough. I have seen much more than enough, my friends. Sorry..."

The woman continued inexorably on. "What I remember best and I have heard others say this... There were shadows on the walls. Shadows of people. A man working on a ladder. A child throwing a ball in the air. The shadows were these people. All that remained of them, burned into the walls."

Mildred stood, her voice strained, unnaturally high. "Think I'll join Doc," she said. "Sorry."

Without a word, Krysty rose and followed her from the room, passing in front of the projector, her huge shadow cutting off the film for a moment, leaving Ryan, J.B. and Jak to watch the rest of the flickering, damaged black-and-white movie.

There wasn't much more.

"Many bodies were melted. Puddles. You understand? Like heated wax, distorted into puddles of sticky fluids. Here and there a skull, or a row of teeth or a complete hand, oddly untouched. Corpses everywhere, and not one that could be recognized. Most were never identified. My husband, three little ones, sister, her husband and two children and my brother and his wife and both my parents. Not one was ever found. I could not mourn. There was nothing to mourn. They had ceased to exist."

The camera had closed in, and a single tear gathered in the puckered corner of one eye, finally releasing itself and trickling down the unmarked skin of her cheek, passing the trembling side of her mouth and plopping onto her kimono.

There was a jagged crackling sound, and the film ended abruptly, leaving the bright silver rectangle of light on the screen, which vanished as the young bearded man threw a switch.

"There," Mashashige said. "Perhaps that explains things better for you."

Ryan tried to answer and found his mouth was too dry. He swallowed hard a couple of times. "Yeah," he said hoarsely. "I guess that it does."

Chapter Thirty-Two

When they got back to their rooms, none of them felt much like talking. And when a servant knocked on the door and asked them if they wished to come down to supper, none of them felt much like eating, either.

After the elderly woman had bowed her way out, Ryan turned to the others. "Know how you all feel. I'm the same. Idea of food makes my stomach heave. But we're planning to leave tonight. Few hours. No idea when we might next get anything to eat or drink, so we have to go down and do the best we can."

Doc shook his leonine head. "Forgive me, old friend, but I fear that is beyond me."

"Me, too," Mildred said. "No good, Ryan. You just can't make us eat."

Ryan sighed. "All right. I won't make you do anything. Rest of us'll be back here as soon as we can. At least drink plenty of water."

When it came down to it, Jak was the only one of the group who managed anything like a reasonable meal.

Ryan and J.B. both chose some smoked ham with sourdough rolls and a cup of the imitation java, even finding that a struggle after the horrific film.

But Jak demolished four rashers of bacon with three eggs over-easy and a mountain of refried beans, following it with two enormous slices of juicy watermelon.

"You sure you've had enough, kid?" J.B. asked. "No space left for thirds?"

"I'm fine. And don't call me 'kid,' all right?"

The Armorer nodded. "Sure thing. Sorry. We going to the rooms now?"

Ryan pushed back his chair, looking at Mashashige, again the only one of the Japanese to dine with them. "Thanks for the food. Thanks for everything."

"You are welcome. You have helped to open my eyes to things that were closed to me, Cawdor-san."

"Then that's good."

"In the morning I would speak with you—with all of you—about Deathlands."

Ryan nodded. "Sure thing. But we all feel like an early night now."

"Of course. Sleep well and tight. I hope that the bugs do not bite."

BY TEN O'CLOCK the castle seemed to be quiet.

Ryan sent Jak to scout around their wing of the building, checking that there was no unusual guard activity. The teenager ghosted back to report that everything was still.

"How we going to do this, lover?" Krysty asked. "Place is sealed tighter than a gnat's ass."

"Two ways. One is to force the main gate. Mean some chilling and a lot of noise, and the chance of pursuit coming right on top of us."

Doc sniffed and wiped his nose on his sleeve. "I am ahead of you on the logistical planning element of our departure, my dear fellow."

"How's that?"

"You know how I detest swimming."

"Only a few yards, Doc."

"In a lake filled with goodness knows what kind of monstrous predator."

"Carp, Doc," Mildred said. "That's all I've seen in there. Big sons of bitches. I'll grant you that. Maybe a giant eel or two, as well."

"Thank you for your support, madam." He paused. "I shall wear it constantly."

The small joke eased the tension, Ryan leading the laughter. "But you're right, Doc. Small swim. I've worked out our best route away from here. Down into the center courtyard, then head toward the main gates, but stop before we actually reach them. There's a tower alongside the one with all the weapons and grens and stuff in it. Has a barred window, locked from the inside, just above the level of the moat. Open that and slip through. Not much moon tonight. Won't take more than two minutes, swimming slow and easy. No splashing, Doc. Out of the water and in among the trees."

J.B. nodded. "Shouldn't be any problem. Unless we meet any sentries on the way. What then? Chill them?"

Ryan considered the question. "Rather not. Mashashige's played the game with us. Take them out if there's no choice. If we can shut them up for a while, I'd rather do that. In some ways I'd like to stay around here and help against his brother. Then again there's the problem of their plans to try and break through into Deathlands."

"His brother might try that, as well," Krysty said. "Sounds like a nastier piece of work than the shogun."

THEY TWICE SAW patrolling sec men, in their red-and-white uniforms, carrying rifles under their arms. But they were able to get back under cover and passed by undetected, through the central court, with its Zen arrangement of stones and plants, and along several more passages. They paused a moment when they felt a slight tremor run through the ground, waiting to see if it was going to turn into a full quake. But it stopped after four or five seconds, and they moved on.

They melted back into the deep shadows as half a dozen more sec men walked by, stepping quietly, keeping totally silent.

Once they'd gone, heading toward the main gate, Ryan stared after them, vaguely uneasy. "Something not..." he began. "Still, let it pass."

It didn't seem to be anything that should concern them.

THE DOOR FROM THE YARD into the tower that Ryan had selected was unlocked. It was about thirty paces from the corner building that held most of the ville's weapons, and the same distance from the main gate.

"Everyone here all right?" whispered Ryan, hidden in the doorway.

Krysty touched him gently on the arm. "Something's not right, lover."

"What?"

"I can feel men close by."

"Guards?"

She shook her head, the bright flames of her hair just visible in the gloom. "Not that. More than that. Got a strong feeling of something wrong."

Ryan knew better than to ignore Krysty's "seeing" power and looked out across the courtyard, straining his hearing, wondering whether he'd heard the scrape of steel on steel.

"Jak, check out the window. See if you can see anything across the water."

The albino had poor sight in the brightness of noon, but his pale red eyes saw fine in darkness, better than anyone else's.

He was gone for only fifteen flying seconds.

"Men. Crossing the lake. Got rafts of driftwood. Look to be about thirty of them."

Ryan looked toward the main gate, his own sight now adjusted to the dim light, seeing a scuffle of movement and hearing a gasp of pain or shock.

"Treachery," he breathed. "Ronin got men inside here, like we reckoned they could."

"They'll open the gates and drop the bridge. And the ville's going to be open to attack," J.B. said. "Be easy for us to get away and stick to our plan. Nobody notice in the chaos of the raid."

Ryan made the instant decision.

"No," he said. "Could reckon we're still his guests. Owe him our help."

"The gateway?" Krysty probed.

"Later."

He sidled out into the courtyard, keeping pressed against the dry timbers of the high wall, the SIG-Sauer drawn and cocked in his hand. Krysty was next in line, followed by Jak, Mildred and Doc. Without a command or a word being said, J.B. automatically took up the rear guard.

The riding moon peeked out from behind a ragged cluster of high cloud, giving a little more light in the yard, enabling Ryan to see a half dozen men in red and white, preparing to lower the bridge to the invaders.

"Let's take them," he said, readying himself to spring and catch the enemy by surprise.

When the world blew up around him.

Chapter Thirty-Three

As he was tossed sideways by the force of the explosion, part of Ryan's combat mind told him that the ronin had gotten in and blown the armory, and part of him was trying to cope with the sudden burst of violence that sent him rolling over the cobbled yard, deafened and blinded.

He instinctively kept hold of the butt of the SIG-Sauer, taking a jarring blow in the small of the back from the walnut stock of the Steyr SSG-70.

Ryan was conscious of bits of wood and masonry thudding all around him. He opened his eye, finding that he could see bright flames and a curtain of billowing black smoke that boiled from the shattered ruins of the tower.

His head was ringing and he could hear voices, echoing around him, hollow and distant.

Someone tugged at his arm, trying to get him to his feet. Rubbing at his eye, Ryan saw that it was J.B., his fedora still miraculously perched on his head. The Armorer was shouting something to him, but the words were distorted.

"Back inside..."

"What?"

"Best get inside. They got a hold."

"How about the others?"

J.B. nodded. "All right. They're all right. You were nearest explosion."

Ryan was standing, coughing at the smoke and dust. J.B. was at his side, holding the scattergun at his hip. A figure in the colors of the palace sec force loomed out of the darkness at them, holding a Nambu 9 mm pistol.

Without a moment's hesitation, the Armorer squeezed the trigger on the Smith & Wesson M-4000, firing one of the murderous Remington fléchettes at the man's midriff. The twenty darts, each an inch long, tore into the stomach, puddling the intestines, sending the invader staggering backward. He dropped his blaster, hands reaching to try to hold his ruined body together.

"How you know he was ronin?" Ryan yelled.

J.B. grinned mirthlessly through the mask of dirt. "Didn't. Wasn't going to wait and find out."

There was another muffled boom, and more of the tower was demolished, what Ryan guessed had to have been some of the store of grens going up.

"Have to get inside," J.B. repeated. "Now!"

THE RONIN HAD ALSO managed to hit the fortress's main power source, forcing them onto emergency lighting, which consisted of dim lamps placed at irregular intervals.

Inside, everything was chaos.

Men were running around, and Ryan could hear women screaming, not short, sharp cries, but a long, high, keening sound that grated on the nerves.

Krysty was waiting inside the doors to the main part of the ville with Jak, Doc and Mildred. She hugged him as he appeared. "All right, lover?"

"Shaken a little."

"Saw you go down like a ton of bricks off the tailgate of a wag," Krysty said, her voice raised above the hubbub of noise that surrounded them.

"Ryan was ever an exponent of the big-bang theory of life," Doc said, his white teeth grinning in the gloom.

"Best try and find the shogun." Ryan looked around. "Where he is'll be the defense."

"Better be good." Jak had his blaster drawn, the metal gleaming in the light of the lamps. "Ronin well in. Done good damage. Take stopping."

Ryan led the way back into the heart of the huge wooden fortress, followed by the others. Nobody tried to stop them or threaten them. Half the sec men were running in short, scampering steps toward the main gates. The rest seemed to be simply running, like ants when the walls of their nest have been broken down by a giant enemy.

"Hideyoshi!" Ryan spotted the balding head of the samurai in the distance, near a cross corridor. "Hey!"

The warrior stopped, his face worried, the scar still making him appear as if he were sharing a private joke with himself. "Cawdor-san? I heard you had fallen in the attack."

"Bit ruffled. Your armory's gone."

"The *yagura* is exploded?"

"Yeah. Ronin are in. About thirty or so. And we reckon that some of your new sec men are traitors to Mashashige. Got real trouble."

The samurai nodded furiously. He was wearing armor above the waist, but he was helmetless, and he gripped his drawn sword in his right hand.

"Lord Mashashige is at the heart of the fortress. There we will make our stand."

"Could try and hit them before then," J.B. suggested. "Take some out."

"If you can."

At that moment Mashashige himself appeared, walking slowly toward them, his face as untroubled as the surface of a summer millpond. He wore, as usual, the loose black kimono, and his sword was still tucked into the wider sash.

"This is what you Americans call 'the crackle,' I believe," he said.

"The crunch," Ryan stated. "Sure looks like it. What plans you got?"

"To gather my men and attack the ronin. Drive them from my walls and slay them all."

It was said as calmly as if the shogun were giving a recipe for pecan pie to a ladies' auxiliary.

"Why not invent a cure for cancer and create world peace while you're at it?" Mildred snorted. "Get real."

He turned toward her. "This is a problem?"

Ryan answered, ticking off points on his fingers. "One, they got in. Two, they blew your armory. Three, from the smoke they started a fire. Wooden building like this could go in an hour. Four, we're certain some of your new sec men are already on the wrong side. And five, they all got blasters. Odds might favor you. Might just favor you. But not by much. You don't hit them now and hit them hard, then you can get out your wakizashi and start cutting open your belly. You and the rest of your warriors."

It was an unusually long speech for Ryan, and the shogun considered it for several seconds.

"You will help?"

"Yes."

"Yet you know of my plan to bring my people into your Deathlands?"

"Sure. You haven't done much to try and hide it from us, have you? After this fight, I'm not saying we'll go along with your ideas."

Mashashige nodded, taking in a slow breath. "I see. This is good. Let us go then and defeat my hen-shit brother."

"Chicken-shit, Shogun," Ryan corrected. "You mean chicken-shit."

"Thank you, Cawdor-san. Go and do what you can. I will rally my people. May our gods go with us."

RYAN'S IDEA HAD BEEN to try to reach a point where they could either ambush the invading ronin or launch a counterattack against them, somewhere near the main entrance.

But it was impossible.

The ville was such a rambling complex, now poorly lighted, with smoke already showing where fires were taking hold, that there was no way to find their way through or to locate any position to commence a fire-fight.

And there was the constant ebb and flow of humanity, with no hope of determining who was for good and who for evil. Jak very nearly shot Issie through the face as she suddenly jumped on him from a side room, weeping, her makeup so smudged she looked like a heartbroken panda. She begged to be allowed to stay with them, as she feared for her life.

"All do," Jak muttered.

THE RONIN HAD ALREADY spread out through the fortress.

Ryan spotted several of them gathered in a side room, where they were handing out ammo to three or four of the turncoat sec men.

"Still got your grens?" he asked J.B. and Jak. "Give them a couple of implodes."

The light was very poor in the corridor where they all waited, but both the Armorer and the teenager fumbled in pockets and pulled out a pair of grens with two-step firing mechanisms.

"Now!" J.B. called, arming his, then lobbing it across and through the paper walls, the dark shape followed immediately by Jak's implode gren.

Ryan turned away, putting his hands over his ears, opening his mouth to minimize the effects of the shock.

There was the familiar, oddly inverted sound of the implode going off, sucking all matter into it like a reverse explosion. But the second gren made a different sound, louder, accompanied by a flash of vivid yellow-and-orange fire.

"Shit," Jak hissed. "Mine was flamer. Couldn't see colors in dark."

The two grens together had done their lethal work, killing or maiming every man in the room, sending a couple of them staggering away, screaming, burning. The fiery grens contained a highly concentrated form of napalm that splattered everywhere and stuck and burned.

And burned.

Ryan squinted at the dazzling inferno, seeing that gobbets of flame had burst onto adjoining walls, starting fresh fires. "Whole place could go unless someone starts fighting it," he said. "Wood's like tinder."

"Reckon the shogun's goin' to be too busy trying to save his life to worry about the fire," J.B. replied. "And we sure don't have the time."

"Best try and get to the center. See if we can hold there."

Doc clapped his hands. "Well said, good Master Cawdor! For if the center cannot hold, then what hope can there be for the rest?"

THEY KILLED THREE MORE of the ronin, or their treacherous allies among the sec men of the castle, as they struggled to find their way through the dark, reeking maze toward the courtyard at the heart of the building.

Behind them they were aware of the roar of the fire as it gathered momentum, fanned by a rising northerly wind that drove the hungry flames deeper into the ville.

"Not going to be anything left to rescue, lover," Krysty panted.

Ryan stopped, struck by the thought that they could end up trapped in the heart of the fortress, with the holocaust swallowing them as it raged by.

"Mebbe we should head for the outside and get into the water," he said.

"The open courts should act as some kind of a break," Mildred stated. "Like they cut spaces in a forest fire. Might slow it down some."

"Yeah. Could be. But if I yell for us to get out, then follow on tight. You're responsible for the girl, Jak."

"Sure."

THEY WERE IN AN ARCADE of *pachinko* machines, running past them when someone opened up with an automatic rifle, sending them diving for cover on the floor. Whoever it was had no skill as a marksman and fired high, ripping through the chrome and glass and bright colors of the games, scattering thousands of the tiny metal balls across the floor.

Ryan didn't risk getting to his feet, surfing on his stomach on the waves of *pachinko* balls, followed by the others, until they were all safely out of the room.

A LITTLE FARTHER ON Ryan almost bumped into one of the few samurai who still lived in the ville, loyal to Lord Mashashige, one of the nameless warriors who had allied himself with the venomous Yashimoto and hadn't even bothered to introduce himself to the outlanders.

Now he was dying.

One of the long war arrows had pierced his neck, from right to left, the shaft standing out by more than a foot on each side. Blood ran down over the collar of his armor, seeping from his mouth and nose.

Ryan came within a whisker of shooting him through the chest with the big 9 mm blaster, checking at the last moment as he recognized the man's tortured face through the coils of choking smoke.

The Japanese knelt, slowly and carefully, as though he were about to dine, one hand touching the blood-slick arrow, his face puzzled. The leather bindings on the heavy armor creaked as he moved, and his helmet, with a heron's beak in inlaid silver, tilted backward.

"What happen?" he mumbled.

"You got chilled," Ryan said.

"You help ronin?"

"No. Where's the shogun?"

The man gestured wearily with his thumb, pointing behind himself. "Some ronin there. Saw Ryuku. Think race is lost, outlander."

"Never over until it's over," Ryan said.

"And the fat lady sings," Mildred added.

"Shogun still alive?"

"Alive, Cawdor-san."

"Sure?"

"*Shinda tsumori.* We all ready for that." He coughed, his whole body jerking with the pain, a lump of blood the size of a fist filling his open mouth, flooding over his breastplate. "We anticipate death."

"Could try getting arrow out," Jak suggested.

But Mildred held up a hand. "No point. Might quicken his passing. That's all."

The samurai looked up at the strangely assorted group, his pain-filled eyes catching the terrified Issie. He pointed a blood-drenched finger at her.

"It is all bad joke," he said very quietly, then slid forward on his face on the floor, the feathered flight of the arrow rasping on the planking.

"Best get on," Ryan said.

A figure in dark blue erupted out of a door on his left, holding a Nambu blaster. For a moment the man hesitated, and Ryan shot him carefully through the center of the chest, sending him toppling backward out of sight.

THEY HAD OUTRUN the flames, but paused in a room where an exotic buffet had been laid out, the platters of food untouched.

"Funny," Doc said, "but right now I think I could do me some eating after all."

Ryan looked all around, head to one side, listening for sounds of danger.

There was shooting, accompanied by screams, but all of it seemed to be far off. As near as Ryan could work out, the corridor to the heart of the ville lay ahead of them, through the room with the food, maybe forty or fifty yards away.

"All right to snatch some food, lover?" Krysty asked, eyeing an oval blue-and-white dish bearing a wonderful array of fruit.

Doc was already halfway through a pastry shell filled with slices of thin meat, covered in a spicy red sauce. "Delicious, friends," he grunted, spluttering crumbs on the floor. "Best I've eaten since Ma Thompson's ice-cold frankfurter and hot parsnip mayonnaise!"

Mildred stopped halfway through a golden sliced pineapple. "God, Doc, you surely do come up with the most bizarre and disgusting thoughts."

Doc looked thoughtful. "Now that you mention it, my dear, Dr. Wyeth, it was a somewhat revolting repast, though I had not eaten for several days at the time."

Ryan drank deeply from one of the cut-crystal vases of fresh ice water, washing away some of the heat and dryness from his throat.

"Better." As Ryan put down the empty jug, he noticed that the sound of the flames was getting closer and the smoke seemed to be thickening. "Time we got moving again," he said.

Mildred wiped her mouth on her sleeve, patting J.B. on the arm. "I'm beginning to think that we might've missed the fat lady, John."

Chapter Thirty-Four

It seemed as if the firefight was more or less over.

The shooting had fallen to silence behind them, though the noise of the fire was getting closer. There was still an occasional shot from ahead of them, toward the heart of the ville, where they believed that Mashashige might be organizing his last line of defense against his brother and the ronin.

They had seen a half-dozen bodies, mostly wearing the red-and-white uniforms of the sec men. Two of them were obviously outsiders, and one was another of the samurai from the fortress. He had been shot several times in the body and was lying bleeding to death, his steel-and-bamboo armor stuck to the floor in the pool of congealing crimson.

"Help me, *gaijin*," he whispered as he recognized Ryan and the others.

Hardly breaking stride, Ryan stooped and touched the muzzle of the SIG-Sauer to his temple and squeezed the trigger, blowing a chunk of skull the size of a saucer off the back of the man's head. The corpse twitched, then lay still.

"The Romans at their most barbaric showed mercy to their doomed enemies," Doc said conversationally.

"Thought they crucified them," Mildred said, unable to resist the implicit challenge in the old man's words.

"But they used to break the legs of the victims with an iron bar to speed their ending." He laughed. "Being the pedantic old Romans, they even had a word for that iron bar. Called it a *crurifragium*. Interesting, is it not?"

"Not," Ryan said curtly. "Not now."

YASHIMOTO APPEARED from the smoke like a demon in an old-fashioned pantomime. The samurai had been cut near the old scar by his mouth and kept spitting venous blood, frothing over his armor. He had lost his horned helmet.

His sword was also missing, and he held a chromed Dragoon Colt in his hand, the huge barrel gaping like a railroad tunnel, pointed at Ryan's chest.

"So, time for farewell, infidel!" he grated. "The die is casted, and it is the eyes of the snake showing."

"Shoot me and the rest of us'll fill you with lead," Ryan said calmly.

Yashimoto leered at him. "That is no dishonor, *gaijin*. The blood debt will be paid to my brother. The ronin are winning. They take many losses, but they will win." He laughed, high and weird. "What will their treasure be? A mountain of ashes and bones. That is all."

Mildred stood immediately behind Ryan, her Czech target revolver already drawn and cocked. It was obvious that the Japanese warrior's nerves were strung tight, and any move would mean a bullet for Ryan. Even though the gun was obviously a predark replica of the old cap-and-ball classic, the odds were that he wouldn't miss from less than twenty feet.

"Where's Mashashige?" Ryan asked, trying to buy time, take the samurai's concentration away for a moment and give one of the others the chance to waste him. The problem was that they had been moving in single file so that he blocked any direct shot. Mildred was right behind him, and Ryan had no way of guessing whether she might be able to take a chance against Yashimoto—until he felt the slight pressure against his right arm.

"He is wounded," the warrior replied, still grinning brightly. "Many are dead and the palace burns. All that is left is to die with honor."

"Then do it," Mildred said quietly.

She had eased the muzzle of the ZKR 551 6-shot revolver under Ryan's arm. Now she pressed the trigger, sending the Smith & Wesson .38 round on its way.

Ryan's body muffled the noise of the shot, making it sound as if it came from far away.

For a moment the woman thought that she'd missed the samurai. He didn't move at all, the barrel of the Dragoon not wavering an inch.

A black spot had appeared on his burnished armor, just over his left breast, and it suddenly began to leak bright crimson, the blood flowing freely, pattering on the stone floor of the narrow corridor.

"Who...?" Yashimoto whispered, puzzled. "Which of you...?" His gaze raked the six friends, settling on the blaster in Mildred's right hand. "Not black bitch...?" He dropped the gun as though he'd forgotten that he'd been holding it.

"Yeah," Mildred said. "The black bitch done for you, you Nip bastard!"

The samurai lay down carefully, his armor rattling, a puddle of blood already spreading below him. He settled himself comfortably on his back and let his head tilt, looking up at the ceiling.

"Not what I wanted," he mumbled crossly, then died.

"Thanks, Mildred," Ryan said.

As THEY MOVED ON again, they all felt a deep vibration run through the ground.

"Quake," Jak called.

"Could just be the building settling as the fire consumes it," J.B. replied.

"Felt like a quake to me." Mildred paused, looking behind them. "Fire's falling back again."

Ryan nodded. "Do what we can and get out. Don't like these tremors. Often a sign of something big coming along."

"WHAT?"

"It's Issie."

Ryan bit his lip. "What's wrong with her, Jak?"

"Says she can't go on."

"Fireblast! Told you that she wouldn't keep up with us. Leave her."

"Not her fault."

Ryan pointed at the teenager, staring into his crimson eyes. "Doesn't matter whether it's her fault or not. You know that, Jak. We all keep up or we all go under."

"I don't think that's fair, lover."

He turned to face Krysty. "We aren't talking about what's fair and what's not. That's for storekeepers in a comfortable little rural ville.

Krysty faced him. "The girl's terrified. Her world's fallen around her ears. She's seeing death up close. Smelling blood. Tasting fear. Look at her. She's trembling like a hunted deer. For Gaia's sake, Ryan!"

He gazed at the young woman, her beautiful kimono smeared with blood and soot, torn at the hem, her painfully bound little feet and her pretty doll-like mask, the makeup smudged and running, with tears streaking her dimpled cheeks. Issie looked up at him and attempted a desperate smile, but it never got without a country mile of her eyes. Krysty was right; the little geisha was shaking like an aspen in a hurricane.

"All right," he said. "Jak, you and J.B. have to help her. But if there's trouble, then you drop her. I mean that. Drop her on the floor and get blasting."

Jak nodded. "Sure. Understood."

THE CENTRAL COURT WAS a calm place in the middle of swirling chaos. It seemed like two-thirds of the fortress was already burning fiercely, only a drop in the wind keeping the flames partly in check.

Mashashige was sitting on a straight-backed chair that had obviously been brought from another part of the ville. He was even more pale than usual and had a blood-soaked bandage wrapped around his left shoulder.

Hideyoshi was at his side, and two other samurai, as well as a scant half-dozen sec men, all of whom looked even more petrified than Issie.

As soon as Ryan led his little band into the smoky, graveled court, the shogun pulled himself upright and bowed to them, though his whole body language betrayed him, showing how much pain he was in.

"I am sorry not to be able to welcome you with proper ceremony," he said. "But I fear that things have become difficult."

"You have seen Yashimoto?" Hideyoshi asked. "He left and has not returned."

Ryan shook his head. "No. Not seen him. We saw a few dead. Sent a few of the ronin to meet their ancestors. But it looks like they could be winning."

Mashashige gestured to his seat. "Do you mind if I show disrespect and sit? This arm is more painful than I had thought. A bullet from a rifle."

"Sure," Ryan said, seeing out of the corner of his eye that Issie had collapsed on the small raked stones, huddling into the fetal position, weeping quietly to herself.

"My brother, Ryuku, will not win," the shogun said. "We are all losers here."

Ryan couldn't find any argument against that. The losses on both sides were so crippling that whoever came out with the most alive wouldn't be able to hold on to any power. And the whole ville would be destroyed and useless.

"Pyrrhic victory," Doc said. "One in which the cost to the winners is so great that they might as well not have fought at all. The Romans again."

"This is, I think, like the last standing of General Custer," Mashashige said quietly. "Or the remembering of the days of glory at the Alamo."

For a moment there was silence, broken only by a burst of gunfire and the crackling of the red-orange flames that flared above the rooftops.

"Why not break out of here?" Ryan asked, surprised at the fatalistic acceptance of defeat from a man he had come to admire and like.

"How?"

"Unburned side. Into the water. Head for the gateway and jump into Deathlands. Just a few of you can't hurt." He didn't mention his plan to destroy the whole mat-trans unit as soon as they'd initiated their jump out of Japan.

"Why?"

"Better than dying."

The shogun smiled gently. "You do not understand us, my friend. If I run, then I am a dead man. Totally unworthy of respect. Better to depart from this dark world on my own terms, with honor intact. Toyotomi Hideyoshi here will aid me in my passing."

His number three immediately bowed low. "I will so do, dear Lord Mashashige."

"Then we might as well leave you." Ryan looked around at the pitiful remnants of the once-powerful shogun's forces. "If that's truly your final decision. No point in everyone sinking with the ship."

Mashashige nodded. He raised his voice and barked an order in Japanese. His sec men looked at him, and at one another. Then all of them bowed to the floor and scampered away in the direction of the rear of the fortress.

He looked at the pair of warriors, who were nervously shuffling their feet. "I also release you from your oath of... What is word I wish, Doctor-san?"

"*Fealty* would do nicely," Doc replied.

The shogun smiled at him. "Thank you for guidance. I shall miss having such teachers of the American way of speaking." He turned to the samurai. "Leave me now. There is no dishonor in saving your lives. Take your concubines and any servants that live, and flee this place of death." He held up a hand as they both began a halfhearted protest. "No. Do not stop for speeching. Time runs faster than a man's hopes. Go."

Like the sec men, the two samurai bowed their way out of the presence of the shogun.

Less than ten seconds after their departure, there was

a long burst of shooting and a scream from that direction.

"Think we missed the fat lady singing after all," J.B. said, readying the Uzi at his hip.

Ryan smiled grimly at his oldest friend. "Not over until it's over. Well, this looks like over to me."

Chapter Thirty-Five

Ryan felt the floor quiver as yet another tremor ran below the fortress. Unlike the others, it lasted for better than half a minute, but never developed into a serious quake. A war banner that was hung from one of the walls of the courtyard fluttered and fell down in coils of bright silk. Mashashige turned to watch its fall, his face showing no emotion.

"That was the flag of my honorable father," he said. "I think perhaps it's an omen."

The shooting had been so close that Ryan realized their retreat toward the safety of the water was barred. The Trader used to say that if you could run, then you ran. If you couldn't run, then you stood and fought.

Now they could all hear many raised voices and the tramp of heavy boots coming from the corridor to the north of the courtyard, the side of the ville farthest from the steadily advancing flames.

Mashashige steadied himself for a moment on the arm of his chair and stood, hand on the hilt of his sword. "It is my brother," he said. "As my guests, I do not think you will be harmed. They will fear your guns. Do not interfere, whatever happens now. And all will be well for you."

Ryan bit his lip. Now that it was all coming down to the wire, the main thing was to focus on survival. If they could all walk safe, then it was worth taking the advice of the shogun. "Yeah, all right," he said.

"We just watch?" Jak asked disbelievingly. "Just stand and watch?"

"Right. Unless we're threatened directly. Then we move and we all move."

A flimsy door was flung open, and fifteen or so armed men burst into the courtyard. Ryuku Mashashige was three or four inches taller than his shogun brother, and at least a hundred and fifty pounds heavier.

He had a long, drooping mustache and fleshy lips, visible under the ornate silver-and-bronze helmet he wore, its top crested with a bunch of heron feathers. He had a sword at his side, but was carrying a Remington 5-round, 12-gauge shotgun.

The gang of ronin with him mostly carried a mixed bag of scatterguns and hunting rifles, with a couple of semiautomatic weapons.

"Welcome to the warm fire of what remains of my humble dwelling, brother," the shogun said, bowing slightly. "It has been a long time."

Ryuku lacked the style and elegance of his older brother, hawking and spitting on the neat rows of small stones. "Fuck long time. Fuck dwelling. Fuck brother," he said, but his eyes and those of his men were fixed on the half-dozen outlanders standing in a loose half circle at one side of the chair.

"Rather a limited vocabulary, would you not say?" Doc whispered loud enough for everyone to hear him.

The shogun spoke, his voice ringing out. "The *gaijin* are all my guests, brother. They will not fight against you and are all to go free."

"And you, brother?"

"I shall take the way of honor. Toyotomi Hideyoshi here shall be my second in this."

Ryuku threw back his head and laughed. "That running dog. I do not think so."

He leveled the shotgun and pulled the trigger, blasting the samurai through the chest, sending him spinning across the room like a discarded marionette with all of the strings cut. Hideyoshi left a trail of blood across the lamp-lit gravel, collapsing in a heap in the corner.

"Gaia!" Krysty breathed.

Ryan's finger whitened on the trigger of his SIG-Sauer, but he held his fire.

The shogun closed his eyes for a moment. "That was a sorry, barbarous, cowardly act, brother," he said finally, his voice as cold as a blizzard's heart.

"You and your honor!"

"It is all there is."

"Fuck that!" Ryuku looked at Ryan. "You. The one-eyed mongrel! I will be generous. Take your scum and leave. I give you fifteen minutes to leave this ruin, and then I will have you butchered as you deserve."

"What about Lord Mashashige?" Ryan asked, his voice calm and gentle, concealing his rage like the dark waters of a mirrored lake could hide a ravening monster.

"What happens to him will happen whether I have you slaughtered or not. His passing will be as slow and painful as I can make it."

One of the ronin muttered something to Ryuku, and he looked past Jak at the cowering figure of Issie. He laughed again.

"The geisha slut stays, as well."

Ryan held up his left hand, silencing the albino, nodding at the leader of the ronin. "Is there anything else you request from us before we leave?" he asked humbly.

"Yes. Your blasters. Leave all your weapons behind, *gaijin.*" He waved a hand. "And go."

He turned to grin at his followers, preening himself at the ease of his victory over the feared outlanders.

"Of course, Lord," Ryan said, bowing.

He whispered out of the corner of his mouth to the others. "On three. One and two and . . . *three!*"

He had picked out Ryuku as his own special target, remembering Trader's comment that not many animals would fight once their heart had been cut out.

The ronin had been grinning, relaxed and triumphant, seeing their arrogant leader in total and absolute command of the isolated, wounded shogun and his pathetically docile handful of Yankee guests.

It wasn't a firefight.

It was a massacre.

Ryan put three of the P-226's 9 mm rounds neatly into the chest of the gloating Ryuku Mashashige, all together in a spot smaller than a playing card. The full-metal jacket burst through the polished medieval armor like a jousting lance through a wet paper bag.

He didn't bother to watch the fat man go down in the dirt. He was too busy blasting at Ryuku's men.

All around him there was the racketing, deafening thunder of gunfire.

J.B. sprayed the ronin with the Uzi on full-auto; Jak used his massive Colt Python .357 Magnum, the rounds blowing chunks of flesh away at close range; Mildred aimed and fired repeatedly, killing a man with every shot, placing each bullet through the forehead; Krysty put her first couple of bullets into Ryuku, then altered her aim with the Smith & Wesson double-action 640, knocking two of the landless, lordless samurai over with the .38 rounds; Doc, his mouth open, screamed "Geronimo!" in hatred and anger as he squeezed the trigger on his beloved gold-engraved Le Mat, the scattergun obliterating three of the ronin from the left side of the helpless group.

"That's it!" Ryan yelled. "Over."

Every one of the ronin was down and done for.

Three or four were still moving, arms and legs flailing and kicking, moaning in shocked, weeping voices. The gravel was ruined, trampled and awash with gallons of spilled blood.

Mashashige hadn't moved from his seat, watching the total butchery without a change of expression.

"Check the doors, J.B., and you, Jak. Reckon we've broken the back of the bastards, but there might be more."

"I think there will not be any more, Cawdor-san. Once you have severed the head of the dragon, its body will not do you much harming."

"More or less what an old friend of mine once said," Ryan replied.

"Fire's coming closer," Krysty warned, reloading her blaster. "Soon take the whole place. Make it dangerous to try and reach the water."

"Yeah. Get the girl up, if she's coming with us."

Ryan turned to the shogun. "Want to come along?"

There was a pause. "It is attractive and I thank you for it. Thank you all also for saving the honor of my home. But now nothing remains. My plans for the gateway are in ruins. Deathlands is safe from any samurai invasion."

J.B. called from the side of the yard, "No ronin, but the fire's getting real close."

"Then we'd best go." Krysty and Mildred had helped Issie to her feet, supporting her between them. There was another throbbing tremor from deep underground, and some of the loose stones rattled against one another.

"All clear!" Jak yelled from the far side of the open courtyard, barely visible through the thickening smoke that was filling the space.

"Then we go. Now." He nodded to Mashashige. "Sorry it didn't lay better." He turned away toward the open door at the opposite side of the body-littered court.

The shogun called him back. "Might I require two minutes further of your time, Cawdor-san?"

"Why?"

"It is personal. Might the others go." He waved a hand to them. "Go with my thanks."

He spoke to Issie. "Do not bring shame on your parents, child."

Ryan hesitated, looking at Krysty, who shrugged. "Get going," he said. "Head for the windows at the flank of the ville. Into the water and all get across together. Chill anyone tries to stop you. Be with you in a minute."

"Sure." A quick kiss on the cheek, and she was gone, followed by the others.

"You want me to help you kill yourself. Act as your friend, now Hideyoshi's gone."

There was a slight nod, with a thin smile. "I knew you would guess. Yashimoto had gone to obtain the special *wakizashi,* but he must have fallen."

"The special dagger?"

"Yes. My sword is too long for the purpose. I know you carry a machete with a suitable blade. A little wide and long, but it will serve. If I might? Yes? My thanks. When I then bow my head, you will act as my *kaishaku* and use my own sword to end matters."

"You're certain?"

"How do you say? Never more so."

Ryan nodded. He finished reloading the SIG-Sauer, then unslung the Steyr and leaned it against the chair. He unsheathed the panga and handed it to the shogun, who took it in his right hand and weighed the balance.

"Heavy. But sharp. Thank you again, Cawdor-san. I do not wish you to be burned alive for helping me from the troubles of this valley of tears. So, let us to it."

Ryan shook hands with him, impressed by the firmness of his grip. He took the sword from the samurai baron, admiring the wonderful feeling of lightness and power in the honed steel.

"If you wish to keep the sword, after..."

"No. Thanks, but I'll leave it with you."

"Then we shall begin."

Behind him Ryan could now feel the heat of the flames on his back and hear the crashing of massive roof timbers falling in the inferno. Time was racing away.

Mashashige knelt slowly on the gravel, carefully avoiding the lake of crimson that glowed almost black in the light of the wall lamps.

He held the taped hilt of the panga in his right hand, easing his wounded shoulder with a passing grimace of pain. He placed the bare steel on the ground for a moment while he unfolded the front of his kimono, exposing the flat, muscular wall of his stomach, then picked up the blade again.

"Stand behind me, friend. And when I nod my head... you must use much strength and aim at—"

Ryan interrupted him. "I know what to do. How to do it. Goodbye."

"May all our gods watch over us, Cawdor-san."

There was not a moment's hesitation.

He thrust the needled point of the eighteen-inch blade in under the ribs on the left side and drew it up and across and down again, following the angle of his ribs. Blood poured over his lap from the wide mouth of the gaping wound.

Mashashige laid down the panga, contemplating the ruin of his own intestines that slurped from the gash.

"Now," he said, nodding.

Ryan had moved to stand behind him, the sword hefted to his shoulders, ready to make the single scything cut, mouthing snatches of a remembered prayer that he should get it right first time and not screw up. Having to repeat the blow was unthinkable.

The sword was the sharpest thing that Ryan had ever seen.

There was a faint jar as it hacked through the vertebrae at the top of the spine, but its momentum was hardly checked by muscle and sinew.

The shogun's head dropped off with a dull thump, rolling twice and settling in the bed of stones, the eyes open, staring toward Ryan. It might have been a trick of the light, but Ryan would always swear that he saw the lips moving, as if the shogun were trying to deliver a message from the other side of the dark river.

Blood jetted several feet in the air, and Ryan had to step back hastily to avoid being soaked by it.

The headless body knelt where it was for several long seconds, before the muscles relaxed their hold and it slumped gently sideways, the flow of blood slowing to a mere trickle as the corpse voided itself.

Ryan laid the elegant sword by the side of the dead man, overcoming a momentary temptation to take it with him. It was one of the finest weapons he'd ever seen, but he couldn't imagine much use in Deathlands for it.

He picked up the panga and looked around for something to wipe off the shogun's blood, eventually using the cotton underrobe of Ryuku Mashashige.

He sheathed the blade, then turned and picked up the rifle, slinging it.

Ryan winced at a wave of heat that came from the burning building, seeing that his helping Mashashige had put his own life in jeopardy from the raging fire.

HE RAN AT TOP SPEED, bursting through the delicate, paper-thin walls, struggling to keep a sense of direction. He climbed stairs and sprinted along corridors, eventually finding himself by a third-floor window that opened onto the dark water of the moat.

Ryan could smell his clothes scorching and leapt into the blackness.

Chapter Thirty-Six

The moat, set defensively around the ville, was brightly lit by the volcano of fire that had once been the all-powerful ville of the shogun. Ryan glanced behind him as he kicked his way across the cold water, heading for the shore where he'd already spotted the others waiting for him, seeing that only one corner of the fortress remained inviolate, and the flames were already licking hungrily toward it.

When he was within a few yards of safety, he had an odd experience.

The surface of the lake rippled suddenly, almost as though some powerful creature had passed close below him. For a moment Ryan had a heart-stopping vision of something like a great white, then the moment passed and he was helped out by Doc and Krysty.

"Did you just feel that strong tremor?" the old-timer asked. "Devilish powerful, was it not?"

"Is it all over, lover?" Krysty asked.

"Over," he said. "Let's move out of here."

IT WAS ABOUT FOUR MILES to the building that they knew held the gateway in its basement.

The wind was blowing the smoke away from them, but they had gone only halfway when the immense glow from the fire began to fade, leaving them in near darkness.

There was no attempt to follow them.

Nor did they meet anyone on the trail.

Issie managed to stammer that the destruction of the ville would be so unbelievable to the local peasants that they would all have taken to their beds in terror that some new Hiroshima was happening.

The young woman was gradually coming out of her own paralyzing fear. She hung on to Jak's hand as she hobbled bravely along, trying to keep up with the hard pace set by Ryan, who had serious reservations about taking the geisha with them, after her short, sheltered, soft life. But it was Jak's decision and he seemed happy enough.

As they moved through the blighted land, they felt two more quakes, each stronger and lasting longer than the one before. The second one made Ryan stop for several heartbeats, waiting for the shifting earth to become stable again.

"Building's ahead," J.B. panted.

Ryan saw it looming through the tendrils of foul-tasting mist that clung to the valley around them.

"Made it," he said.

Then the quake struck.

It was a vicious, stabbing, surging tremor.

The ground seemed to shift sideways by six or seven feet in a single violent movement, throwing all of them off-balance into the dirt.

Ryan went down hard, yelping with pain as the bolt of the Steyr rifle dug into the big latissimus dorsi muscle just below the shoulder blade.

The dark, overcast sky rolled all about him, and for a few seconds he completely lost his sense of direction. The air was filled with the instantly recognizable sullen roaring from below the earth, like some enraged primeval beast roused suddenly from millennia of hibernation.

Someone was screaming.

Issie?

It had to be her. The voice was too high and shredded for either Krysty or Mildred.

The quake lasted less than a dozen heartbeats, stopping just as quickly as it had started, leaving the head ringing, ears hurting from the noise. The ground was still again, and Ryan was swiftly up on his feet, rubbing the bruise on his back, calling to the others.

"All right? Anyone hurt?"

"I'm fine, lover."

"All right, bro. Sudden and sharp, that."

"Jarred my wrist," Mildred said, "but I'll live."

"By the Three Kennedys! The planet has been taking a most ferocious laxative. I fear that it has given me a minor nosebleed."

Jak didn't answer immediately. Ryan saw the flash of white hair in the blackness, stooping over the screaming figure of Issie, trying to calm her.

"She hurt, Jak?"

"Scared. Be fine."

"Sooner we jump the better. Let's get in and then place the grens. Destroy the gateway for good and all."

"Main entrance is open," the Armorer said.

The quake had jerked one of the heavy iron gates off its hinges, leaving it crumpled on the ground, the driveway to the house open and unguarded.

The path to the front porch, with its overgrown yews, was furrowed by the tremor, some of the cracks several inches deep. The wickerwork sofa had completely fallen from its couplings and lay on one side by the door.

Ryan was first there. He tested the handle, finding that it was open, and looked back to beckon the others to hurry. J.B., Mildred and Krysty were already at his heels. Doc strode a few paces behind them, swinging his swordstick like some Parisian boulevardier taking a summer stroll, dabbing at a worm of blood from his nose with his familiar swallow's-eye kerchief.

Jak brought up the rear, one arm around Issie's waist, almost carrying her.

They were still about twenty yards from the relative safety of the house, by the dried fountain, when the quake bared its teeth again.

It was by far the strongest of the tremors and seemed to have its epicenter directly beneath them. There was enough light from the cloud-veiled moon to make out the ground rippling like water as the dirt became liquid. The large house rocked violently back and forth, and broken glass showered from the upstairs windows.

Ryan, Krysty, Mildred and J.B. clung to the rails of the porch and to one another. Doc was flung sideways, reaching out with his right hand and grabbing at the bottom step of the creaking balcony.

But Jak and Issie were stranded in the middle of the shifting holocaust of noise and violence.

His hand was torn from hers, and he was sent staggering and rolling to the left, into the borders, managing to tuck in like the trained acrobat that he was.

Issie was less lucky.

As everybody watched in helpless horror, the ground opened some distance beyond the spiked iron gates, the crack widening as it rushed toward the house, like the gaping mouth of Hell itself. Flames burst out, and the air was filled with the choking stench of sulfur.

Issie lay sprawled in the dirt in the path of the crack, paralyzed by infinite fear, her eyes wide open, staring toward the opening earth.

Ryan broke free from Krysty and tried to power himself toward the young woman, but the shifting ground defeated him and he stumbled across Doc, falling over himself.

The noise was indescribable, like the wailing of ten thousand banshees. Out of the corner of his eye, Ryan could just make out Jak, on hands and knees, fighting to get to Issie, his mouth open, screaming soundlessly at the top of his voice.

The Japanese geisha also had her mouth open, and she was flattened out, as if she were trying to press her body into the earth for safety.

But the quake wasn't to be denied its victim.

The great crack reached her and swallowed her up. The last glimpse was of one hand, fingers scraping in the dirt, digging a furrow as the opening sucked her down.

There was a hollow roar, and the earth closed again like a gigantic trap.

And the silence flooded back once more.

Doc found his mind swamped suddenly with a memory of a tall, beautiful, young blond woman who had been snatched away from him in a somewhat similar manner. "Lori," he whispered, and tears soaked his cheeks.

Now the only sound was Jak's yelling, his voice breaking in anguish as he crawled to where the crack in the driveway had slammed shut. But there was scarcely a sign of where she'd been taken, just a fine network of cracks that seamed the surface of the ground.

"Nothing to be done, Jak," Ryan said, pulling himself to his feet and helping Doc up.

"Least it was quick," J.B. added, shaking his head. He took off his glasses and started to polish them.

"Oh, fuck it, fuck it..." Jak moaned, rocking back and forth, running his hands through the tangled mane of snow white hair.

Krysty went to the distraught teenager and took him in her arms, holding him tight, his head on her shoulder as he sobbed out his loss.

"That was a mean mother of a quake," Mildred said quietly. "Poor kid."

Ryan didn't know whether she meant Issie or Jak, and didn't feel like asking.

"One more like that could wreck the house," he said, aware of how loud and harsh his voice seemed to sound. "And it's goodbye to the mat-trans unit and goodbye to ever getting home again to Deathlands."

Even in his rage and misery, Ryan's words penetrated to Jak, and he broke away from Krysty, wiping his eyes on his sleeve. "It's right, Ryan," he said. "Must go. Nothing here stay for. Nothing."

THE INSIDE OF THE HOUSE was badly damaged since they had last been there a few days earlier.

The shrine by the entrance had tumbled, and the little brass statue of the grasshopper was lying on the floor, three of its spindly legs broken off. The beautiful stained-glass picture of the cherry blossom and the stork that had decorated the front door had shattered into a hundred brilliantly colored shards.

Ryan led the way toward the air-lock door, through and along to the elevator.

"Where we going to put the grens?" J.B. asked.

"They've only got twenty-second timers, haven't they? Not all that long."

The Armorer nodded. "Right. We don't really know how long it takes for a jump to be properly initiated. Feels like thirty seconds or so before we become unconscious. Might be a deal more than that before we actually get to jump out of there."

"Grens could go off while we're in midjump," Mildred said. "That what you're saying, John?"

"Right, love. Could put them in the elevator shaft when we're down there. Seal it off tight and also bring the house down on top of everything."

"That would bury us snugger than a pharaoh in his sarcophagus, would it not?" Doc asked.

"Sure would," Ryan replied.

"And if something malfunctioned with the mechanism? What then? Then it will a long goodbye and a big sleep for us all. As Mr. Chandler would have said."

Ryan didn't know who this Chandler guy was, but Doc had a point.

It could be rather like sawing off a branch that you were sitting on.

"Mashashige won't be invading Deathlands," he said. "Nor will any of his men. Nor his brother."

"But there'll always be someone else who'll find the house and the gateway," Krysty protested.

Ryan sighed. It was tempting to take the grens with them back to Deathlands, where they could always find a use. But, Krysty was right. Everything that they'd seen in what remained of Japan pointed toward lethal problems over the next few years. And if the gateway should still function . . .

There was an obvious risk to themselves, but a greater risk for the future if they didn't act now.

"Use them in the house," he decided. "Last burner and an implode. Last pair of implodes can go up in the elevator at the final moment before we go to make the jump. We can check that everything seems all right in the gateway first."

Nobody argued against the plan.

When they stood in front of the elevator, Ryan almost expected Dean to appear and eagerly ask whether he could press the controls, as he always used to. During the exciting time in Japan, Ryan had put his son to the back of his mind. Now they were heading home again, he wondered how the boy was getting on up in his Colorado school.

But he set that aside and pushed in the code himself—six, two, eight, three, four and one.

The door slid open and he stepped in, pressing the button to hold it open. "J.B., use your burner and the implode. Jak, keep yours for the last minute. Set them for the full twenty and then get in quick."

The Armorer set the timer on the scarlet-and-blue implode and lobbed it out through the interior door into the hallway, following it immediately with the burner. He closed the doors and stepped smartly into the elevator.

Ryan pushed the Down button, and the cage began to drop.

"Quake now and we're deep in the ordure," Mildred commented.

Ryan was looking at his chron, counting down the seconds. It was on eleven when they reached the bottom of the shaft and the door hissed smoothly open.

As they were entering the mat-trans control area, the tiny digits flickered around to twenty.

There was a faint vibration from above them, and a few flakes of plaster fell from the cracked ceiling. Ryan noticed even at a cursory glance that the control area had suffered from the recent quakes with some consoles dark and several ceiling lights off.

One thing that had been worrying him was how they would actually jump to Deathlands, whether the ordinary last-destination button code would do the trick.

But he noticed something they'd missed on the way out. There was a sheet of paper taped to the door by the control panel, with a list of American regions on it.

"Want me to do the last grens?" Jak asked.

"Sure." The earth trembled and another light went off. "Do it now. Krysty, we could copy this list, take it with us, and see if it operates from other gateways. Give us control over where we want to jump to."

Doc shook his head. "I fear, my dear friend, that it would be fruitless. The codes differ from redoubt to redoubt. I remember that from my time with the whitecoats. Just pick a place and enter it."

Jak came running back. "Sent them up in elevator," he said. "Got about fifteen. Closed outer door. Give protection. But should go quick."

"Right." Ryan scanned the list. "How about Tennessee? Haven't been there for a while."

"Do it, lover," Krysty said nervously. "Got a bad feeling that something's going wrong."

Like an echo to her words, they all felt a rumble that made the floor shake.

"Grens," Mildred said hopefully.

Jak sniffed, counting to himself. "Not time. Coming up... Now."

They all heard the distinctive noise of the pair of implode grens, far above them, though it was muffled by the sec doors into the gateway.

The sound was overlaid by the thunder of a quake, the noise all around them, as if the walls of the gateway were about to crumble in at any second.

"In," Ryan snapped, punching in the digital code for Tennessee, not waiting for everyone to sit on the floor of the orange-walled chamber. He stepped in and slammed the door firmly shut to trigger the jump mechanism.

Everyone knew what to do.

J.B. had taken off his fedora and placed it on his lap, carefully folding his glasses and placing them safely in a pocket, the Uzi in his lap, scattergun within reach. He held Mildred's hand. She reached out for Doc, who had slowly creaked his way down, laying the ebony swordstick at his side, stretching out his aged knee boots.

Jak, red eyes swollen from crying, sat next to Doc, pressing his skinny back against the armaglass wall.

The rumble was becoming much louder and more insistent as Ryan finally seated himself alongside Krysty, having unslung the rifle and placing it by his side.

"Here we go," he said.

"Sayonara, my friends," Doc whispered, his voice sounding small and far away.

The disks in floor and ceiling were beginning to glow brightly, and the familiar white mist was gathering above their heads. Ryan felt his brain being scooped out of his skull and whirled around and around.

"Tennessee," he breathed, his last sentient thought one of pleasure that they would very soon be home safely in Deathlands again.

At that moment the big quake finally arrived.

An old enemy develops a deadly
new train of thought...

THE

Destroyer

#103 Engines of Destruction

Created by
WARREN MURPHY
and RICHARD SAPIR

The railways have become the fastest—and surest—way
to get from here to eternity. Could the repeated sightings
of a ghostly samurai swordsman be linked to the
high-speed derailments that are strewing the rails with
headless victims? Suspecting the train terror is merely a
decoy, Remo Williams and Master Chiun become
involved, only to find they may literally lose their heads
over an old enemy.

Take
4 explosive books
plus a
mystery bonus
FREE

**Bolan's war takes retribution to
the Amazon killground**

DON PENDLETON's

MACK BOLAN.®

JUNGLE LAW

A ruthless conglomerate has embarked on an extermination
campaign—death squads are hunting down and executing
the native peoples of the Amazon. For Mack Bolan this
modern-day holocaust requires only one response—exact
justice in blood, and demonstrate the grim realities of the
jungle to those who finance genocide.

Look for it in April, wherever Gold Eagle books are sold.

**A flare-up of hatred and violence
threatens to engulf America**

BLACK OPS #2

ARMAGEDDON NOW

created by MICHAEL KASNER

The Black Ops team goes where the law can't—to avenge acts
of terror directed against Americans around the world. But now
the carnage is the bloody handiwork of Americans as Los Angeles
turns into a powder keg in a sweeping interracial war. Deployed
to infiltrate the gangs, the Black Ops commandos uncover a
trail of diabolical horror leading to a gruesome vision of
social engineering....